WICKED JENNY

WICKED JENNY

Matt Hilton

**SEVERN
HOUSE**

First world edition published in Great Britain and the USA in 2025
by Severn House, an imprint of Canongate Books Ltd,
14 High Street, Edinburgh EH1 1TE.

severnhouse.com

British Library Cataloguing-in-Publication Data
A CIP catalogue record for this title is available from the British Library.

ISBN-13: 978-1-4483-1393-8 (cased)
ISBN-13: 978-1-4483-1392-1 (e-book)

This is a work of fiction. Names, characters, places and incidents are either the
product of the author's imagination or are used fictitiously. Except where actual
historical events and characters are being described for the storyline of this
novel, all situations in this publication are fictitious and any resemblance to
actual persons, living or dead, business establishments, events or locales is
purely coincidental.

All Severn House titles are printed on acid-free paper.

MIX
Paper | Supporting
responsible forestry
FSC® C013056

Typeset by Palimpsest Book Production Ltd., Falkirk,
Stirlingshire, Scotland.
Printed and bound in Great Britain by TJ Books,
Padstow, Cornwall.

Praise for Matt Hilton

"A finale of gut-clutching violence"
Booklist on *Death Pact*

"Hilton grabs readers from the outset of this superior
standalone thriller"
Publishers Weekly on *The Girl in the Smoke*

"Trust Matt Hilton, author of the popular Tess and Po thrillers, to
come up with some nice twists"
Booklist on *The Girl in the Smoke*

"Hot conflicts rage in the freezing cold"
Kirkus Reviews on *Cold Fire*

"Just right for the Hammett and Chandler crowd"
Booklist on *Fatal Conflict*

"A riotous action read"
Booklist on *Collision Course*

"Action galore"
Kirkus Reviews on *Collision Course*

About the author

Matt Hilton worked for 23 years in private security and the police force in Cumbria. He is a 4th Dan black belt and coach in Ju-Jitsu. He is the author of thirteen novels in the Joe Hunter series, and ten in the Grey & Villere thrillers.

www.matthiltonbooks.com

Dedicated to my wife Denise

ONE

Something felt wrong.

Carl Butler walked tentatively. In contradiction to his tiny steps, he kept his hands firmly wedged in his jacket pockets, trading balance for warmth. His chin dug deep into his collar, and he breathed deeply out of his open mouth. His gaze darted around.

The cobbles sparkled underfoot, slick from a recent downpour. The skeletal trees had practically shed their foliage, with only the most determined leaf clinging on. The fallen leaves formed decomposing mounds in the gutters and in gates and doorways. The cobblestone path had been swept, but some leaves had found their way back and made it treacherous underfoot.

He had taken this shortcut home from his local pub on dozens of occasions, sometimes even in darker and wetter conditions than these and it hadn't bothered him. But tonight was different.

Yes, tonight felt wrong.

Wrong in an uncanny sense, at which Carl would normally sneer. He didn't believe in ghosts, goblins or anything else that plagued the imaginations of simpletons. Yet the small hairs rising on the back of his neck, the goosebumps causing him to itch from coccyx to collar, argued that maybe he was more of a simpleton than he'd care to admit.

Something followed him, and if not evil in a supernatural sense, then it followed with evil intent.

Shadows flitted between the trees.

He convinced himself it was only the movement of the foliage on the opposite side of the canal, casting their shadows over the water to his side. It wasn't much of a theory as the trees on his side were backlit by street lamps, on the far side all was in darkness.

'Somebody there?' he demanded.

The instant he spoke he regretted it.

If somebody was lurking, his words might draw them out, and no good could come of it.

He'd heard that the homeless sometimes bedded down around there, using the adjacent woods for shelter. The last Carl wanted was for some drunken wino to accost him and demand money from him in the dark.

He picked up his pace, wobbling as he proceeded on the slippery stones.

The damp atmosphere robbed the sharpness from the slaps of his footsteps. The sounds of distant traffic were muffled.

It was as if his eardrums had compressed.

Something stirred the water.

A fish, a diving bird?

Carl halted, staring down at the murky depths. It was black, and impenetrable. Nothing lived down there in the polluted depths. On the surface there was still sluggish movement, and the meagre light falling through the trees made it look like an oil spill.

Rat, Carl decided.

Yeah, must've been a rat. One of those big ol' water rats that have no fear of cats, dogs or human beings.

He shivered in revulsion.

If there was one thing he hated more than deep, murky water, it was deep, murky, rat-infested water.

He moved on.

A titter arose behind him.

His compressed eardrums flattened the notes, but they still had a feminine quality to them. What kind of woman would be out there in the wee small hours? He immediately thought of the homeless people that made camp across from him, but he doubted any woman chose to hide out in the depths of the woods where she was more vulnerable than ever, not unless she counted herself among the dangerous ones. Perhaps the laughter arose from the adjacent street, where tipsy revellers wended their ways home, exactly as he did.

The laughter rose again, before it was broken by a series of bubbles and plops.

Carl halted again and leaned over the side of the canal. He swore, because again something had stirred the surface. Did the fucking water rats around here have the voices of sirens, designed to lure the unwary into the filthy water?

Carl snorted at the idea.

But he didn't turn away.

Something was just below the surface, there beyond the front edge of his vision.

He leaned further, trying to make out what it was that slithered past less than a fingertip's depth below the surface.

The water settled.

Carl frowned.

His face must have caught an errant beam of light from the street lamps, because reflected on the surface he could see the palest of countenances . . .

Deep, dark eye sockets.

An open mouth, teeth glistening darkly.

He reared back, croaking in horror.

It wasn't his face reflected in the oily surface, it was another's.

He spun, wrenching his hands out of his pockets, about to run.

Something struck him on the back of his skull, sharp and pin-pointed.

It felt like a bullet had pierced his head.

His strength puddled under him as he collapsed.

On his hands and knees, he craned up, trying to see over his shoulder.

Something loomed there in silhouette, holding something aloft that dripped water and slime dredged up from the bottom of the canal . . . or maybe it was the blood from his shattered skull.

'You've done something very bad . . .'

Carl's voice was trapped in his chest, so it wasn't him that spoke.

An arm rose, and against the faint lamplight were two fingers too sharp to be wholly natural. Each was tipped with a hooked talon. The arm slashed down.

TWO

1988

Hot and sweating, Andy Miller braced his feet on the mound of dirt. Flying ants filled the stifling air; so did other missiles. He swung a stick but usually a second too late behind the clods of earth being hurled up at him. When he did manage to knock aside a divot, it still exploded and covered him in dirt. It was in his hair and up his nostrils, and crumbs of earth had invaded his collar and trickled down his chest. His T-shirt, tucked into his jeans, collected it in the fold of material. Andy tried yanking his shirt free, only to be pelted by more sods.

'Pack it in, all right?' he yelled. 'This isn't funny.'

'It is from where we're standing,' Carl Butler laughed.

Carl threw another handful of grass and dirt.

'Pack it in!' Andy swung pointlessly at the muck. It showered him. 'Stop chucking stuff. If I go home filthy my mam will go mental and give me a hiding.'

His plea only encouraged his friends. Johnny Wilson crabbed across the field, seeking loose turf to rip from the ground. He hauled back on one divot that was as large as Andy's body, and if it struck him would probably take his head off. Luckily, Johnny hadn't the strength to hurl it at him, and Andy took the opening to escape. He leapt down and ran, throwing a few choice insults at the others. Johnny hooted in triumph, and tossed handfuls of dirt after Andy. When he failed to hit his fleeing pal, he turned his missiles on those nearest him. More insults, curses and hysterical laughter pierced the hot air. Andy slowed now he wasn't the object of torment. One of his friends was on the ground – Johnny probably – and the others piled on top, stuffing dirt and grass inside his trousers. *Who needs enemies when he has pals like Carl Butler and Johnny Wilson, Brian Petrie and Gavin Hill?*

Abruptly the trio on top launched away, and beyond them Andy watched Johnny scramble up, digging his hands into his waistband and extricating what had been stuffed in his underpants. He chased the others, yelling in mock outrage and chucking the dirt at their backs. Andy joined the pack, running and shouting insults with the best of them. He took it back; his friends were the best any thirteen-year-old boy could wish for.

Somewhere during the race across the field, Johnny caught up, fell in with the others, and joined the pushing and shoving match as they jostled to climb a rickety stile. Brian made it over first, while Gavin and Johnny struggled for room and fell in a tangle of limbs on to Brian. Carl bowed, made a sweep of his arm for Andy to go next: the instant Andy accepted, Carl rushed to beat him over. The boys wrestled for dominance, Carl first to clamber over the wooden steps. On the cinder path alongside the field, they hurtled towards the shortening shadows of the trees ahead.

Another stile was negotiated with similar unnecessary effort and then the group raced through the woods, whooping and hollering. Birds took noisy flight, their wings beating at the foliage. Something larger crashed through the undergrowth, and Andy halted, his breath caught in his throat. He clutched his stick, but what use would it be against a charging beast? What kind of animal large enough to make that racket lived in these woods? He didn't fancy being charged by a deer with a set of antlers the size of a coat rack.

'Oww!' He instantly forgot about the danger posed by woodland creatures, shying away from another jab of Carl's knuckles in his shoulder. He swung his stick, with no intention ever of hitting his pal. Carl pulled a face, rolling his tongue in his bottom lip.

'You Mongol,' Andy called him.

'You're not meant to use that word any more,' Carl countered.

'You can still say it,' Andy said, without a trace of irony, 'cause it's the name of people from Mongolia.'

'Do you know what they call a div in Mongolia?'

'That's easy. They call them Carl Butler.'

Carl made the face again, this time adding to its ugliness by crossing his eyes and emitting a moan. Then without warning he launched another jab at Andy's shoulder, making sharp contact and then charged off. Andy had completely forgotten his reason for halting. Already his friends were a good distance ahead. 'Hey! Wait for me.'

His pals started chucking things again. This time it was in an attempt at knocking a crow's nest out of a tree. Andy wasn't a saint, and not beyond the same senseless destructiveness of other thirteen-

year-olds. He snapped his stick over his knee and dropped one end.
With a more manageable length in hand, he lobbed it into the tree.
He missed the nest and the stick caught on other springier twigs.
He shrugged off the miss: besides, his friends were already on the
move and he jogged after them. Johnny – lagging behind the others
once more – tossed a final handful of pebbles, nowhere near the
nest this time, but guaranteed to hit Andy. Andy bit his bottom lip,
bent and scooped up a clod of hardened dirt, and threw it at Johnny.
'One hundred and eighty,' he crowed when the dirt exploded on his
friend's back.

The boys ran on.

They came to a halt, their progress blocked by a five-bar gate.
None of them moved, but stood looking. Beyond the gate there was
a shallow valley that ran as straight as an arrow shot. Had it not
been for the trees and bushes encroaching on each side Andy might
have seen where the decommissioned railway line met the distant
horizon. However, the overgrown foliage blocked his gaze within a
hundred yards. It was hot, airless, but beneath the canopy of trees
existed a microclimate; it was dank and cool and smelled of decay.
The old railway lines were now a series of connected ponds and
muddy hollows. Reeds stood tall and the murky black water was
covered by blankets of green algae and duckweed.

It was weeks since Andy and his friends had last visited the ponds
– back then it was to collect frogspawn, now the surviving tadpoles
would have hatched, and gone through metamorphosis to froglet,
perhaps even to fully fledged frogs. Whatever stage they'd achieved,
the boys intended to find them. Carl Butler had designs on any of
the amphibians they could capture, and had brought a handful of
plastic straws to test his unpleasant plan. The other boys, Andy
included, would help with his experiment, whether or not they
wanted to. Carl was their friend, but none of them knew why they
put up with his bullying.

THREE

Andrew Miller – Present Day

Fear demanded loyalty, as could a blackened eye or split lip. So, it's not difficult to grasp how I'd fallen into line and followed Carl Butler's hare-brained and often nasty antics. Within an hour he had us all attempting to inflate frogs by inserting the straws in their bums and then blowing. In hindsight it was a horrible thing to do to the defenceless creatures. As was shooting them from Gavin Hill's catapult and watching them flail their tiny arms and legs like Kermit from the Muppets, before they smacked into the trees. My friends hooted and hollered in amusement, and to my shame now, I hooted and hollered along with them, despite the nausea in my gut and the sense that the torture we were inflicting was awful and probably *wrong*.

I've often wondered at what age a child is most impressionable, and when a burgeoning serial killer ferments murder in their minds. Small children can be horrible, and they are not beyond torturing their siblings or friends, or tormenting animals, but I think the turning point is at much the same time as when puberty hits. Some thirteen-year-old boys – and girls – can inflate the skin of a frog, pull the legs off a spider, or knock fledgling chicks out of a nest with thrown stones, with glee, and grow more fervent about inflicting pain. Others are sickened and turn away from those acts, often promising to never harm another living creature as long as they live. I'd like to say I'm of the latter category now, but during that hot summer day in 1988 I definitely hadn't fully discovered such compassion.

The juvenile Andy isn't the same person as the adult I grew into. I recall his memories, but it's as if I'm accessing the recollections of a third party, not my younger self. Recollecting the way in which those poor frogs were blown up, skewered on the end of plastic drinking straws stolen from our local Wimpy makes me ashamed, though at the time I laughed as cruelly as the others. Something approaching shame did assail me, but only when I looked up from stomping a froglet to its death in the muck to see a pair of girls watching from the tree-crowned embankment: a Golden Retriever stood at their side, staring balefully at us. The girls' expressions were more stricken.

Thirty-five years later I squirmed under a similar look of horror. This time I hadn't been committing frog-icide but was evidently responsible for something my wife found equally disturbing. All I was doing was eating my breakfast.

'What's wrong, Nell?' I asked as I set down my fork.

She didn't immediately answer. Instead, she pushed her face into her palms, and moaned. I reached across the table and touched her elbow. She drew it away from my touch, raising her head. Her eyes brimmed with tears. 'Nell,' I tried once more, 'what is it?'

'Aren't you listening, Andy?' she sobbed.

'Listening to . . .' Ah, the radio played, tuned to a local channel. As we ate our breakfast it was simply background noise to me, kind of similar to how my wife's often meaningless breakfast-time chatter didn't impinge in my thoughts. I don't know though, perhaps the radio announcer's words had found a way into my psyche, and was responsible for casting me back to 1988.

'I don't believe he's dead,' Nell cried.

'Neither do I,' I said.

It was difficult to believe, but Carl Butler, someone I'd once liked and loathed with equal passion, but had always accepted was my friend back then, couldn't be dead.

The radio announcer claimed that his body had been found by a dog walker, and that he appeared to have been the victim of assault. No specifics were gone into, probably because the police didn't want to release any evidence they could pursue in the subsequent investigation. It would have been odd enough for them to name the victim, if he hadn't been found days ago, and his closest relatives already informed of his murder.

Once, I would have learned sooner of his passing, but we'd drifted, parted by the years and a wedge that had been forced between us. There was a time when I could've believed the relationship I had with my friends was almost psychic, because we were so familiar with each other that we could read our emotions without asking, could end each other's sentences only half-muttered, and could sense when the pack was about to move, or run, or even fight if circum-stance dictated. Had Carl been murdered back then, I'm pretty sure that young Andy would have sensed his passing, maybe as a stinging pain in the heart, or as a nauseous flipping of his stomach contents, or something else, but adult Andy hadn't felt a thing.

'We can't be certain it's him,' I tried, but Nell only wept harder. I tried once more. 'Surely there are other Carl Butlers living in this city.'

'In all the years we've lived here have you heard of another?'

'No, but . . .' I shut up because I wasn't helping.

To be honest, I was kind of befuddled, my mind not working properly as I tried to make sense of the news.

Carl couldn't be dead. He just couldn't.

And yet, undeniably, I knew that he was.

Not only was he dead, but by all accounts, he'd been beaten to death, murdered.

I stood up from my breakfast. There was no possible way I'd eat it now. But all I did was stand, looking across at Nell, watching her watching me with tears rolling down her cheeks.

'Why are you upset?' I wondered, suddenly angered. 'It isn't as if you had a kind word for him while he was alive.'

'How can you say that? Carl was our friend.'

'No, Nell. Carl was *my* friend and you never liked him. In fact, you once said you despised him. You wouldn't let him come to the house, and only ever called him choice names if I mentioned him.'

'You're being unfair, Andy. You're only picking and choosing times that suit your version of events, not mine.'

'Tell me a time when you welcomed him here, then,' I said.

'There were plenty of times,' she said.

'I can't think of a single one.'

'That's because you're confused. You know you get that way. You've just had some terrible news, and you're reacting by lashing out at me! It's unfair, Andy. You are being unfair to me!'

'My friend has been murdered, and somehow you manage to make it about you? Jesus-fucking-Christ, Nell!'

She stormed out of the kitchen. I could hear her muttering and swearing under her breath as she tore through the house, slamming doors and drawers. I allowed her to vent, because yeah, I suppose I had lashed out and maybe I was at fault.

I found my phone where I'd left it on charge and typed Carl's name into the search bar. Immediately I was rewarded with a list of links to online news sites. Now that the victim had been named by the police, the media wasn't being shy in sharing photographs of him. Mostly a picture of a smiling Carl Butler was positioned under a shouty grab line. For a few seconds I held on to the hope that this was some other Carl Butler, and that my childhood friend was safe and sound at home. But my wish that another pitiful soul shared his name was dashed the instant I looked at the face in the photos. Back as a thirteen-year-old, Carl had reminded me of a ferret, with his beady eyes and long pointy nose, sticky up blond hair and equally sticky out ears. Over the decades he'd filled out, his face becoming chiselled rather than weaselly, and growing into his ears. His pale hair had receded, and his beady eyes had gained crows-feet to match the deep lines from his cheekbones to his chin. It was Carl all right, somehow managing to make his smile sarcastic, the way he always had as a boy.

'What happened, Carl?' I asked. 'Who did this to you?'

No one answered. No voice from above, out of the ether or anywhere else. The only sound was Nell still calling me names from another room in the house. After a moment she began weeping loudly, and I was unsure if it was at Carl's demise, or that I'd upset her by shouting. I thought about seeking her out, to apologize, and maybe seek mutual comfort in an embrace, but grief overwhelmed me. It came upon me like a tidal surge that completely submerged me and snatched the oxygen from my lungs. Dropping my phone, I clutched at my shirt front, dragging my collar clear of my throat, but it didn't help. My knees folded and I sat down, not even aware that I dropped all the way to the floor with my back against the kitchen cupboards.

Tears flowed from me, and my face contorted, and I let out a bellow of denial. I must have cried out several times more, because despite being mad at me, Nell came and she huddled over me, pressing her forehead to mine, and together we grieved, more for our lost daughter, Rebecca, who had drowned during a holiday break in the Alps than for our friend who once boasted that he was going to live forever.

FOUR

'I can't think of anything worse than living forever,' Andy said.

'Why, what's wrong with having eternal life?' Carl countered.

'My great grandma lived to ninety-two,' Andy pointed out. 'She'd gone blind, couldn't hardly hear, and couldn't get out of bed to go to the toilet without help. Can you imagine how helpless we'd be even fifty years older again?'

'I won't be sick and weak like your great granny, I'll be invulnerable.' Carl beat at his keeled chest with the ball of a hand. 'Who'd want to live forever if you were just lyin' there droolin' and shittin' yerself? I'm going to invent a pill that keeps me young, fit and healthy.'

'Is that right, Carl? You'd best stick in at school then, cause last I saw you were doing crap in chemistry.'

'I don't need to be good at chemistry, not if I just get some scientists to make the pill for me.'

'Because they're going to do that. O-kaaay . . .'

Out of nowhere, Brian Petrie slapped Carl across the back of the neck with a long stick broken off one of the bushes. The stick was green, and thin and held no weight, but it certainly stung.

'There can be only one!' Brian announced in a poor attempt at a Scottish accent, holding the stick up alongside his face as if it were a sword. He'd been attempting Shuh-shuh-Sean Connery impressions ever since they watched that movie about head-decapitating-immortals on a crappy pirated VHS tape.

'Ow, you . . .' Carl cringed, rubbing the red welt on his flesh. Then he sprang after Brian with a yell, and Petrie dashed away laughing uproariously, and they both splashed knee-deep through the frog ponds.

Andy watched them, but their stupid antics couldn't hold his attention when he again spotted the girls and their dog. The Golden Retriever stood with its front paws in one of the ponds, nose close to the murky water. The girls had both picked up sticks and they prodded and lifted up strings of almost neon-coloured duckweed. He recognized the girls from school, albeit they weren't in his form and were a year older. He knew that the blonde one was called Melanie, but couldn't put a name to her ginger friend. It didn't matter, because he was only interested in Melanie. He watched her, and liked the way she leaned back and flicked her hair behind her ear. He also liked the way her breasts pressed against her T-shirt.

Johnny Wilson knuckled Andy's shoulder.

'Give over, Johnny-boy!'

'You give over, you perv. It's kind of obvious that you're letching over Melons Melanie. Not unless you've got the hots for Ginge.'

'Give over,' Andy repeated.

'You'd better hide your stiffy, Andy, before Ginge sees it and thinks she's on a promise.'

Mortified, Andy glanced down, dreading to see a protrusion at the front of his shorts. There was none, though he couldn't deny a stirring feeling deep down.

'Made you look, you dirty duck,' laughed Johnny and danced away from a kick Andy aimed at his backside.

The girls looked over, then huddled together whispering, and laughing at something they found funny: him, Andy realized.

Heat bloomed in his cheeks, and he turned his back on them. Johnny continued to taunt him, but then Gavin pounced on Johnny and they both ended up sitting in the water. When Andy glanced back, the girls had moved closer; their dog danced at the edge of the ponds, tongue lolling as Johnny and Gavin tried to extricate themselves from the soupy mud and clinging pond weed. Despite being soaked to their waists, Carl and Brian laughed at their friends' predicament.

'Look what you did, Gav!' Johnny yelped. 'We could catch some kind of disease off of this manky water.'

'D'you hear of many typhoid cases around here, like?' Gavin challenged.

'We could get some kind of lurgy!'

'Don't talk rubbish.'

'He's right.'

All eyes turned to the girls. It was the red-head that had taken Johnny's side.

'What do you know?' Gavin sneered. 'Are you some kind of doctor or what?'

'No. I don't need to be a doctor to know that playing in dirty water can't be good for you.'

'It doesn't really matter. Do you want to play doctors and nurses with us?' Carl totally ignored the girl in favour of eyeballing her friend, Melanie. 'What do you say, Melons?'

'Dream on,' Melanie said, and Andy's blush grew brighter.

Carl stuck his fist up inside his T-shirt and thumped it back and forward. 'Oh, go on,' he said and stilled his fist, 'before you break my heart.'

'How corny,' said the red-haired girl.

'Shut up, Ginger Nut,' Carl sneered. 'Nobody was asking you, you ugly git.'

The girl's face fell.

'Don't talk to my sister like that,' Melanie snapped.

'Why?' Carl scowled down at the Golden Retriever. 'What you gonna do, set Scooby-Don't on us. Gertcha!'

He aimed a prod at the dog with the toe of his soaking trainers.

His kick didn't land, but the dog still shied away. He set up another kick and it yelped and bolted for cover behind the girls.

'Hey!' Melanie shouted. She clenched her fists by her sides.

'If you don't want to play with us, you can go away.'

'You don't own these ponds,' the red-head said, her voice a few octaves higher than before.

'No, but I can still duck your bloody head in them if you don't bugger off. Johnny, Gavin, we're already soaked. Help me get her.'

Neither of the boys obeyed. Andy stood in Carl's way.

'What?' Carl grunted.

'Let her be,' he told Carl.

'Why? I thought it was her sister you were more interested in.'

Andy glanced quickly at Melanie, and his face was still scalding hot. It was Melanie he liked, but what better way was there to make a good impression with her than to stand up for her sister?

'I'm not going to let you duck either of them,' Andy said.

'Oh, is that right?' Carl looked away from Andy, raising his eyebrows at Johnny and Gavin. He spun back too quickly for Andy to react, his tight little fist smacking Andy directly in the mouth. Immediately Andy fell back, holding his face, feeling blood and saliva drip through his fingers. Carl chased him, aiming another fist, but this time Brian got between them. 'Lads, lads, lads, we're supposed to be mates, right?' he said.

Somehow, Carl managed to turn the blame on Andy, as he often did with all the other boys. 'Some mate he is when he chooses a squinty-eyed little ginger minger over his friends.'

'Some mate you are splitting my lip,' Andy replied, spitting bloody saliva between his feet.

'It's nothing. A scratch.'

'Yeah, well try it again and I'll give you a worse scratch,' Andy promised.

'You and whose army?' And just like that, it was over. The fight was done, dusted and forgotten.

In the meantime, the girls had shown good sense and moved away, allowing the stupid boys to carry on the way stupid boys often did.

Brian watched them sagely. He touched Andy's wrist and said: 'You're better off forgetting about Melons, Andy.'

'Why's that then?'

'She's the school bike. From what I heard she's got the pox.'

FIVE

Andrew Miller – Present Day

The rule isn't universal, but put a group of some thirteen-year-old boys together, and they'll say the most horrible things to and about each other. They'll invent nasty untruths about people, they'll brag and boast about their non-existent sexual prowess, about how many people they've beaten-up in fights, and they'll make up lies to fit their personal or group agendas. Young Andy wasn't much different to any of his peers, except he was approaching a level of maturity where he could recognize that most of what was said was complete twaddle. When Brian announced that Melanie had a venereal disease, Andy scoffed at the idea while also bemoaning *what if?* Inside his developing brain, it was I, Andrew, that reassured him that Brian was talking utter rubbish. Five minutes beforehand, Brian had not the slightest idea who Melanie was, and had based his summation on the horrible sexist nickname he'd overheard Carl calling her. If Andy had allowed him to go on, Brian would've got round to swearing he'd slept with her before, and worse, that she was useless at it.

Whereas Carl had been an overconfident child, unafraid of arguing his opinion, or throwing around his fists, Brian established his position in our little gang as both protector and clown. He was notorious for issuing poor impressions, telling jokes that only he found funny, or conducting himself in a manner that wouldn't have been out of place in a Three Stooges skit. Sometimes his clowning could have a slightly sadistic edge, as in when delivering a stinging whack of a branch to Carl's neck, or it was designed to cause the most trouble possible for his pals. Brian wasn't beyond chucking a stone through a window, causing them all to flee in fear of the consequences from an irate householder. As he aged, he didn't exactly mentally mature, not that he had learning difficulties or anything else as dramatic, only that he never quite grew out of a teenager's antics.

As mad as it sounds though, Brian has remained my closest friend of the bunch. I'd had it out with Nell, about why she didn't like me inviting Carl around to the house and, to be honest, it hadn't happened very often. When we were kids, I'd put up with him, had gone along with the gang mentality, but we had never been friends in the proper sense of the term, no affection existed between us whatsoever. Not then and certainly not prior to his murder. My outburst at Nell had been more to do with shock and grief than any true feelings I felt at the loss of Carl. No genuine friend punches you in the mouth without the slightest provocation. It was different with Brian. For all his daftness he could be annoying, but I couldn't help feel affection towards him.

It was horrible watching his eyes water and his bottom lip tremble. I couldn't help tearing up myself, and saying, for possibly the hundredth time since learning of Carl's death, that it was hard to believe he was gone.

Brian said, 'Look at me. Why am I upset over losing that nasty little bugger?'

In unison, we said, 'Because he was our nasty little bugger.'

Ordinarily we would have laughed at the synchronicity, but it wasn't the time or place. We were standing in the front office at our local police station being eyeballed from behind plexiglass by a civilian receptionist. It was a woman, maybe our age, late forties, but wearing a back-combed beehive hairstyle that was fashionable back in the 1950s, bright dabs of colour on her cheeks, lips and upper eyelids. She had glasses, but they dangled on a lanyard between her huge breasts: she regularly squinted, then widened her eyes to their maximum, bringing us into sharper relief. For some reason it appeared she didn't enjoy what she saw. She had not been on duty when we'd arrived earlier, so had no idea what we were there for. I smiled, then waved off the question forming in her mind, and I ushered Brian out the station. A minute ago, we'd been buzzed out through a secure door, more or less given a similar bum's rush by a couple of detectives after we could offer them nothing useful in their investigation. When I was first contacted to supply a statement, I'd worried that, somehow, I'd become a suspect and it was a ploy by CID to grab me. I was mildly relieved when Brian had phoned to say he'd been invited into the police station too, and did I want to attend at the same time. As chief administration officer at Heatley's Office Supplies, I held a little clout, so I wangled a couple of hours off work at the end of shift and picked up Brian en route to the nick.

We couldn't tell the detectives much, except that Carl Butler had been a lifelong friend, albeit we hadn't seen much of him in the past couple of years. He'd married, divorced, got a second wife, but they also divorced. Yes, Carl was a bit of a womanizer – that was a detective's description, not ours – and liked to play the field as if he were still a young man, but as far as we knew he wasn't currently in a relationship. The police already knew where he lived, where he worked and where he drank, but hoped we could add a few finer details: they were trying to piece together his movements and behaviour, to determine if he'd come across his murderer before, or if the incident was as random as it had appeared.

Outside, we stood in a car park chock full of vehicles. Sycamore trees formed a boundary, and partially hid the station from the main road. Leaves swirled on the breeze, an indication that autumn had arrived. Brian took out a pack of cigarettes and lit up, without offering me one. I'd given up smoking years ago, but could have smoked an entire pack just then. I averted my gaze from him, feeling my stomach gurgling as I fought down old cravings.

'Did you hear what that copper said?' Brian asked after two or three draws on his cigarette.

The coppers had asked about a lot of stuff without giving much away in return.

'About the hammer,' Brian said.

'A hammer was used on him?'

'Weren't you listening?'

'Yeah,' I said, 'but there were also times I was caught up in my own thoughts.'

When the subject of Carl's assault had risen, I'd deliberately blocked the terrible images swarming past my mind's eye. Apparently one of the coppers had dropped in a pertinent point not yet released to the press. Perhaps it had been deliberately inserted into our interview to see if it got any kind of reaction from us; perhaps we were being considered as potential suspects. Maybe if I'd heard, something in my reaction would have betrayed me.

'Did you tell them about . . .'

Before the words were out of my mouth Brian had shut me down. He began walking away, flicking ash and sparks, and I was forced to follow. When we'd arrived together in my car, there had been no vacant spots in the car park so I had been forced to find a space several hundred metres away. Brian headed for where I'd parked.

Only once we were out of sight of the station did he offer me a cringe of apology. 'Sorry about that. I was unsure how sensitive their CCTV system was and didn't want to be overheard.'

'What are you worried about?' I asked.

'You know . . .' he leaned close, ensuring only I heard. His breath was rank with cigarette smoke. 'The bloody hammer?'

I shook my head. 'Something that happened thirty-odd years ago couldn't possibly have anything to do with Carl's mugging now.'

'Can't it?' He sounded doubtful.

SIX

'Better keep away from the water, or ol' Ginny Greenteeth will come out and snatch you,' Brian announced, then cackled and wriggled his fingers as though they were talons grasping at prey.

'Get stuffed,' the red-headed girl called from the opposite side of the frog ponds.

'I mean it,' Brian pressed on. 'Ginny comes for the naughtiest boys and girls, and from what I hear you've both been very, very bad.'

'Yeah, they've been a couple of slags,' Carl added.

Andy clucked his tongue, and tried to send a silent apology to Melanie. She didn't even look at him; she was more interested in scowling at the boys teasing them. 'You'd best run home before it's dark, little babies,' she said, 'or you're going to be late for bedtime.'

'Ha!' said Brian. 'I'll bet that if you aren't in bed by midnight, you have to go home.'

Carl, Johnny and Gavin all whooped it up, as if Brian had said the funniest thing; Andy was mortified. If Melanie couldn't see past the others, she might never give him the time of day again.

'Don't pay any attention to this lot, Melanie,' he called. 'They're only kidding.'

'No we're not.' Carl crouched, scooped up handfuls of duckweed and then flung them across the pond at the girls, causing them to squeal and retreat up the far embankment. The Golden Retriever cowered at their sides. 'Go on. Git! Or ol' Ginny will drag you underwater.'

'You're all a bunch of horrible little shits,' the red-head snapped, including Andy in her summation.

'Come on, Poppy,' Melanie said, and took hold of her sister's hand, 'they're not worth wasting our time on.'

'Poppy! What kind of name is Poppy?' Carl cackled.

'Don't you get it?' said Gavin and tapped his hair. 'Poppies are red.'

'She should be called Copper Pubes, then,' Brian said, and his three stooges howled in laughter. Andy chewed his bottom lip.

The pack set off running, yelling and hooting, and as if they were beasts of the savanna, Andy fell in with them compelled by forces beyond his control to follow the herd. He didn't holler though, he checked back to see how the girls had been affected by Brian's nasty jest, but they'd already turned their backs. The boys scrambled over the five-bar gate and ran out into the open field beyond. It was several hundred yards before they'd reach the first of the stiles. By the time they reached it the group had fallen into smaller factions, with Andy finding himself teamed up with Gavin and Johnny.

'How come they're sisters?' Johnny wondered as they ran.

Breathless, Gavin supplied the only possible answer he could think of. 'They must be twins.'

'They aren't twins,' said Johnny. 'I mean look at Mel's melons compared to Poppy's tiny ones and . . .'

'I don't mean identical twins.'

'What do you mean then . . . they're unidentical?'

'Unidentical isn't even a real word, you nugget.'

'He means non-identical twins,' Andy inserted, and Johnny nodded at the correction. 'But I don't think they're twins at all. Maybe they're half-sisters, and have the same dad but different mothers.'

'No wonder they're a pair of slags when even their dad can't keep it in his pants,' said Johnny.

'He must be blind to stick it in Poppy's mam,' Gavin decided, 'if she's as ugly as her daughter is.'

Johnny laughed.

'Maybe their dad's the one with red hair,' Andy said.

'No, because Mel would be another ginger . . .' Johnny reached the stile first, and as he clambered over, he lost his breath entirely. Hands on his knees, bent at the waist, he coughed, sounding like a sea lion.

Once Andy had scaled the fence, he set a flat hand between Johnny's shoulder blades. 'You all right?'

'Must've swallowed some of that pond weed,' Johnny said, then coughed again. Gavin joined them. Soon Brian and Carl caught up. Carl remained on top of the stile for a while, as if claiming dominion over his friends from the loftier elevation.

Johnny continued to bark.

'Slap his back,' Gavin told Andy.

Before he could help, Carl said, 'Kick him in the nuts, that'll stop him from hacking up his lungs.'

'Get off,' Johnny said, and swiped away the hands of his friends. As if by magic, his cough disappeared and he set off running again. The others followed into the woods. Carl got close enough to kick Johnny's heel, and their friend went down face first in the dirt. Seconds ago, they were concerned he might choke to death, but causing him to crash to his face at a full gallop was permissible. They all laughed, Andy included, as they raced past. Johnny scrambled up and gave chase: he laughed too.

A hard clack sounded.

It could've been a distant crow scarer, or even a shotgun blast. It didn't impede too much on any of their minds, until a nearer, sharper and louder clack brought them to a halt.

They were in much the same location where Andy had halted at the sound of something large rushing through the underbrush on their journey to the frog ponds. Again, Andy experienced a sense of crawling anticipation in his bowel.

'Over there,' Gavin proclaimed. 'It's only Divvy Nixon.'

They all turned and spotted a burlier lad, several years older than they were. A 'divvy' in local slang meant somebody of low intellect, an idiot, and it wasn't uncommon to give people the cruel slur as a replacement forename: most of the male teachers at their school were known to the kids as Divvy-this or Divvy-that.

'He's not a divvy,' Johnny argued pathetically, 'he's my cousin.'

'There you are then,' said Carl. 'It proves being a divvy runs in your family, cause you're a divvy as well.'

'Piss off. You're the divvy.'

And just like that a squabble erupted, showing exactly how they all could act like divvies. Andy stood aside, taking no part in the pushing and shoving match that erupted. He watched the genuinely called Ian Nixon as the big lad was alerted to their presence and turned to glare at them. He clutched a claw hammer in his right fist, obviously the source of the clacking noises resounding through the woods. What he'd been doing with the hammer Andy couldn't tell for sure, but there were several bright spots on tree trunks where the bark had been knocked off: it was probably just wanton vandalism.

'What're you lookin' at?'

Nixon had directed his challenge directly at Andy.

Andy's voice peeped. 'Nothing.'

'You lookin' to get a smack round the head or summat?'

'What you got to hide, Nixon?' Carl called, the squabble having been put to rest now that Nixon was a better target for him. 'Have we discovered where you stash your nudie books or something?'

'Yeah,' Gavin joined in. 'We probably disturbed him from having a toss.'

'Little bugger.' Nixon aimed the business end of the hammer at Gavin. 'Say that again and see what you get.'

'Tosser,' said Gavin.

Carl stuck his tongue in his bottom lip and mimed an act of sexual self-gratification. He also called Nixon a corresponding name.

'Right,' Nixon shouted and swung the hammer over his head, 'who wants it first?'

Johnny yelped, and cried out. 'Ian, no, it's only me, your cousin Johnny Wilson. My mates are only funning with you.'

'Some cousin. It makes it worse that you're taking their side,' Nixon snarled.

'Who'd take the side of a divvy?' Carl asked, and laughed when Nixon swore.

Holding the hammer aloft, Nixon charged towards them.

'Run!' somebody shouted, but it was unnecessary.

They sprinted away, laughing, crying out in mock alarm, and shouting back insults at the big lad who had no hope of actually catching them. By the time they'd clambered over the next stile and on to the cinder path, the threat from Nixon and his hammer was left behind.

SEVEN

1988

I
t was getting dark by the time young Andy finally dragged himself home. His mates had all gone for tea hours ago. He hadn't a watch, but had learned to judge the time quite well by when the street lights flickered to life. It was summer, the lights didn't come on until after ten p.m. and even then they weren't really needed unless it was a new moon or overcast. As it had been for a couple of weeks now, the skies were clear, and he could see the first stars dotted above the eastern rooftops. The orange streetlights would blind out those weaker stars before long, but not the brightest or the planets Venus and Mars. Many kids his age had no interest in the stars and planets, and to be fair Andy was no Patrick Moore but he could spot Ursa Major – the Great Bear – aka the Plough or the Big Dipper, and if he turned directly south he could easily locate Orion's belt, and from there pick out the rest of the constellation, which would ultimately point to Canus Major: in all his years though he was yet to identify the Pole Star, usually because light pollution from the city washed that part of the sky a sickly hue.

His dad didn't personally interact with him very often. His dad worked, put his wages in Andy's mam's purse to pay the bills and make ends meet, and then he spent the rest of his time watching football on TV, or if it was a special fixture, he'd be down at his local, watching football on the TV there. He'd ensure that Andy's needs were seen to, that he was fed, bathed and dressed neatly, but rarely face to face. Instead, he'd sit and read, or do the crossword, and barely say two words to his son. There was once though when he caught Andy lying in the garden, peering up at the evening sky.

'Do you know how to tell a star from a planet?' he'd asked.

'That's Venus,' said Andy, pointing at one bright speck in the heavens.

'It is,' said his dad. 'Stars twinkle, son, the planets are steady lights.'

And Andy discovered his dad was correct. Stars were suns and made their own lights, therefore they twinkled, while the planets and moon reflected the light from our sun.

'If you intend to make something of yourself in life, don't be a planet, be a star,' said his father.

'What, like a movie or pop star?'

'Yeah. Either of those would work. But what I meant was you should always aim to shine, not reflect what everyone else is doing around you. They're conforming, you must scintillate.'

This was coming from a man usually so dull an observer could be forgiven for thinking he was absorbing the light.

He wondered if his dad was drunk, or secretly in the closet.

He was a deeper thinker than Andy had taken him as before.

They were alike in that respect.

'Don't make do with the life I have, son,' he went on. 'You want something, reach and take it.'

'Yeah, Dad. Thanks for the advice. I will.'

His dad would sometimes be lost in his own thoughts, and mostly it was as if Andy's mere presence was enough to annoy or aggravate him, but he also cared for the boy more attentively than he could say his mam did. If Andy was late back for instance, his dad would ensure a plate was saved from tea time and left warming in the oven. His dad would ensure his trunks were wrapped in a towel, ready for when his class went to the baths for swimming lessons. He'd ensure that Andy's school uniform was clean, pressed if necessary, and hanging up and his shoes were polished.

If it was left up to his mam, none of those things would happen, and yet to listen to her, anyone would believe she toiled like an unpaid slave from morning to night. Andy regularly stayed out late purposefully so he didn't have to interact with his mam. If she noticed him, it was because she was angry, and if she was angry, he could expect to be her sole target. Dad didn't stand up for him then; he knew better than to get in her way, but also understood that her rage lasted much shorter if she was allowed to exhibit it so he wouldn't prolong Andy's torment . . . usually she burned out before Andy was too physically hurt.

Andy's Raleigh Grifter was waiting for new inner tubes. It had been waiting for weeks, set on its saddle and handlebars alongside the house. The chain hung loose and in need of oil. The bike wasn't new when Andy got it, and he'd ridden it and performed tricks on it for the past three years. His dad had promised new tubes, but hadn't come through yet, but Andy didn't make a fuss. Times were hard, and besides, he was holding out for a newer bike at Christmas. Maybe that was his dad's game, and he was waiting to play Santa Claus, and would present Andy with a new BMX Burner, like most of his pals had owned for several years already.

His parents didn't have the spare cash to outright purchase a brand-new bike; they would have to chucky it, meaning pay for it in weekly hire purchase instalments. Half of their possessions were only partially owned on what was commonly referred to as the never-never and the rest were practically worn out. He stood for a moment, regarding the bike in the dimness, wondering if it ever would be ridden by him again. He touched his mouth. It was swollen and sore, and had bled quite a bit: Carl's fault, the sneaky little weasel.

Andy was bare-chested. His shirt had been ruined, first with all the crap his mates had chucked at him, then from getting wet and muddy, then lastly being speckled with blood. Rather than wear it home, he'd discarded it, with the plan of getting in the house and upstairs to his bedroom before anyone noticed.

Indoors he thought he'd made it. The lights were off, but not the telly. It was showing a sitcom about a poor family from Liverpool: they always pooled their money as a family, and were much better off than the Millers who only had one bread winner. It was playing later than expected, unless his mam had recorded the show earlier on VHS and had taken the opportunity now to catch up.

'What time do you call this to be traipsing in?' she demanded from where she sat in her easy chair.

'Uh, I dunno, Mam,' he answered,

'Ten past bloody ten,' she told him. 'It's not the weekend, you've school in the morning. Have you done your homework?'

'Uh, yeah, Mam. Done it earlier.' He was lying. He fully intended scribbling down something that would satisfy his English teacher during home room first thing at school before registration.

'Where's your bloody shirt?'

'I, uh . . .' He hadn't come up with a contingency, fully expecting to slip by his parents unnoticed.

'You've lost it?'

'I took it off because it was so hot,' he said, 'and I had it pushed into my jeans. It, uh, must've fallen out on my way back.'

She stood, and marched towards him.

Andy was tempted to run, but he held his ground. Run and she'd pursue, and his punishment would be worse.

She hit the light switch.

'Look at you, your back is red raw from sunburn. Are you stupid, boy?'

'No, Mam.'

'You can bloody fool some but you can't fool me. Why are your jeans so wet?'

'I, uh, got pushed in the beck at the park by some big lads.'

Without warning her hand cracked across his cheek.

His already sore mouth began bleeding again.

She dragged him around, one hand on the nape of his neck, carelessly rubbing the blistered skin off. He squirmed in torment, cried out in pain, but knew better than to physically resist.

'You've been down those bloody ponds again, haven't you? What have I warned you about going near them and coming home soaked?'

'We weren't at the ponds,' he lied.

Slap.

'We weren't, Mam, honest.'

'Honest, is it? Was I born yesterday?'

He didn't reply. It was pointless. Her tongue had squirmed from the corner of her mouth as she set her jaw.

'Have we got money to burn? How are we supposed to afford new clothes if you're just going to throw them away?'

'I didn't throw my shirt away, I lost it.'

'Dirty little liar!'

She struck him with her balled fists, and with her open palms. Always she took care to beat him where he wouldn't bruise too much. His body was already dotted with tiny fading yellow bruises, scuff marks and minor abrasions. He also had a split lip. Anyone querying why he was so beaten-up, he had a ready-made excuse in his bully Carl.

He didn't like her, but he didn't hate his mother.

Strangely he even loved her. He'd do anything to protect her. Her abusiveness towards him would be their family secret.

She was to be pitied, he supposed, considering there was definitely a screw loose in her head. There but for the grace of God go I, he thought, as her hand slashed repeatedly across his bare back and buttocks.

She could be overzealous in doling out punishments, but he supposed he deserved what he got, after all he had blatantly lied, and knew he'd behaved badly.

EIGHT

Andrew Miller – Present Day

I tried clearing my head of the terrible images that paraded across the internal screen of my mind, but it was pointless. I didn't dwell on my own beating at my mother's hands: there had been too many times to differentiate between them. Instead, I kept picturing Carl, cowering, crying out for mercy as he was repeatedly beaten with a hammer, the claw end ripping his skin and pulping the flesh and bones beneath. Then it wasn't Carl's face I looked upon, but those of Melanie and Poppy. Brian said very little on the drive back to his house, but he'd already said enough to cast my mind back to memories so vivid that some of them must have been false, planted there by young Andy's imagination to endure the decades that separated him from me. We never ever saw Ian Nixon with the hammer after he chased us away, and certainly didn't see him wield it against the girls, but in my memory I always pictured it how it must have been found, the claw end clotted with brains and bloody hair, after their killer was done with them.

I dropped Brian at his front gate. He'd married and lost his first wife, Trisha, to cancer. His second long-term partner was called Joyce, and was ten years his senior. She mothered Brian at the best of times. She was waiting for him in the open doorway, clutching at the front of her sweater with arthritic fingers. For a moment I envied the look of love Joyce and Brian exchanged as he slumped up the garden path towards her and she came outside to meet him. My Nell never showed that kind of affection towards me. Not since after we lost our teenage daughter, Rebecca, and there were only the two of us left behind in our family home. She said she didn't blame me for allowing Rebecca to travel through Europe without us chaperoning her, that it was not my fault that we weren't there to pull her from the lake when she'd got in trouble, and that I should not blame myself because she had drowned, but I didn't believe her.

Brian said something to Joyce, and they both turned to regard me.

I watched them through the car's open window.

'Do you want to come in?' Brian asked.

'No. I'd better get back; Nell will be wondering where I've got to.' Nell actually wouldn't have given my absence a second thought but I hadn't shared my marital problems with anyone else, not even with my best friend. I'm pretty certain that Brian knew that Nell and I were in trouble and not getting along, but rather than pry, he was the kind of friend to wait until I was ready to share my problems. Perhaps he thought now was the time.

'You sure, Andrew?'

'Yeah. I'm sure.' I gave them a little dismissive wave of my hand.

'We'll have to get together,' Brian said. 'Maybe wait until after the funeral, but you, me, Gav and Johnny should get together, do a bit of reminiscing, have a few laughs, y'know . . . down a few pints in Carl's memory.'

'Yeah,' I agreed, with no real enthusiasm. 'After the funeral. We should.'

Brian nodded, gave Joyce a hug, which she reciprocated, and then they turned and walked holding on to each other inside the house.

I drove away.

My car was pointed in the opposite direction to my home. I contemplated driving, just keeping on going, and not caring where I ended up, as long as it was far away from this horrible situation. My resolve lasted all of about fifteen seconds, and then I found the entrance to a cul-de-sac and I used it to perform a turn and headed back the way I'd just come. As I passed Brian and Joyce's house, their front door was resolutely shut: I pictured Brian, with his head on Joyce's lap, while she ran fingers through his hair, soothing him with softly crooned words. The other day, when Nell and I sat in the kitchen, foreheads touching, it was possibly the most intimate we'd acted in years, or maybe it was the prelude to a headbutt Nell was setting up. No, I had to stop finding vindictiveness in everything that Nell said or did. The loss of our old friend had upset her possibly more than she'd ever expected and it was in genuine need of comfort that she'd returned to me. While I'd blubbered about our Becky, she'd crouched, holding the back of my head, pressing our brows together, and I can't now recall how long it was before she'd disengaged and left me there in the kitchen. In the days that followed, she mainly kept her distance, and only spoke in a polite but perfunctory manner. I imagined that on my return I could forget the kind of welcome home extended to Brian by Joyce.

Finally able to block the awful images, I negotiated the streets and other traffic in a numb daze, with no recollection afterwards of taking turns or stopping for red lights. Brian had suggested a reunion with our other school pals, to which I'd distractedly agreed, but my enthusiasm hadn't grown since. At thirteen years old I'd have died for them – not necessarily given my life in sacrifice, but I'd fought bullies on their behalf and could easily have been beaten to death or bashed my skull open on the tarmac – but by the time we were sixteen we'd already started drifting apart as new friends and girls inserted themselves into our circle. Gavin stayed on at Sixth Form then went off to another town to attend college; Johnny got a job washing dishes at a motorway service station, on a rota of early shifts one week and late the next, and pretty soon the only time I saw him was if I randomly bumped into him in town. By the time I was nineteen, I'd met Nell, got her pregnant and we married when I hit twenty-one: after that neither Gavin nor Johnny were part of our social circle, though I understood that their friendships with Brian had endured a bit longer. In the intervening decades, I'd maybe been in the same room as Gavin a handful of times, Johnny even less. I knew them as boys, not as the adults they became, and who knew, maybe they felt I was practically a stranger to them now, as I did them?

I drew my car to a stop outside my house. I'd barely migrated beyond the same neighbourhood I'd grown up in. Instead of in the council housing estate – now run by a housing association – I'd purchased one of the larger private houses on what was a secondary route out of Carlisle that formed the estate's northern boundary. I could claim to live in a more affluent postcode, but was close enough to cling to my roots when nostalgia demanded. As the crow flew, I lived less than half a mile from where Carl was murdered. For no other reason than it was so close, I pushed the car into gear and pulled away from the kerb, again seeking somewhere to turn safely.

Part of the city was dominated by Victorian-era textile factories, most of them converted to executive apartments, student accommodation, or split into individual units housing small start-up businesses and established cottage industries. Several chimney stacks towered into the heavens, now capped and smokeless in this greener era. When those factories had been working at full throttle they had been serviced by the railway and also the canal and aqueducts that had survived modernization. For perhaps fifty years, the canal had died, become a dried-out bed, a receptacle of trash, burned out stolen cars and abandoned shopping trolleys. With the reclamation effort, the canals had been turned from their once functional industrial use, to recreational. Sections of the canal had been refilled, the paths and locks fixed and spruced up but, alas, no effort had been made to maintain the area after the economic crash of 2008, and it had slipped back towards neglect. With its cobblestone towpaths and leafy backdrop, the canal could still claim a certain amount of beauty, but only until you checked out the toxic water and found it mostly silted up and the domain of blue algae, pondweed, used condoms and discarded fast food wrappers.

I parked my car and walked to where I believed Carl's body was found. If ever the police had strung up crime scene tape, or a forensic tent, there was no sign they'd ever been there. The cobbles were damp underfoot, and rotting leaves made drifts. There were crushed drinks cans and broken glass in some openings: it surprised me because I thought the police would have hoovered up everything in search of the tiniest piece of DNA or other forensic evidence, but in hindsight the area was so contaminated that it would have been a useless exercise.

I walked, following the edge of the canal, and allowed my mind to wander wherever it ended up, feeling that perhaps I'd sense that old connection I'd had with my friend when we were kids. It was kind of stupid in hindsight, and I was lucky I didn't slip on the cobbles or stumble off the path into the canal because there were times when I walked in a fugue with my eyes closed. No sixth sense alerted me to where Carl's life ended. Instead, it was the relative cleanliness of the cobbles compared to everything else nearby that told me. There the crime scene investigators had swept and picked the place clean, even between the cobbles themselves. I'd pictured a gory death for Carl, and perhaps they'd washed the cobbles afterwards too, to rid them of blood.

I stood looking down at the ground.

Earlier, I couldn't get his face out of my mind, but then I couldn't picture my old friend, not as an adult. Instead, I saw him lying at my feet as a thirteen-year-old, skinny, with sticky out ears and a buzz cut, a nose as pointed as his chin and an Adam's apple that protruded like a karate master's knuckle under his skin. He lay sneering up at me.

'So much for wishing for eternal life,' I muttered down at his shade, and watched as his face morphed into a look of sorrow. 'You weren't as invulnerable as you hoped, eh, old friend?'

He, of course, didn't reply, only melted away, so that I was again only looking at recently swept cobblestones.

I turned to the canal. Across on the other side, the wilderness had crept back into the city. A woodland sprawled between the canal and still active railway lines. Under skeletal trees, bramble bushes dominated, and were recipients of wind-blown rubbish that hung like celebratory bunting on the thorny tendrils. Between the bushes were pale snatches of colour, some from the tents or sleeping bags of rough sleepers. I probably wasn't the first to wonder if Carl had been assaulted by one or more of the dangerous ne'er-do-wells mingling with the other homeless. If any of them had been responsible for murdering Carl, I thought they'd have hightailed it long before the police could begin rounding them up as suspects. Still, it gave me pause for thought. Maybe I shouldn't hang around there too long, in case I became a victim.

I turned and was about to return to my car.

Beside me the canal water gurgled.

There was no current apparent, no detectable flow whatsoever, so I couldn't fathom what had caused the sound.

Looking down, all I could see below the oily surface was a dense growth of weed that had been left to choke up the waterway. It would conceal most things smaller than a small car: had the police not dredged the canal for clues, or was it already clear to them who was responsible for beating Carl to death? Maybe they had a prime suspect and just weren't saying, so that they didn't spook them into fleeing before they could be apprehended.

I peered again into the unfathomable depths.

I stepped back.

It was as if a fist had formed in my gut, after grabbing my stomach between its fingers and squeezing.

Why I experienced such an onset of foreboding, I couldn't clearly say, but there was some kind of evil promise in the murky water that sent me scurrying to get back to the safety of my car.

I arrived back at it with a cold sweat on my brow and my guts still in a knot. Before clambering inside, I stood with one arm braced against the roof and vomited between my feet. Little came up; it couldn't from what felt like a constricted stomach, only stringy bile that burned my throat and gums. Once I'd purged as much as I could, I climbed shakily into my car and sat groaning as I clenched the steering wheel with both hands.

Some minutes passed before I'd regained enough control to drive safely. I turned the key in the ignition and the engine thrummed to life.

Also, the radio came on.

I don't recall having listened to the radio on my journey into town, but couldn't swear one way or the other, because at first I'd been too lost in memories and afterwards in a daze.

One thing I was certain of though was that the volume had not been turned up to the max before: Freddy Mercury belted out at ear-bleeding volume, demanding to know who wants to live forever.

Scrambling to turn down the radio, my hands felt as if they belonged to somebody else. Finally, with the question ringing inside my head, I sat in near silence again, stunned by what had just happened. I had never believed in portents, or in messages from the dead, but just then I could swear I'd been a recipient of both.

NINE

1988

I t was unusual for the entirety of Andy's school year to be gathered in the assembly hall, despite the echoing room's intended use. Normally an assembly would comprise a single form, but that day, it was as if the entire school had gathered there. The last time that Andy could recall being there with hundreds of other kids was when all the eleven- and twelve-year-old boys had been pulled together and shown a projected film about the birds and the bees. It had been a hilarious hour spent in assembly, where boyish ideas were dispelled, and the teachers in attendance stood with their cheeks red with embarrassment. The girls had attended a differently slanted presentation, and had left clutching little brown bags with a secret gift inside, one that the boys could only speculate about. Plus, there was that time approaching Christmas when a military band had come into school to entertain them with carols and some ancient big band music that Andy had found exhilarating but wouldn't admit to his friends; without exception his mates followed the pop trends, so presently they were into Bros, Rick Astley and Phil Collins rather than Glenn Miller.

On those previous visits to the assembly hall, the atmosphere had been different, more joyous and excitable, but that day Andy had followed a queue of sombre boys and girls inside and taken a seat without uttering a word. Chair legs still scraped softly, and coughs and sniffles sounded though they were subdued: it was almost as if the subject matter was common knowledge. Andy thought for a moment that somehow they were all in trouble, considering the two detectives standing with the headmistress, waiting to mount the stage. Already he had spotted other uniformed police constables in the school, which to be fair wasn't that unusual because dozens of his council estate peers could be badly behaved and the coppers often came into school to give them dressings down. Also, he had passed a trio of girls being ushered into the administration block by a teacher, all of them in floods of tears, and ashen white with shock. Maybe those girls were in most trouble and the rest of the year had been gathered to receive some sort of stern warning.

No. That couldn't be it. The teacher with those girls had been sympathetic, and had even taken one girl under her arm to almost carry her inside the office area. The detectives and uniformed coppers wore frowns and grimaces. Something bad had happened more like, and they'd all been brought together to hear the shocking news.

Andy bent forward in his seat, checking to both sides. Although they were mates, the five of them weren't all in the same form. Brian, Gavin and Carl were together in a different form, so had been seated with their class in another part of the hall. Johnny was in Andy's group for assembly – but attended different lessons on rota from him – so should be nearby. He spotted him about five seats up to his left. Johnny also sat craning forward, his hands grasping his knees as he peered back at Andy. Andy mouthed, 'What's going on?' and Johnny mouthed back, 'I haven't a clue.'

Andy looked for a hint in the two detectives standing beside the stage. They were in conversation with the headmistress, Mrs Hanford, but despite his attempts at lip-reading, Andy couldn't make out what was being said by either party. A boy in front of Andy turned to whisper to the next boy along and Andy heard him mention *murder*. Andy jabbed the boy's shoulder with his fingertips, drawing his attention.

'Did you say there's been a murder?' he asked.

'It's just what I heard on the local radio,' said the boy, and wiped his nose with the back of his wrist. 'Summat to do with a lass being found with her head bashed in.'

'No way,' said Andy. 'Who?'

'How should I know?'

'A lass from our school?'

'Aye. Why else d'you think the rozzers are here?'

A shudder rode over Andy. He sat open mouthed.

The boy was about to expound on what he'd heard but Mrs Hanford and the detectives were on the move. The headmistress clapped her hands swiftly, calling for order. Andy had been unaware that they weren't the only ones wondering what was going on: the volume had swollen to a babble. Immediately it cut off, the abrupt silence leaving Andy reeling a little.

A teacher, Mr Morris, appeared from over Andy's shoulder. His breath was rank with coffee and cigarettes when he snapped, 'Sit back and pay attention, boy.'

'Uh, yessir. Uh, I mean sorry, sir,' Andy blustered.

'You're holding up the whole school, Miller,' Mr Morris continued, which was a complete exaggeration but Andy knew not to answer back. Divvy Morris was quick on the draw and could chuck a blackboard eraser the length of a classroom and hit you square in the head. When unable to hurl his trusty missile he was equally heavy-handed when dishing out after-school detentions.

Andy sat upright, back rigid, and stayed that way until Mr Morris grunted and moved off to deal with another pupil he decided was causing a delay. His stinking odour hung in the air around Andy for several seconds afterwards. Andy finally grimaced and squinted to check where Morris had got to. He fanned a hand under his nose, even as he resettled his backside, which was still smarting from the beating his mother gave him the night before.

On the stage, Mrs Hanford coughed loudly, drawing everyone's attention. She wasn't the most effervescent of women at the best of times, but that day she looked extra sombre. Without any preamble, she said, 'Today is a very sad day for our school. Perhaps you have heard by now that something very awful happened last night, and we sadly lost a star student, a friend, a sister and, to her parents, a much-loved daughter. I cannot stress how upsetting it is to hear of the senseless attack on not one, but two of my pupils, by a person or persons unknown at this time. It was a devastating assault, which has left one girl fighting for her life and the other dead. Understandably several of you will be upset by the passing of your friend, and if you need to speak to somebody, designated teachers are ready to meet with you and listen to your concerns. Some of you might be frightened by what has happened, worried that it might happen again.' She glanced quickly at the detectives, ensuring she wasn't speaking out of turn. 'So, if you wish to talk your fears through, again your teachers will be available.'

Again, Andy had been unaware that the volume in the assembly hall was rising. Several girls had begun weeping, and one of them verged on hysterics. She was led, sobbing wildly and staggering from the hall. Other boys and girls threw around questions but any answer was pure conjecture. Andy again looked for Johnny, but his friend was obscured from sight by the other boys seated between them. He tried to hear what the boy in front had to say, but beyond hearing about a murder, he was clueless about who had died, and who was still fighting for their life. He looked again at the head-mistress, whose voice had never faltered. Andy had missed her last couple of statements. Ordinarily she wouldn't tolerate this amount of chatter during one of her infrequent assembly talks, but she'd allowed it due to the dire subject matter. On her behalf, Mr Morris and Miss Thompson, a grim-faced gym teacher, called for calm and silence. The hall quietened, but Andy was still aware of noisy gasping breaths, and it was seconds before he realized the sounds emanated from inside his own chest.

'School will be closed today. Any student that doesn't require counselling should go directly home, and hand your parents one of these notes.' Mrs Hanford wafted a pink slip of paper – obviously dozens of the notes had been prepared in advance of the assembly. 'It explains why school is temporarily closed. On it are handy tele-phone numbers should your parents require further information. I'll now hand you over to Inspector James, who wants to say a few words . . .'

Inspector James was a big man, dressed from head to foot in shades of grey, even his shoes. His hair was grey too. Andy thought the inspector made an ideal detective, or even better, a spy, because he looked as if he could blend in anywhere and would be very difficult to spot or separate from a crowd. His partner was a seriously skinny man with a huge chin and thinning hair. His height had obviously got him accepted into the police force because he stood well over six feet, almost a head taller than the inspector: it was surprising that he had made CID when he would definitely stand out in a crowd. Of course, Andy was under the assumption that CID work was all done clandestinely, sneaking around, rather than about gathering witnesses and evidence. The skeletal detective stood to one side, hands clasped over his groin, and stared, Andy thought, directly at him. Andy squirmed. Probably every boy within fifty feet of Andy thought they were the sole object of the detective's scrutiny.

Inspector James spoke with a smoker's rasp. He reassured everyone that they were safe from harm, that the police were following several leads and they hoped to capture the perpetrator of the assault within hours. However, he asked that, for the time being, they all returned directly home and stayed indoors unless it was absolutely necessary to be outside. He asked, but made it sound like an instruction, an *order*, that they stay well away from the riverbank, the woods, and the decommissioned railway lines on the northern side of the estate. He must have known that he'd have been better off waving a red rag and expecting a bull to slink away in the opposite direction.

Even if he hadn't openly named the victims, the inspector's request more or less told Andy who had been attacked, and which of the sisters, Melanie and Poppy, had died and after everyone filed out of the assembly hall, he sought out his friends, having already concluded their next move.

Seconds after arriving home and thrusting the pink slip into his uncaring mother's hand, Andy sped off, still clothed in his school uniform, to rendezvous again with Carl, Brian, Gavin and Johnny, their destination the frog ponds.

TEN

Before returning home to Nell, I drove from the canal to the entrance to a country lane, called a "lonning" locally, that we used to take to access the river and the adjacent frog ponds. I could drive the car no further, as the lonning had been absorbed into a recently erected housing scheme, and was closed to the public by a metal barrier. I sat there in my car, ruminating, casting back my thoughts to connect again with my younger incarnation.

In hindsight, I'd say that the murder of Melanie was the first time I – that is, young Andy – had any close experience of violent death. Before that I'd had elderly family members pass, but being so young I hadn't been included in the grieving or funeral processes, protected from them, I suppose, by my parents. I barely knew Mel, had mostly fancied her from afar, pretty much the same as my mates had. But having been in her close proximity the day earlier, having personally spoken with her – albeit she'd been on the defensive at the time and largely scorned me – I felt closer to her than I had to any of my elderly great aunts or uncles who'd died during my lifetime. Had she not been at the frog ponds at the same time as we were there, her death would have still come as a shock to me, but it wouldn't have had the same visceral effect as it did.

I don't know what we hoped to achieve by sneaking to the ponds, because it was highly doubtful that Melanie's body was still there, and beyond maybe spotting some crime scene investigator bloke – actually, back then they'd have been called a 'SOCO' or 'scenes of crime officer' – poking about for clues, there'd be nothing of interest to see. Carl and Brian hoped to spot something grisly, whereas the rest of us were more withdrawn. I felt sick to my stomach, and my extremities shivered continuously: I was probably experiencing an adrenaline dump. I wouldn't have turned back for anything though, because in my mind I had to return to the place of Melanie's murder to assure myself that it was true and not some wild dream I was stuck in.

Of course, on our walk there, we weren't as excitable as we had been the day before. We spoke low, almost in whispers, relating the few morbid details we'd each picked up from overhearing other conversations and there were long periods where we didn't communicate at all. The first buzz of activity occurred when we approached that part of the woods where we'd disturbed Ian Nixon in whatever madness he'd been up to, and almost anticipated him chasing after us with his hammer again.

I'd say it was in the back of our minds prior to that, but it was only as we'd approached the clearing he'd made under some overhanging boughs, that the idea fully coalesced that Nixon was probably the one to attack Melanie and Poppy, and I went along with the consensus: after all, he had the weapon, the anger and the madness to assault the girls. For a motive, what more did he require other than lust?

We crouched, peering under the branches into his den. Under a tarpaulin, he'd set up an old easy chair, cut a log to serve as a table, and had several bottles of who knew what stashed in a rusted metal box. Carl hadn't been too far wrong yesterday when assuming we'd come across where Nixon hid his collection of nudie books; he'd pinned pictures of topless models cut out of the papers and wrapped in cellophane to the trunks of several trees. At that time – thankfully, I suppose – Nixon wasn't there. We were still several hundred metres away from the field next to the frog ponds, but he had to have spotted the police activity in the area and made himself scarce.

'Can anyone see his hammer?' Brian had asked, kind of confirming that I wasn't the only one to finger Nixon for the crimes.

The blood drained from Johnny's features. He'd turned on us, eyes bulging, and started screeching at us that Ian was his cousin, and despite his odd behaviour he was incapable of such horrendous violence: that's my adult description of his response, when in truth it had been wilder, with lots of swearing, snot and flying spittle. Johnny's denial was somewhat expected, but of the rest of us, there wasn't one that had any doubts. The issue was what we must do about our suspicions.

Maintaining loyalty was very important to us in those days. Nobody wanted to be a grass, to be the person to run squealing to the coppers, but that was only when a crime was perceived as low level, like shoplifting a chocolate bar, or chucking a stone through a greenhouse window, not when it came to the really serious stuff like rape, child molestation or murder. Not that knowledge of any of those subjects had ever tested us before, but there wasn't much stopping us from fleeing directly to the nearest copper and blabbing on Nixon. Not much except for Johnny, that was. Johnny called us all the names under the sun the second we mentioned reporting our suspicions concerning his cousin. I know that, even to this day, three and a half decades later, Johnny's family still holds some resentment towards us for pointing the finger of blame at 'their Ian', but what else were we supposed to do?

It turned out that one fourteen-year-old girl had been struck unconscious by repeated blows of a blunt instrument to the back of her head; this was Poppy, who had to be placed into an induced coma in order to heal. The second teenaged girl, Melanie, endured a worse assault, where she was also beaten with a blunt instrument, but her attacker had grown more aggressive and switched to the claw end of his hammer after her dog, the elderly Golden Retriever, had tried unsuccessfully to save its mistress. The dog survived its beating, but poor Melanie had not. Few knew the extent of either girl's injuries at that time, only that Poppy was hospitalized while Melanie had perished. We agreed there was no way that we could allow Nixon to get away with hurting them so awfully. If we'd learned before then that Melanie had suffered post-mortem sexual assault, my friends might have hunted down Ian Nixon and stoned the bastard to death. Hell! Given the opportunity, I might have taken his weapon and buried its twin hooks in his twisted brain!

We almost turned back from the ponds after that, knowing fully that going to the scene of the crimes wouldn't help anyone except to appease the ghoulish fascination of a bunch of teenagers. But that fascination was too powerful to deny, so we left Nixon's den and re-joined the cinder path that took us to the stile and entered the open field. Ahead, the woods and five-bar gate were over the next rise in the landscape, so we couldn't tell how far the police had set up a cordon, or if it was still in place. I recall approaching the scene, walking on the balls of my feet and almost incapable of taking a breath. As the gate hove into view there was no sign of police or SOCO yet but there was a single figure hunched over, his forearms hanging over the uppermost bar as he peered down into the narrow valley left when they decommissioned the railway.

'Is that *him*?' Gavin croaked.

There could only be one person that Gavin referred to. I recall thinking it must be him, because didn't all murderers supposedly return to the scene to gloat, to taunt or to relive the thrill of their crime?

We must have struck up a racket, because the figure snapped a look at us, and then darted away, heading for the cover of the steep, wooded bank of the river that paralleled the frog ponds. There he could easily lose himself in the woods, or even wade across the wide but shallow river at that point. He didn't have to do either, because we turned and fled back the way we'd just come, certain that the murderer was on our heels and our brains were about to be bashed in.

The lonning I was now parked at used to be a thoroughfare between the estate and a railway marshalling yard, and the ground adjacent to the river had been dominated by warehouses and engine sheds: they'd all been decommissioned along with the railway, and had been demolished in the following years: mostly the rubble had been left where it fell, and was an eyesore and danger to the local community, but an adventure park to their children throughout the 1970s and 1980s. I remembered that we took a break, seated on a sloping slab of concrete from which bent rebar protruded at its edges. Brian had tapped out a drum rhythm on one of the longer bits of metal, causing it to thrum: the sound seemed to synchronize with my heartbeat and soothed me. By comparison it annoyed Carl and he batted at Brian, although Brian just took the weak slaps in his stride. Gavin looked as if he was about to throw up, and Johnny couldn't sit still and kept on rolling on his back and extending his legs in the air, while moaning loudly. I felt sorry for Johnny, because his loyalty to his family was being tested by his loyalty to his best mates.

Not for the first time, Gavin had opined, 'We have to tell someone.'

Without rising from his back, Johnny croaked: 'That's all right for you to say, Gav, but my dad's gonna go spare with me. Ian's his brother's son, my dad's nephew, *my cousin*! I don't know about yours, but my family doesn't squeal to the pigs about their own.'

'Yeah, mine don't either, Johnny,' Gavin agreed, 'not usually, but then again we don't have nutters and murderers in my family.'

Johnny didn't answer, just swiped blindly with an arm that missed Gavin by a mile.

'I always knew there was something wrong with him,' Carl had said. 'You only have to look at the divvy to know he has a few screws loose and is a nasty big bastard.'

Yeah, I thought but didn't dare say out loud, *we could say the same about you Carl, except you aren't big, just a nasty little weasel.*

'Wouldn't surprise me if he's done something like this before,' Brian said without dropping a beat on the rebar.

'Yeah,' Carl agreed. 'His den looks like it's been there for ages; he's probably lured little girls there before and touched them up.'

'Fuckin' nonce,' Brian called Ian.

'Kiddie fiddler,' Carl added.

We had no evidence to say that Ian was responsible for touching any little girls, because we had no idea that the post-mortem sexual assault on Melanie had occurred until later on, but that didn't stop us from surmising. In four of our minds, Ian had already been judged guilty of the foulest of deeds possible, and even Johnny was beginning to come around to the idea that his paedo cousin didn't deserve his silence.

'What are we gonna do?' I wondered aloud.

'We have to tell the rozzers,' Brian said.

'Are we going to the cop shop then, or should we just flag down the next bobby we see?' asked Gavin.

'Maybe we should do an anonymous phone call,' Johnny suggested, and I understand now that it was because he could later claim to have had no part of squealing on his cousin if challenged by his dad or uncle.

'You got any dosh for the phone box?' Carl demanded.

'No.'

'Didn't think so.'

'We don't need cash to make an emergency call,' I reminded them.

Brian shook his head. 'Yeah, but by the time we tell them everythin' they'll probably send a black maria to the telephone box and nab us. Do you want them grabbing us and taking us to the nick?'

'There's no other way around it,' I said. 'We can't just send an anonymous tip to the police and expect them to go and grab Nixon. We all have to stick together and tell them individually what we saw yesterday or they aren't going to believe us.'

'Do I have to tell on him?' Johnny groaned and finally sat up. His eyes were glossy with unshed tears.

'You'd only be saying what you personally witnessed,' I pointed out, 'not saying that you'd seen Ian attacking Mel and Poppy. It's down to the police to prove he hurt them, because you won't be saying that, only that you saw him with a hammer near to where the murder took place. Surely your dad won't be annoyed with you because of that?'

'You obviously don't know my dad.'

Carl sneered. 'If he's half as nuts as your cousin, you've got a bloody right to be worried.'

As per usual, Carl was taking a cruel dig at an easy target, but judging by the crestfallen look on Johnny's face, he had hit a genuine nerve. Back then, in the late eighties, there was already a wind of change blowing, and it was less likely for teachers, or for parents, to resort to corporal punishments, as they had in previous eras, but there were still some neanderthals dotted in among the gentler new romantics and gender benders whose first recourse was to rely on their fists to pound home a message. My father never lifted a hand to me, not then, not before, but my mother could be quick on the draw with a slipper or spatula when she deemed me in need of a lasting lesson, which was quite often, and woe betide me if her tongue protruded from the corner of her mouth because that signified I was in real trouble; perhaps poor Johnny was the recipient of similar lesson reminders from his old man.

I'd rested a hand on Johnny's shoulder and squeezed reassuringly. Like I had, he'd come straight from school so was wearing his nylon blazer, pullover, shirt and tie, and was sopping with sweat. It wasn't as blazing hot as it had been the previous day but he wasn't the only person to swelter in full school uniform: it's funny how I can recall the tiniest of details now, such as the beads of perspiration that clung to my forehead and shivered on my eyelashes, but I can't remember what exactly we argued to bring Johnny around, but shortly after we vacated the demolition site, he followed us without any further resistance to the nearest telephone box.

The phone booth, the quintessential red metal and glass box, had been located less than fifty metres from where I'd parked my car in the present. It had long ago been removed, no longer a feature in an age of smartphones and instant messaging, yet I still pictured our small group shuffling towards its ghost, with Carl and Brian tussling for the right to be the one to make the 999 call to the police. I saw my friends as a bunch of insubstantial shadows, dim recollections of the distant past, and yet I could clearly picture young Andy, who actually reached the box first and dragged open the heavy door. As he stepped inside, I could instantly recall the acrid stench of urine and damp cardboard that all the telephone boxes seemed to smell like on our estate, and those smells set off explosions of other recollections in my mind.

ELEVEN

A sound dragged me back to the present, my memories evaporating like morning mist under the sun's rays. I sat for a few seconds, wondering what I was hearing, and couldn't tell exactly. It was almost a rhythmic thrum, the way in which Brian had set up a beat on that exposed rebar all those years ago, and I looked all around expecting to find somebody standing alongside the car and drumming their fingertips on the roof.

I couldn't see a living soul.

I glanced at both wing mirrors, then rose up in my seat to get a better angle to check that nobody was crouching down by either rear wheel. The rhythm was broken by a long, drawn-out screech.

Snapping out of my seatbelt, I scrabbled at the handle to throw open the door. Before I could pop the lock, the screech curtailed, but I still fought out of my seat and pushed to my feet. I turned, expecting to find a surly crow or beady-eyed seagull or some other hooligan of a bird-species on the roof but it was bare. There were some dots of white faeces, but they were dry and not something deposited in the last few seconds. Another screech sounded, and I could swear that something metallic was being dragged across the paintwork on the far side. Shouting wordlessly, I charged around my car, ready to kick or punch or whatever else it took to protect my property.

I stumbled to a halt.

There was nothing there.

No animal with talons. No malicious little kid with a set of keys. Not even a piece of loose wire or debris that might have been pushed against the side by the breeze.

'What the bloody hell's going on?' I asked the ether.

Nobody answered.

But from the driver's side the screeching returned . . .

I hurtled around the bonnet, again fully expecting to discover the vandal, but again there was nothing there. Yet the screech continued, and for a second my pulse slowed a little, thinking that the sound must, of course, be a mechanical fault of the vehicle itself. But no!

What could it be? The car had been parked, the engine turned off, for a good length of time by now: these sounds weren't natural settling sounds of a cooling engine or slowing fan. As I bent forward, frowning deeply, I could almost trace the origin of the sound and it was definitely from the exterior shell of the vehicle. I followed the noise, mind rebelling in disbelief, as the screech tracked over the rubber seal and on to the glass of the rear driver's side window. For the briefest time, I'd swear that I watched an invisible talon scratch across the glass, before I lunged, crying out, and fumbled to grasp whatever taunted me. My hand slapped the glass and nothing else. I stepped away, staring, listening, gasping, and there, reflected in the glass was . . . some*thing*.

I can't describe what I saw very well. It was a glimpse of move-ment, of something stick-thin, with a wild mane of weeds that appeared to writhe as if with life, and then it was gone and I saw only the reflected clouds and the thin branches of a nearby tree. So fast was the glimpse that it had barely registered, before the stick figure had disappeared, and in the next instant my logical mind convinced me that I'd only spotted the movement of the tree and fitted the image to what I expected to see. OK, I could accept that, but the bloody reflection of branches was not capable of making screeching sounds on the car's paintwork!

I scrambled to get back inside, and I hit the central locking button. Starting the engine, I reversed the car out of the dead end and spun it in a tight crescent to face the exit on to the main road. During rush hours, the traffic could stand nose to tail on that road out of town, and during the rest of the day the movement of traffic was almost constant. I was lucky not to crash when I ignored the give way signs and sped directly out onto the road. I'd avoided going home before, but after that weird occurrence there was nowhere else I'd rather be. I broke several speed limits and regulations before I again pulled up outside my house on the boundary road on the opposite side of the estate. Still bewildered, ashen faced and feeling as if my bowel was about to empty into my trousers, I abandoned the car at the kerb and rushed indoors.

Inside, I threw the door shut, and then my body against it.

Nell wasn't home.

Unsurprising.

I had not expected a welcome home the way Brian had received one from Joyce, but right then even Nell's presence in the house would have helped me dispel the uncanny sense that something had pursued me all the way across the housing estate and rushed up behind me directly to our front door. As I held the door shut, I could almost imagine that stick thing on the other side, leaning forward, its Medusa-like hair snaking against the door, its eyes peering, trying to discern me through the security peephole. I avoided checking that it wasn't peeping back, for fear of finding my fears were true. I waited, anticipating the screeching to begin again, or the thrum of its fingertips beating a rhythm on the PVC door, but all I heard was my own ragged breaths, and strange tiny animalistic sounds that shamed me.

Stepping back from the door, I fisted my hands by my sides.

'If you're there,' I said, 'you can fuck off and leave me alone.'

It was a pathetic announcement, and if my cowardice hadn't totally embarrassed me before, it did now. With nobody around to see my beetroot face, I turned and headed for the stairs and went upstairs at a run and hid for a while in the bathroom with the door bolted.

When Nell returned, I allowed her to get settled before emerging. I flushed the toilet, though I'd seen to my bodily functions a while ago, so she wouldn't know how long I'd spent in the bathroom. Going downstairs, I announced myself, and heard her respond from the kitchen.

'Oh! You're back,' she said by way of greeting.

'Yeah, sorry if I took a while,' I said, 'but I'd rather a lot on my mind and I needed some thinking space.'

She shrugged off my half-hearted apology. She held out the mop she'd dug out of the adjoining utility room.

I took it from her before asking what she expected from me.

'You made the mess,' she said, 'so you can clean it up.'

'What mess?'

She raised her eyebrows in silent question.

'I genuinely don't have a clue what you mean,' I told her.

She snorted dismissively and crooked a finger for me to follow. I dutifully fell in behind her.

She led me to the front door, and I still had no idea what mess she was referring to.

Until she opened the door and I saw it.

The door's normally white uPVC was streaked with thick clods of mud and weeds. Somebody – some*thing* – had drawn filthy hands up and down the door and on the front stoop had left a dirty puddle. It had begun to dry, but there was still enough of it wet enough for me to catch a waft of odour. It stank like a swamp, or maybe the filth churned up from the bed of an unused canal.

'What is this?' I croaked.

'Your mess,' she reiterated.

I shook my head. 'No, Nell. This has nothing to do with . . . '

She walked away, heading along the path to the gate. Even as I fell in again behind her, I could see the drying footprints, faded now, but still obviously having been made by whomever had drawn their dirty hands all over the front door. At the gate, Nell stopped and crossed her arms under her chest. Once more, she appraised me with arched eyebrows, waiting for an explanation.

I had none for her.

My car was where I'd left it at the kerb, but now there were dirty handprints on the driver's door and the roof. There was muck on the driver's window, both outside and in, and when I checked inside it was on the steering wheel and seat too.

I stepped back, my mouth hanging open. I still held on to the mop as if it was some kind of weapon I could use to fight off whatever insanity I was involved in.

'Come on, Nell . . . what's going on? Is this some kind of joke or what?'

'A joke, Andrew? Really? That's all you've got to say? I don't know what you think it is, but it isn't very funny.'

I shook my head. 'It wasn't like this when I parked it.'

'Wasn't it?' Again her eyebrows arched, but this time she pursed her lips and gave a sidelong tilt of her head. I followed her gaze, looked down at myself and the shock was almost as physical as a sharp knee to the testicles. From mid-shin, my trousers were sopping wet, my socks were baggy with moisture and my shoes were plastered in foul-smelling mud.

TWELVE

Gavin Hill

Gavin spied the old shop that used to be the best fish and chip shop in the city. The owners were Italians, Mr and Mrs Giovannini, and they deep fried delicious but affordable food, and they used to have a fountain that served milkshakes long before they were a popular staple at the big name fast-food outlets, or hot Vimto if you preferred. Their shop closed in the mid-1980s, and was put to diverse uses over the intervening decades. Now it was an outlet for e-cigarettes and vaping products. As Gavin drove past he could swear he could smell the lingering odour of frying fish, but it must surely only be in his head. He pictured himself along with his little gang of friends all huddled at the front, reading the handwritten menu board in the window and deciding what delights they could purchase with the few coins they'd managed to scrape together. A favourite had always been 'tattie scones' – a slice of par-boiled potato deep fried in batter – or if they'd enough between them a sharing portion of chips and scrapings – the rogue bubbles of batter lifted out of the searing oil – wrapped in newspaper. Back then, Brian had been the one with the money, but it was because he was a working lad, helping the milkman with his deliveries around their estate, so he always got dibs when it came to finishing off the scrapings adhered to the greaseproof paper. Brian was often up before the crack of dawn, and often out 'dossing around' with his mates until close to midnight, but a lack of sleep didn't seem to slow him down. Not then, things might be different these days.

Aye, we've all got older, and slower, Gavin thought as he caught sight of himself in the rearview mirror. He wore gold-rimmed glasses, from behind which extended crows' feet all the way to his hairline. His hair had been allowed to grow shaggy and voluminous, and he'd partially pulled it back in a tail at the nape of his neck. His moustache and beard were cultured – once upon a time he'd have been called a Beatnik, now he'd be classed as a hipster – and unbeknown even to his closest friends he dyed them to conceal the white hairs from creeping in. Loose skin hung like a lizard's wattle beneath his chin.

The car bumped over a sleeping policeman, bringing his attention back to the road. He had forgotten about the traffic calming measures erected to slow down the car thieves that once plagued the estate, but only served to damage the suspension of careful drivers' vehicles. Everyone knew that car thieves enjoyed the thrill of bouncing over the speed bumps, considering they were on a joyride that usually ended with them torching the car. Back in the eighties, most people were lucky if they owned one car per household, now it was as if every man and his dog had a car parked at the roadside. He couldn't see any pedestrians whatsoever.

The road took a shallow bend, then went steeply downhill. Gavin permitted the car to coast along, gathering a little gravity-assisted speed. The sleeping policemen were staggered on the hill, and Gavin allowed the car to slew first one way then the next so that only one side of the vehicle was elevated at a time, and enabled it to keep moving. Briefly he wondered at the thrill those ne'er-do-wells felt when ramping stolen cars off the tops of the speed bumps, and he was tempted to hit the next one full on.

A woman stepped from between two parked cars.

Gavin cried out, and stamped on the brake.

The car continued moving, rubber juddering for traction on the shiny tarmac.

The woman faced him, her hair forming a reflective halo around her head, casting her features in shadow. He could see the whites of her eyes and the glistening of saliva on her tongue and teeth as her mouth opened in . . . no, not fear, but an exclamation of anger.

Gavin rocked forward in the seat, forcing his foot down, hands gripping the steering wheel. Finally, the car screeched to a halt, and not a half-second too soon. The woman still faced the car, almost in challenge, with its bonnet pressed against her upper thighs. She slammed down both palms, the heels first, and it was as if someone had struck the car with twin cricket bats. The car rocked on its chassis, front to back, and as she craned forward she glared unadulterated murder at him.

'Oh, God!' Gavin spluttered. 'I'm so, so sorry. Are you all right . . . are you hurt?'

She didn't reply directly. She craned an extra few inches, and her twisted visage came into full relief. Her lips writhed at first, then they slithered almost closed: there was something uncanny about the way her words slid out in a liquid whisper, yet they resonated inside his skull. '*I hear you've been very bad.*'

'What. No. It was an accident. I didn't see you till . . . uh,' he stammered to a halt.

The woman had drawn back from the car, almost as if she'd lost all interest in him. For a second he thought . . .

'Hey, wait. Don't I know you? You're . . .'

He slapped a hand down on his seatbelt clip, trying to unhitch it, and his eyes were off her for no more than the length between two heartbeats. As he pulled out of his belt and tried to exit the car, she had disappeared.

He scrambled out, believing her obscured behind the cars parked opposite. Even outside the car, he couldn't spot her. He darted across between two parked cars, and checked the pavement on the far side. No sign of her.

She can't have returned to the other side of the road, surely? He had to check before he'd be satisfied. He jogged across the road, and again looked for her on the pavement beyond the parked vehicles.

Where could she be?

Thinking logically, she could have perhaps gone inside one of the houses on the street and closed the door, except his eyes were literally off her for a second, no more, so he couldn't fathom how she could have moved so rapidly.

He threw up his hands.

At least he could be confident that she was unhurt, and he wouldn't have the police knocking on his door later to arrest him for a hit and run accident. Even if they did come, he could argue he wasn't the one to flee the scene, but the victim. Except, wait! She wasn't the victim because he hadn't hit her at all; she was the one to strike his car. He should have her charged with criminal damage.

With that thought he went to the front of his car to assess the damage caused. Astoundingly two delves formed impact craters in the metal. From the central points of the delves the paintwork was crackled and longer cracks radiated outward. But that was not all. The woman must have been digging in soil or mud seconds before he almost ran into her, because she'd left behind twin filthy hand-prints on the paintwork.

THIRTEEN

One thing I was certain of: the mud can't have manifested out of my memories for me to daub all over the place. In the following days I turned the mystery over in my mind, trying to come up with a logical conclusion and in the end I managed to convince myself that I must have got muddy when I was down by the canal, inspecting the scene of Carl's murder. I'd been spooked – not literally, I argued – and fled back to the car, got shaken a second time by the tune that blasted from the radio, and drove to the lonning. Without noticing, I must've already had the mud on me, and managed to get it inside and out when seeking whatever the hell had made the thrumming and screeching noises. Back home again I'd practically abandoned my car in the road, in a hurry to get inside, and on the front step I must have shed the dirt without noticing, and wiped smears on the door while distracted and fumbling to unlock the door.

It was a feasible explanation.

It was also complete and utter nonsense, but what was the alternative?

I'd spent time in the bathroom. Without painting the most lurid of images, I'd sat on the loo with my trousers round my ankles. I know for a fact they hadn't been wet or muddy, and neither had my shoes been filthy, because they hadn't left a single mark on our fluffy white pedestal rug or laminated floor. In a daze, I hadn't gone about cleaning the bathroom, made it spick and span to my wife's exacting standards without cleaning myself up first. When I asked Nell if she'd noticed the muck on me when she first saw me enter the kitchen she'd just written off my question as if it was obvious. Yeah, I must have been dirty. I'm convinced that if she'd seen me treading more dirt through the house she'd have had me standing in my boxers and bare feet right there in the kitchen and my filthy clothes would have gone into the washing machine. She wouldn't have had me follow her to the front door and deposit more crap on the hall carpet.

Anyway, a bucket full of soapy water and the mop did the trick, and my clothing got tossed in the washing machine, and that was the end of it.

The passing of a few days blunted my fascination with the incident. Besides, Nell had already made up her mind that I was the culprit, and was simply redirecting from Carl's murder as a coping mechanism against grief. Maybe she was right. She refused to discuss the mystery any further, she'd solved it according to her, and I'd nobody else to talk with so the weird incident was put to rest, alongside the other strange and disturbing things that had led up to it.

With Carl's death obviously being subjected to a criminal investigation, there was no early release of his body for burial. After initially hearing about his murder, I'd asked for a few days off work from my administrative job and been granted them on compassionate grounds, but my employer, Norman Heatley, hadn't given me carte blanche to take off weeks on end. I returned to work at his Business-2-Business sales company, selling consumables such as office supplies and equipment and employee workwear. The mundanity of it actually helped to further shove the weird stuff to the back of my thoughts. Within a week, if anyone had asked about any of it, I would've chuckled at the absurdity.

Things were different the evening after, following Brian turning up unexpectedly at my front door. He'd walked across the estate in a light drizzle. When I answered the door his hair was wet and flattened to his brow, and the shoulders of his jacket were soaked through. He was unshaven, some of the hairs white on his chin, and he had bags under his eyes that could have held a weekly shop from one of the less expensive supermarkets. His trainers squelched as he shifted awkwardly under my scrutiny. Also, he smelled. Not so much unwashed, but there was an unpleasant odour hanging over him that instantly threw back my mind to the week before when last I'd lingered in that doorway. I checked him for mud or duckweed, but thankfully there was none.

'Am I intruding?' Brian ventured.

'What? Eh, no. Course not, pal, you're always welcome here.'

'Is Nell home?'

I instinctively looked over my shoulder. Nell was out, in town, meeting with her older sister for coffee, cake and, no doubt, a good old moan about my shortcomings as a husband. His words made me wonder if she'd turned him away in the past, the way she'd instructed me to turn away Carl on a few occasions.

'Are you here for me or for Nell?' I wondered.

'You,' he confirmed. 'It's just what I've got to ask you, well, I don't think that Nell would understand.'

'If you've come for a loan of money you've come to the wrong place.'

I said it as a joke, but Brian's eyelids flickered and he dipped his chin into his collar. I worried I'd hit a sore nerve.

'It's not about money.'

I didn't reply. Only waited.

He looked up again, his mouth pursed tightly.

I looked back.

'You gonna ask me inside or not?' he said

It struck me that I had held him at the threshold too long. I said, 'As long as you're not a vampire that needs an express invitation to enter.'

Again, I was joking, hoping to lighten things with levity, but my words went right over the top of his head. This was once the boy whose favourite movie had been *Fright Night*, from which he'd quoted incessantly to a point where I could have recited the entire script myself.

As he moved past me, I again caught the smell of standing water off him: considering he was soaked through to his bones by now I suppose it was hardly surprising. I closed the door and moved down the hall after him. Unbidden, Brian made for the kitchen and sat at the breakfast counter. He knew me so well, and my addiction to strong coffee. I had a half jug in my coffee machine. I poured us both a mug and Brian helped himself to sugar, spooning in five heaped spoonfuls. 'Hasn't Joyce warned you about diabetes?' I only half-joked that time.

'She isn't speaking with me.'

'What? No way. I thought the two of you were all loved up.' I entwined my index and middle fingers in a demonstration of how tightly I perceived their relationship. In reply, he held up his same two fingers and gave me 'the vees', eliciting a grunt of laughter from me.

'We fell out a few days ago,' he admitted, 'and she'll barely look at me, let alone listen to anything I've got to say.'

'Bloody hell, Bri, welcome to my world. I've got one just like that.'

'You and Nell are going through a bad patch?'

'I thought that you'd sussed that out already,' I said.

He grimaced. 'Yeah, well, Joyce did mention it . . . before she stopped speaking with me, that is.'

'We're not on the verge of divorce or anything,' I said. 'Things have just been kind of strained since we lost our Becky. I'm unsure if Nell blames me for what happened but, well, I do. I can barely look her in the face without being overcome with guilt and . . .' I shut up, waving off my problems. Brian had obviously come seeking help with his, so I shouldn't be piling my burden on to his wet shoulders.

'All this crap with Carl must've dredged things up again?' he wondered. He couldn't have known how inappropriate his words were, not when rescuers had used ropes and grappling hooks in order to snag and then draw Becky's lifeless body from the bottom of an Austrian lake. She was only seventeen, and it was Becky's first time holidaying without her parents. Nell had been against allowing her to travel through Europe with her college friends, but this was just prior to the UK leaving the European Union, so possibly her last opportunity to do so freely. I'd argued that what was the worst that could happen, gave Becky the warnings about unwanted pregnancy and the dangers of too much alcohol, and gave her my blessings to travel. She'd drowned in a lake in the Austrian Alps, and we learned we'd lost our beloved only child when some intuition had Nell telephone Becky and one of her failed rescuers answered the call.

Whenever I think about my daughter these days, it is always with deep melancholy, and not a little shame. It's every parent's nightmare to lose a child; losing one to an illness is terrible enough but out of their hands, when the child dies through a totally avoidable accident . . .

I hid my frown from Brian while dragging over a stool and sitting so that we were diagonally opposite at the breakfast counter.

'What's troubling Joyce?' I asked, prompting Brian to change the subject back to him.

'I've been seeing a woman.'

I jerked upright.

Brian grunted. 'Huh! I should be so lucky. No, it isn't like it sounds. I mean, I keep on spotting this woman lurking, as if she's stalking me or something, but when I look directly at her she has disappeared or it's an entirely different person.'

'So why's Joyce upset at you?'

He pushed the damp hair back off his forehead as he thought how best to explain. 'I've seen this woman off and on for weeks now, when I'm awake and even when asleep. I've dreamed about her, and apparently the other night the dream turned a bit' – again he shoved back his hair – 'well, let's just call it a bit mucky, eh?'

'Mucky like?'

'You know, Andrew. You don't need me to spell it out.'

'Jeez, Bri. Fellas our age tend to be past having wet dreams.'

'It's the first I've had in about twenty years. Fuckin' problem was it was when Joyce was still awake and she saw and heard everything.' He grunted once more in embarrassment: despite men being encouraged to discuss their personal problems more, it still wasn't easy for us to talk through stuff like this without chagrin. 'She wasn't mad because I, well, you know . . . she was mad that I called out another woman's name as it happened.'

'Ha! No wonder she's giving you the cold shoulder. Whose name was it . . . wait, not your first wife's name?'

'It wouldn't have been as bad if it had been Trisha. I've never hidden anything from Joyce when it comes to Trisha. She knows that I loved her, love her still to be honest, and if she hadn't died I would still be with her today.'

'You may think she's OK with it, but you don't know what's really going through her head,' I tried.

Brian shook his head, a little angry with me for challenging his take on his relationships. 'Nah, Andrew. I love Joyce, too, just in a different way to what I did with my first wife.'

I knew it was time to keep my mouth shut and let my friend take the reins. Picking up my mug I downed half the steaming brew. I looked wide-eyed over the brim at him, encouraging him to continue.

'It feels a bit weird admitting who I was dreaming about,' he said, and again pawed at his wet hair: it stood up now like a cockatoo's crest.

'Tell me it wasn't Joyce's younger sister,' I taunted.

'No.' He grunted, and a tiny smile crossed his mouth before disappearing. I wondered if indeed he'd entertained fantasies about sleeping with Joyce's prettier, younger sister in the past. 'Worse than that in a way. I blame what happened with Carl and reminding me about the hammer attack Ian Nixon made on those two girls.'

'Hang on, Bri. You've been dreaming about Melanie?'

He grimaced and twin spots of colour bloomed in his cheeks. He shrugged. 'Before you accuse me of being a complete perv, she isn't a teenager in my dreams. She's a fully grown woman, probably our age, still beautiful, and doesn't even look much like she did back then. The strangest thing is, I knew who she was, even though she has never given her name.'

'Our brains do funny things,' I said, and almost blurted out how my memories had been screwing with my waking hours, never mind while I've been asleep.

'Aye. You don't expect it to punish you for your past, though,' he said.

'What do you mean, "punish you"?'

'Well, as if my missus falling out with me isn't bad enough, within seconds of doing the deed, the dreams change from pleasurable to nightmarish. As soon as we finish, Melanie *changes*. She goes from being an attractive middle-aged woman to a crone. No, it's worse than a crone, or hag. She turns into this horrible creature that only vaguely resembles a woman, like she's made out of rotting sticks and slimy weeds and shit. Y'know, like her parts have been dragged up from the bottom of a lake and assembled into a humanoid shape.'

Oh, I could picture that horror, all right.

How could I tell him that I'd possibly seen the very same creature reflected in the window of my car, and that it had followed me home to scratch at the front door to get inside? If I admitted to it, then I'd also be forced to admit I was going crazy. No, we'd both be forced into admitting that we must have had our screws loosened by the murder of our childhood friend. How else could we both be seeing the same hallucination unless it was a case of mass hysteria?

'You are probably right about Carl's murder bringing it all back to the fore about Melanie. Before this, when was the last time you thought about her?'

Brian shook his head. 'I can't say I've given her murder much thought since we were teenagers,' he admitted.

'Me neither. So, yeah, I'd guess a psychiatrist might say we are imagining her while trying to process what happened to Carl.'

Brian glanced sharply at me. 'You're also dreaming about her?'

'No,' I lied, because, if the truth were told, then I probably had subconsciously apportioned the strange stick creature to my memory of the murdered girl. 'But I've had several weird and uncomfortable dreams since hearing about Carl.'

'Good. For a second there I was afraid that bloody Freddy Krueger was playing games with us and collectively getting in our heads.' Brian laughed, to show how absurd the notion was. Personally, I couldn't find any humour in the idea, even feared that there might be some truth in a collective invasion of our thoughts, so I could only raise a strained smile.

'Forget about Freddy. This isn't only about dreams,' I pointed out. 'You said you'd seen the same woman when you were out and about, but when you looked directly at her she disappeared?'

'When I think about it, I can't really have seen her, only somebody vaguely similar.'

'That's what I think too.'

'The few times I thought I was being watched, and looked, there was maybe a blonde in the crowd. Maybe that was all it took for me to think about Melanie, what with her being in my dreams lately.'

'That's probably it,' I agreed.

'The strangest thing is that I thought I saw her before I started dreaming about her.'

'Sounds like a self-propagating problem,' I said. 'Like the chicken and egg. You saw somebody for real who reminded you somehow of Melanie, and you used her image to populate your dreams. Once you'd subconsciously used her face for Melanie's, it was the one that you expected to see when looking for a stalker . . . or sexual partner when it came to your erotic dream.'

'Hark at Clement Freud,' he grunted.

'I think you mean Sigmund?'

'Nah, definitely Clement. You remember the bloke that looked like his bloodhound dog, Henry?'

This time I couldn't help laughing; it burst from me in a guffaw. This was the Brian Petrie I knew and had loved as much as a brother when we were youngsters. We exchanged further good-natured insults, and it helped raise the gloom we'd been under. When Nell finally returned home, it was to a house filled with our laughter.

FOURTEEN

An inquest would be held later, but with the post-mortem completed, the coroner released Carl Butler's body so that funeral arrangements could be made. His cremation service was a low-key affair, a little over a fortnight after he was killed. Perhaps it was indicative of his surly nature that he had few friends, and even most of his family members stayed away. His parents attended the service, albeit with dry eyes and an impatience to be elsewhere. Carl had younger brothers, three of them, but only one turned up to pay his respects. I recalled Little Ricky from when we were kids, but I'd already been a teenager when he was still a toddler, so he was practically a stranger to me then let alone now. He scowled a lot, and sniffed but not through grief, more from habit. I could see Carl in Ricky's thin features and build, and decided he was probably another aggressive little bully with a small man's chip on his shoulder. I kept clear of him and his wife and the twin ferret-faced girls who were obviously theirs. Both of Carl's ex-wives had shown up, and were seated shoulder-to-shoulder, and they appeared friendlier towards each other than they'd been with Carl towards the end of their respective relationships. A bunch of Carl's workmates had turned up from the tyre factory, but I got the impression they'd attended Carl's service as an excuse to take the rest of the afternoon off work, than through any affection towards the dearly departed.

The family took up the front row, while Carl's workmates had filled a couple of the empty chairs on the same row and most of the next. I was seated two rows back, next to Nell. Joyce sat beside my wife, reconciled for the time being with Brian, and Johnny and Gavin and their partners completed the row. I hadn't met either of my school friends' partners before, and didn't know if they were wives, girlfriends, common law spouses, life partners, temporary hook-ups, or simply friends with benefits, the choices seemed so many to me these days. Behind us, the seating area was mostly empty, but for random people seated here and there, of which I thought a couple might've been familiar enough to have been other school pals, but not ones from our immediate circle. Distractedly,

I wondered if one of those strangers behind us was an undercover detective on the lookout for Carl's murderer turning up to gloat. I began turning none-too-discreetly around and weighing up the mourners, trying to spot a policeman, or a killer. All I deduced was that Carl didn't warrant interest from either parties, and got an elbow in my side for my trouble. Nell handed me a tiny leaflet detailing the order of service. On the front was a grainy photocopied image of Carl. It was the same image used of him on most of the websites I'd visited the day I'd first learned of his passing. Inside, I saw that the order was short and to the point. Carl wasn't religious, and certainly didn't enjoy hymns. A celebrant officiated, and Ricky was there to offer a eulogy to his big brother, then Carl was going to be played out to music while the curtains closed around his coffin. There was no mention of a wake, or even a suggestion that the parents would like the mourners to join them for a drink in his memory afterwards. It suited me, because the last thing I wanted was to spend time with people that barely cared that their eldest son had been brutally slain, any more than I wished to trade untrue pleasantries about a man we all knew could be *unpleasant*.

As promised the service was short. The funeral celebrant was a rosy-faced woman in her fifties, who made the best of the scant details she'd been given about Carl. Giving way at the lectern to Ricky, she stood with her hands folded at her tummy, and smiled encouragingly at each of the lame anecdotes he delivered in a voice unused to public speaking. Some words were then read by the celebrant, and I didn't catch whose words they were, but took them to be something standard read at funerals. Then it was time, and finally I allowed my gaze to be drawn to the coffin on the catafalque to our left: I'd purposefully avoided looking at it since taking the briefest glance before getting seated. Suddenly the enormity of what lay inside that pale little box hit me. It contained only the shell of my friend now, but also all the memories, good and bad, we'd constructed over four decades, and the sting of unshed tears burned my eyes. Something as big as my fist wedged itself in my throat, and a burning sensation spread across the back of my head. Alongside me I heard sniffles, and understood that I wasn't the only person in our social group to be affected.

'I'll now allow you a minute's silent reflection in order for you to say your personal goodbyes to Carl,' the celebrant said, and for a second I thought she had directed her words directly at me. I glanced at her, and mouthed, 'Thanks'. She nodded and smiled, and once again folded her hands at her middle.

As I stood, with no recollection of getting to my feet, I similarly cupped my hands at my waist, though it wasn't in prayer. My mind was blank of memories. I think I actually counted down the seconds, until the celebrant's voice broke the hush and she recited the committal and the curtain around the catafalque began to slowly close. A faint crackle issued from a speaker, and I steeled myself for the music that would send Carl on his way. After the other weird happenings since Carl's murder, I was ready for another message from beyond the veil of death, but instead, a melancholy dirge sounded, a chamber music piece I didn't recognize, and I thought Carl would have spat if he knew what his parents would choose as the soundtrack to his final journey. While the music droned and the curtains continued a stuttering closure around the coffin, we waited until the family had exited and then the remainder all began filing out. We were funnelled down a narrow corridor to a side door, where Carl's father and Ricky stood, taking each mourner's hand and shaking it briefly. The two Mrs Butlers and the twins huddled in the dimness behind them. Carl's workmates all made small talk, causing the queue to back up, and I stood shuffling my feet while Nell nudged me in the side to keep moving. I made it to the front, and shook Carl's father's hand: it was limp and cold and the old man didn't even meet my gaze. Had he done so, I doubt he would have recognized me, and certainly not recall afterwards whether I'd attended the service or not. Little Ricky shook my hand next, said, 'Thanks for coming, I know he was your mate from way back.'

'I'll miss him,' I said, and then I was pressured to move on by those in the shuffling column behind. I waited a moment while Nell shook hands with Ricky, and then stepped outside. Already Carl's work pals had formed a noisy group to plan their next move; some of them had lit up cigarettes and smoke coiled towards the grey heavens. As I turned back, I found Nell wet-eyed. She dabbed at her face with a tissue. 'You OK?'

She sniffled, but nodded, then offered a strained smile. 'It's always difficult until the service is over,' she said, repeating words I'd heard at every funeral I'd ever attended. 'But things should get easier. From now on we should only remember the good times.'

'Yeah, that's right,' I agreed, knowing fully that it was a blatant

lie. I'd have a lot more bad memories to work through before my
mind could know peace again.

Brian and Joyce joined us, Brian fishing out a packet of cigarettes
and offering them around, despite none of us being current smokers.
He lit up and aimed a plume of blue smoke at the overcast sky. He
fed his left arm around Joyce's waist, and she leaned her head on
his shoulder: this so soon after making up and they were as close
as ever. By contrast Nell was at arm's length from me. She turned
and observed as first Gavin and his partner, and then Johnny and
his, exited the side door. It was unlikely they'd seen any more of
each other than they had of me or Brian over the years, and yet
they'd gravitated together on arrival. They exchanged words briefly,
then approached us together.

'I'm pleased that's over with,' said Gavin, using a handkerchief
to clean the lenses of his gold-rimmed glasses.

'Me too,' said Johnny. 'We can put it behind us now, eh? Get on
with living . . .'

We shook hands and hugged, and we each introduced our better
halves. Instantly I forgot the names of the two women I'd just met.
'Are you going on anywhere after here?' Brian asked collectively.
'Maybe we can go get a drink together, have a few laughs about
the old days?'

I checked with Nell and was surprised to find she didn't pull a
face at the idea. I was also surprised that Brian was only now voicing
the idea of getting with our friends; we'd agreed that a get together
should be left until after the funeral, but I thought he'd have raised
the idea with them before now.

Gavin checked his watch – an expensive gold model – and then
shrugged. 'Got somewhere in mind?'

Johnny spoke with his partner, and the vaguely familiar-looking
woman nodded at his request. He said, 'Carl's local was the King's
Oak, but it's a bit of a dive; how about we go somewhere else?'

I noted that Johnny had looked directly at me, as if I should make
the decision on where to go. Or maybe he was only waiting to hear
if I'd be joining them. 'We could always go to the Manor House,'
I suggested. 'Drink there's half the price it is in town.'

We'd each earlier followed the hearse from Carl's parents' house,
so had travelled in separate vehicles, now parked adjacent to the
crematorium. We headed to our respective cars, gave brief waves
and then fell into another motorcade as we headed to a local social

hub, where a modern community centre, complete with a public bar, function rooms and a gymnasium, had been erected adjoining an eighteenth-century manor house. The manor had once sat at the epicentre of a country estate, before the city spilled over and absorbed it within its perimeter. Where once there'd been fields, several housing schemes had sprung up. Back in the 1980s our housing estate had gone through a period where it was designated the roughest in the city. The council had tried tidying it up, but failed, and soon some of the businesses and services began pulling out and poorer families moved in, some bringing drug addictions and criminality with them. Our own community centre fell into disrepair, so we began travelling across to our neighbouring centre to a weekly youth club and discotheque, on the hunt for girls and laughs. It was where I'd first met Nell.

We entered the bar and found it already packed with Carl's workmates. Their factory boasted its own social club, but they could not go there for a drink without being expected to return to work. It was noisy and there wasn't a free table in the small bar, so I urged our group next door into what used to be a lounge where food was served alongside the alcohol. We pulled a couple of tables together and arranged eight chairs around them; as an afterthought Brian grabbed a ninth chair and set it at a place of honour at the head of the tables. 'That's Carl's spot,' he declared and we all slowly clapped at the idea.

A hatch that opened on to the main bar area allowed us to order a round of drinks, and soon we each had a half pint glass of beer or wine before us. One of the others ordered crisps and peanuts, and we made a little buffet out of them. We spent more than an hour exchanging anecdotes and stories about Carl, with most of the edges blunted so that he didn't come across as the sour little bully he could be. We ordered another round and shifted on to other subjects, but largely they all harked back to when we were children. It was about then that I noticed that Johnny was growing quieter and more withdrawn by the second. He got up to visit the loo and I took the opportunity to go and talk with him.

Johnny had aged, as had the rest of us, but his slight build wasn't much more than I recalled from when we were boys. His dark wavy hair was flecked with grey, and he'd had his ears pierced since he was young, but otherwise he had barely changed. A faint aroma of tobacco hung around him, but it was sweet unlike the acridness that

Brian occasionally was blanketed in. As I sidled up next to him at the urinals, he gave me a pinched look, then knocked his shoulder against mine. I knocked him back and he staggered half a step, and had to catch himself before wetting the floor. We each laughed. 'If anyone comes in, they're going to get the wrong impression about us,' he said.

'You're right.' I made space and then unzipped at another urinal two over.

'It's been a while since you made me piss on my shoes,' he pointed out.

'Too long,' I said and we laughed again.

It had been one of those stupid boys' games that we played whenever we were in the school toilets: sometimes the shoulder knocking had turned into full-on wrestling matches and a floor awash with pee. We were too mature and sensible to let such games get out of hand now.

'Do you remember that time you all grabbed me and put my head down the toilet and Carl flushed the chain?' Johnny asked.

'I never did.'

'You did.'

'Maybe I was there but I didn't . . .'

'Maybe, but you didn't stop the others from bullying me, either.'

'It wasn't bullying it was . . .'

'Banter?'

'Exactly. But you're right. We did some pretty horrendous things to each other back then in the name of "having a laugh". I'm surprised we ever stayed friends.'

'Yeah,' he acknowledged the point.

Again he looked melancholy as he zipped up and went to the sink to wash his hands.

I finished and went to stand beside him, waiting my turn.

'If I ever did anything truly bad to you,' I said, 'then I'm sorry.'

'Nah, don't worry about it.'

'I know but . . . well, I mean it, Johnny.'

'Do you know what the very worst thing you ever did to me was?'

Lately I'd thought back on how Johnny had been held down while his boxers were stuffed with dirt, and how I'd chucked stuff at him with the others – exactly how he'd chucked things at me by way of reciprocation – and how we'd . . .

The realization caught my breath in my chest. After exhaling in a stutter, I said, 'It was forcing you to go along with us and blame Ian for attacking Melanie and Poppy, wasn't it?'

He nodded, and his dark eyes lost their sheen.

'All the knocks and scrapes, the kicks and slaps and nips, the practical jokes played on me, even having my head stuffed down the loo and being waterboarded, well, they didn't bother me, not really. It was all part of our coming of age, and I'd bet each one of us has a similar story to tell where we each thought we were the victim. But yeah, being forced to go against my own blood . . .'

'In hindsight we could have spared you having to tell the police about him. It can't have been easy on you.'

'It wasn't. Believe you me,' he said. 'It was fucking awful, and it only grew worse.'

Yes. He was right. I understood where he was leading, and the depth of horror he'd endured in the following weeks had had little to do with his father or uncle discovering he'd been one of the grasses to blame Ian. The accusations of us five young boys had ultimately led to his cousin Ian's death.

FIFTEEN

A ndy found Gavin at their local playing park. He was sitting on a death trap contraption known to the boys as the 'witch's hat' but that passed as an acceptable children's ride then. It was like a huge rusted metal shuttlecock, with wooden bench seats at the bottom, perched on an upright pole, and could be spun around and up and down simultaneously. Many taller kids had experienced crushed knees when lying belly down on the seats and the brute of a toy had slammed down on their bent legs. Andy joined his friend without greeting. The witch's hat swayed under his weight. The bench seat had lost all but a few dried flakes of paint, and was covered with graffiti, some of it dug into the wood with penknives. Andy's name could be found scratched into one seat, though not the one he currently sat on. He traced a fingertip around a lewd and crudely drawn female form with breasts outrageously depicted the size of melons. It took a few seconds for the connotation to hit and he snapped his finger away as if jabbed by a wooden splinter.

Gavin allowed his feet and arms to droop, sitting precariously at the edge of the bench seat. He burped, but otherwise didn't acknowledge Andy's presence, though it was obvious he was aware of him. He'd recently finished a can of Ginger Beer, and dumped the flattened can between his hanging feet.

'Did you hear?' Andy asked softly.

'Me and Carl warned you he was nuts,' said Gavin.

'You don't need to be nuts to commit suicide, only desperate.'

'Or feeling so guilty you can't take the shame.'

Andy grunted in acquiescence.

'Anyone seen Johnny?' Gavin asked.

'Don't know.'

'We should go round and check he's OK.'

'Yeah,' Andy agreed, but neither of them jumped off the witch's hat.

'I haven't spoken with him since we were at the nick,' Andy said.

All five of them had gone to the police station together, to tell them what they knew about Ian Nixon's den and how he'd chased them away from near the frog ponds with a hammer the same day that the girls were attacked. Being youths, the police had been under certain constraints about taking their statements, and had to call in what they termed 'responsible adults' to ensure they were treated correctly and in line with the recent change in Police and Criminal Evidence rules. Johnny had begged that his parents weren't involved, but he hadn't much say in the matter and the last time Andy saw Johnny was after they left the station and he was dragged roughly away by his red-faced mother.

Andy had bet that poor Johnny was in for a hiding once he was handed over to his even less understanding dad. Hell, Andy wouldn't put it past Mr Wilson to give them all a beating if he could get his hands on them. Andy was under no illusions, if Johnny's dad chose to give him a smack, his own dad wouldn't get between them. His dad wasn't a fighting man, in fact he was a bloody wimp, while his mother would probably egg Wilson on.

'I'll let you knock on his door,' Andy offered.

'No way.' Gavin dropped off the bench seat, and sent the soft drink can spinning with a swift kick. 'We'll go round the back and shout for him. If his father's home at least we'll have a chance to run.'

They went directly to Johnny's street, then took a narrow cut between the two end houses that accessed a series of allotments. Back there, Johnny's father kept his pigeons in a purpose-built shed, so had cut a hole in the back hedge around their garden to allow him easier access. Occasionally the boys had used the way to and from Johnny's house after sneaking there while skiving school. When the adults were out, Johnny's mother kept the doors locked but was usually lax about leaving windows off the latch, and several times the boys had sneaked inside through the kitchen window, out of sight should the school board man come knocking.

They crept through the allotments, skirting each separate plot in which the tenants raised potatoes and turnips – *real* turnips, the large purple and orange vegetables southerners referred to as swedes – and even tomatoes under wooden frames and thick sheets of semi-opaque plastic. They kept one eye on Mr Wilson's pigeon loft, and another on the gap in the hedge. Reaching the gap they crouched, one each side, one knee lowered and holding tight to a fistful of privet.

'Can you see him?'

Andy was unsure if he meant Johnny or Mr Wilson.

He shook his head, because he couldn't see anybody.

Gavin leaned out a few inches more. He scanned side to side, then up and down, then withdrew. Peering directly at Andy, he whispered, 'It doesn't look like anyone's home.'

Andy took a turn, and had no argument.

'Hang on.' Gavin scraped around at his feet and came up with a handful of twigs and tiny clods of dirt. Then moving like a ninja out of one of those chop-socky pirate videos they all eagerly watched, Gavin slipped through the gap, worked his way around the garden to a point where he could chuck his burden without being seen through the kitchen window. He cast it underhanded, and the detritus rattled against Johnny's bedroom window above him.

Andy spotted shadowy movement in the dimness behind the glass. He showed Gavin a thumbs-up, and Gavin sidestepped so that he could crane up for a better view. Johnny eased open the largest bedroom window and leaned out. He quickly glanced behind him, before putting a finger to his lips.

'Are you coming out?' Gavin asked.

'Shhhh!' Despite his admonishment for silence, he gestured, miming with his fingers that he'd have to sneak out, and by all accounts one or more of his parents was home, in a ground-floor room.

Andy wasn't surprised when Johnny clambered up on to the window sill and climbed outside. Within a few feet of the window there was a drainpipe. Johnny reached for it and then swung out, bracing his feet flat to the red brick wall. He shimmied down with simian ease. He ducked, staying below the kitchen window, and joined Gavin. They both began creeping along the garden, staying close to the hedge to the adjoining house, while Andy beckoned them, watching that all was clear.

A hand grabbed Andy's shoulder, yanking him backwards.

He yelped, and the strength drained from his knees.

Terrified, he turned, expecting to find an enraged Mr Wilson.

'Bloomin' hell, what're you two doing creeping up like that?' he croaked.

Brian and Carl grinned at him.

'Almost shat his pants, the poor laddie,' said Brian in some strange accent that Andy couldn't place. He was eating a bag of pickled onion Monster Munch. He grinned, showing gums clogged with orange goo.

'By the smell of things, he did,' added Carl.

Andy ignored him and spoke directly with Brian. 'I thought you were Johnny's old man.'

Carl snapped a stinging slap across Andy's earlobe. 'Nah, that's how it would've felt if Mr Wilson had caught you.'

'Pack it in, Carl,' Andy snarled, while massaging his painful ear.

'You're lucky we weren't Johnny's dad,' said Brian. 'We've been sneaking up on you for ages, and would've grabbed you minutes ago if we wanted.'

'So why didn't you?'

'We had to give Johnny a chance to sneak out, and besides, I wanted to finish these.' He meant his baked corn snack.

Andy snorted. Johnny had needed only a few seconds to scale down from his bedroom, not minutes.

It didn't matter. All that mattered was that Johnny had made it outside without being seen by his parents and had reunited with his best pals.

The five of them filed along the edge of the allotments to the narrow path at the corner and then made it on to the street. Immediately they set off running, to any destination that wasn't Johnny's house.

They gravitated back to the playing park, but this time the witch's hat and the towering banana slide and swings were ignored. Through the middle of the park a beck wound between steep banks and under bridges, and they took shelter from the beating sun under one of the arches. There was barely room to crouch under the arch, balancing on the brick ledges only a few inches above the gurgling stream. Out of sight and earshot of other kids using the park, they could speak in private.

Johnny had already been pressed for answers on the way back to the park, but other than confirming that his cousin was dead, he had not gone into detail. Carl and Brian wanted to hear every gory point, while Gavin and Andy tried to steer them so that they didn't upset Johnny. Having escaped his bedroom by scaling the drainpipe, and risking getting in trouble if his parents found out, it appeared that Johnny wanted to share what had happened. Maybe he needed to, so that the burden of guilt didn't rest on his narrow shoulders alone.

'They took him across to Barnard Castle,' Johnny explained, 'on remand.'

Being taken to Barnard Castle demanded no further explanation for any of them. Although the town in County Durham was a beautiful, historic market town complete with a surviving medieval castle, its name was more synonymous to them for its 'borstal'. Cumbria, where they lived, had its own young offender institute, but it was reserved for lower-level criminals . . . the serious ones, the hard bastards and repeat offenders, were all sent across the A66, to the Castle.

'Bet you the other inmates ate him alive,' said Carl. 'My Uncle Jimmy was inside for eighteen months. He said there wasn't a day that went by when he didn't get a good hiding. Said the only ones safe from beatings were the spinners who had rooms to themselves.'

'Who are spinners?' Gavin wondered. 'The kiddy-fiddlers?'

'Nah,' said Carl, the font of all criminal knowledge. 'Back then, the nonces were called champs, because champ rhymed with tamp, y'know as in tamper? Spinners are the space-heads, the nutters, the loonies.' He rotated his index finger next to his head and went, 'woo-woo-woo.'

'It's a good nickname for you,' Brian said. 'Spinner Butler, it's got a ring to it.'

'Righto, *Champ* Petrie.'

Carl and Brian wrestled a moment, feet braced on opposite sides of the stream.

'Pack it in, will yous?' Andy demanded. 'Let Johnny talk.'

'Yeshhh,' Brian said immediately in his silly Connery impression. 'There can be only one!'

Some of the boys sniggered, and Andy thought the sound was like the chittering of rodents. Sweat had broken along his hairline, and it had nothing to do with the stuffy heat they crouched in. Next to his straining feet, the beck swept by, the water gushing through the pinch point caused by the bridge. The beck water smelled tainted, but from experience, Andy knew it was alive with water beetles, leeches and newts. Years ago, gardens had been planted to beautify the park, and to that day generations of kids had mostly respected the haven, so most of the trees and shrubs had survived. At certain times of the year, birds' nests could be found among the foliage, and Andy had spotted several foxes and hedgehogs rooting between the bushes. The park was an oasis at the heart of their sprawling estate, despite the rides that would be more at home in one of

Torquemada's torture chambers. Since they were little kids, Andy, Johnny and Brian had hung about that park together, using the arches below the bridges as dens or simply as shelter from the elements. Andy had experienced his first kiss there with a childhood sweetheart called Jilly Black, crouching in the evening dimness under the same arch they used now. And yet, he suddenly felt unwelcome, almost as if they had invaded the domain of somebody extremely precious over their ownership of the space. He checked out his friends, but except for Johnny who looked devastated, the others seemed unfazed. Unconsciously, Andy pawed at Brian's shoulder for stability, then grasped hold of his friend's school sweater when his hand wasn't knocked aside.

Once Carl and Brian settled down, Johnny continued his story. It proved short and ended somewhat inevitably.

He had been arrested, but not yet been charged in the killing of Melanie or assault on Poppy, but it made no difference to his fellow inmates. Ian Nixon should have been protected. He wasn't. During his first day of remand, he was physically assaulted on four different occasions. On day two scalding hot soup was thrown over him as he waited to be fed. On the third day, his lifeless body was found by the guard tasked with evening lockdown. Somehow, Ian had unpicked the nylon stripes from the sides of his tracksuit bottoms, and formed a loop and running knot from them. Secured to the top of his bed frame, he'd slumped to the floor, and it worked perfectly as a hangman's noose.

'He hung himself?' asked Gavin, open mouthed.

'He was hanged,' Johnny corrected him with a nod.

'That's what I just asked,' said Gavin with a frown.

'No, you nugget,' said Johnny, and he'd obviously been saving words up to have his revenge on Gavin. 'They're *un-identical* terms.'

Despite the unease he felt, Andy chuckled.

'What? Saying hung's wrong?' asked Carl. 'So when the chicks all say I'm well hung, they've got it wrong.'

Brian leaped on the opportunity. 'I've seen you in the shower, Carl . . . the chicks have definitely got it wrong.'

'You wouldn't like it on the end of your nose as a wart,' Carl shot back.

Again, the two seemed set for a wrestling match. Under the bridge there was no room. Andy interjected quickly: 'When a person is strung up they are hanged by the neck, not hung.'

'Hark at the wannabe novelist,' Brian said.

'I'd rather we listen to Johnny,' said Andy.

'I don't know what else to tell you,' Johnny said, his head lowered. 'Ian was taken into remand, and now he's dead, so I suppose that's the end of it.'

'Yeah,' Carl grinned. 'Think about it, though. It means we won't have to go to court as witnesses now. At least some good has come out of it, eh, Johnny?'

'So, Ian's death is a good thing, is it?' Johnny set his jaw. It was one of the few times that Andy had ever seen him confront Carl without fear.

'If it means he doesn't get to bash in any other girl's head with a hammer, aye, I'd say it's a good thing.'

Putting across his point that way, none of them countered his argument.

SIXTEEN

B ack in the lounge at the Manor House once more, I could sense that the close camaraderie and faux joviality was beginning to wear thin, especially between our respective spouses and partners. Nell and Joyce had met fleetingly in the past, but had little in common. It seemed that, even though they'd palled up at the crematorium, Gavin and Johnny's female friends weren't much into each other's crack – the local term for gossiping – and had nigh-on begun ignoring each other in favour of swiping through their respective social networks on their phones. I acted as an intermediary: Brian had kept in touch with Johnny and Gavin over the decades but from a distance, while it was apparent the other two had been that little bit closer, so having spoken quite intimately in the toilet with Johnny, I felt as if I was the weak glue just barely keeping us all together.

'Anyone for another round,' I asked, and picked up my empty glass.

She wasn't the only person to screw up her nose, but I also caught a scowl from Nell, and the pursing of her lips. She said, 'Don't forget, you're driving.'

'I've only had a pint. Another won't harm anyone.'

'You could lose your licence,' she countered, 'and then what?'

'I won't. I'm allowed two.'

'That's a misperception,' she said.

I had to bite my tongue from correcting her with, '*No it's a misconception*,' but wasn't totally convinced I'd got things the right way around. It's one thing acting facetious, but you have to come from a position of supreme confidence in your knowledge. Besides, it'd only be argumentative for the sake of it, as it had become our default mode of conversation since I apparently allowed our daughter to die.

Gavin stood, and he clapped his palms to both thighs; a sign he was ready to leave. 'I'm also our designated driver,' he said, and more or less chose Nell's side by adding, 'I'd best not have more than one pint. It's been so long since I last had a drink that my head's already spinning.'

'I guess it means "that's it" for us too,' said Johnny and he stood. His partner peered up at him from her phone screen, and when he extended his hand, she accepted it and was drawn to her feet. Johnny looked at me, and said, 'We promised the ladies we'd get some lunch after we left here.'

'Yeah, good idea,' said Brian and indicated the half empty crisp and nuts packets strewn on the table. 'Bit of a poor buffet at this wake, wasn't it? You got anywhere to eat in mind?'

Johnny and Gavin exchanged looks. It was obvious they had no plans of extending an invitation to join them to Brian and Joyce, and my friend read the situation in a split-second. He put on a fake smile and said, 'Don't forget, the best chippy in town is at the top of Duke's Heart Road.'

The takeaway shop he referred to had closed back when we had been kids, and its closure had been a sore point for years afterwards whenever we had to walk elsewhere for fish and chips. Mention of our favourite chip shop got the lads laughing and reminiscing again, but it didn't slow down anyone from pulling into their coats and heading for the exit.

'Funny you should mention Duke's Heart Road,' Gavin said, and his next words brought the other three of us to a halt. 'I was driving along it the other day, trying to avoid those savage sleeping policemen and out of nowhere this woman stepped in front of me. I nearly hit her, but I managed to stop with inches to spare. Craziest thing, she slammed both hands on my bonnet and glared at me. She whispered, but I swear I heard every word: "*I hear you've been very bad.*" And d'you know what? She looked different, older, but I could swear I knew her from someplace . . .'

'Melanie,' Brian croaked.

Annoyance flashed over Joyce's features at mention of the name, confusion over Gavin's.

'Melanie Bishop,' Brian clarified. 'The girl that was murdered by Johnny's cousin, Ian.'

'What are you on about?' Gavin asked.

'Have you lost it, pal?' Johnny asked.

'No. I don't mean it's really Melanie. It can't be. But it is what she would look like if she hadn't died.'

I gripped my friend's shoulder, cautioning him with a gentle squeeze. The problem was that he turned to me as his ally in madness. 'Andrew has seen her too. She looks like Mel, I'm telling you.'

'I didn't see anyone that looked like Melanie,' I said quickly, feeling as if I was betraying Brian somehow, 'just thought I saw a woman that followed me home and wiped mud all over my front door.'

'Not this nonsense again,' Nell snapped, throwing up her arms. Without waiting for me she stormed out of the lounge. She didn't hear Gavin's next words, that kind of vindicated my story.

'What's that about mud?' he asked. 'C'mon. Follow me. There's something you have to see.'

As we left the Manor, I could see Nell standing alongside our car. Her arms were crossed tightly under her breasts, and her face was pinched as if she was sucking a pickled gherkin. She glared an instruction at me to hurry, but I ignored her, and instead followed as Gavin led the bunch of us towards his parked car.

'Look,' he said needlessly.

There were twin indentations in the bonnet of his car. Centred over each was a palm print. The stains looked like dried mud.

'I've tried washing those off but, well, as you can see it was useless.'

I bent over the car to inspect the prints more closely. 'They're only mud, they should wash off without any problems.'

'It looks like mud, but touch it,' said Gavin.

I held a fingertip over the nearest.

'Go on,' Gavin prompted, 'it won't harm you.'

I nodded, but still didn't lower my finger. I partly expected this to be some prank, for Gavin to lure me into dipping my finger into dog shit . . . except we weren't thirteen years old any more.

Brian practically shouldered me aside. He touched the stain, then inspected his fingertip. He grunted, showed it to me: it was clean, no residue whatsoever adhering to his skin. 'It's as if the original paintwork has somehow changed colour to resemble mud,' he said.

Gavin nodded.

Johnny sniffed loudly. 'A bit of elbow grease will move that.'

I pressed past Brian to dip my finger in the furthest indentation, and even rubbing back and forth I couldn't remove any of the smear. I wondered if the impurities had always been there on the bonnet, and had only been brought to Gavin's attention after the strange incident with the woman.

'There's something weird going on,' Brian intoned.

Gavin frowned, while Johnny purposefully took his partner's hand

and began walking away. He looked back over his shoulder. 'Hey, we should do this again sometime, huh? But maybe when the circumstances aren't as sad.'

'Yeah,' I called after him. 'Don't be a stranger, eh?'

Gavin clapped his hand on Brian's shoulder, then reached to shake hands with me. I took his hand in mine, and he gripped on tightly, then leaned in close so only I could hear. 'Whoever it was we saw' – and I'm positive now that he was obliquely confirming what Brian had said about her resembling an adult Melanie – 'I think Johnny has seen too, he just won't admit it in front of Helen.'

Helen was the name of Johnny's partner, I now recalled from when introductions were made. But her name wasn't what was important just then. 'There's somebody stalking us? Why?'

He shrugged. 'Can't say I was stalked. I drove down Duke's Heart Road on a whim, kind of on a nostalgia trip after hearing about Carl, and she walked out in front of me. It was purely random, not something she could've planned. I dunno, maybe I put a familiar face to her from my memories. I'd passed our chippy, and I'd been thinking a lot about Carl, and about the rest of us when we were boys, y'know?'

'A minute ago you made out she didn't look like Melanie.' Brian stood, his face screwed like a wrung dishcloth. Apparently, he could hear more than Gavin had tried intimating to me.

'She didn't, Bri. Melanie Bishop died, remember? This woman looked more like an adult version of her sister, the red-headed girl.'

'Poppy?' Brian and I said simultaneously.

'Yeah,' Gavin agreed. 'Except, I learned later that Poppy was only her family's pet name for her. Turns out she was an orphan, a foster kid at first, and she was adopted by Melanie's parents.'

'Explains why they looked so unalike,' I said.

'Yeah, and how they could be of similar ages and not be twins,' Brian added.

'I felt sorry for her,' Gavin went on.

'I felt more sorry for Melanie,' said Brian and earned another scowl of disapproval from Joyce.

Gavin nodded. 'Everyone felt bad for what happened to Mel, but Poppy was mostly ignored, as if it didn't matter that she'd also been beaten half to death and was in a coma for weeks. Must've been hard on her when she woke up, losing her adoptive sister like that, then practically being brushed under the carpet as if she was nothing.

I tried to find her a few years after when I came back from college,' he admitted, 'but as soon as she'd turned sixteen she'd supposedly left the Bishops and gone off down south. I spoke with her adoptive parents, but they weren't interested in her any more, and it was as if the feeling was mutual. They told me that when she left she'd reverted to her original name, Jennifer Seeley, and wanted nothing to do with them again.'

Johnny pulled up alongside them in his car. He didn't say anything, only peered with expectation at Gavin. Gavin aimed a thumbs-up at him, then said, 'Well, I'd best be going. It's been good catching up again lads. Like Johnny said, we should do it again, just under a different situation.'

We briefly shook hands, and then he got in his car, with his partner bombarding him with questions I couldn't hear. Johnny hit his horn in a short bleat, and I'm unsure if it was in goodbye to Brian and me, or to hurry Gavin up. He pulled away and Gavin followed.

I could have cut the atmosphere between Brian and Joyce with a karate chop as we walked across the car park to our vehicles. They didn't speak, but it was obvious that their reconciliation was still on unsteady ground and that Melanie remained a bone of contention between them. Joyce, normally a placid and genial woman, even scowled daggers at me as if I'd played some part in Brian's nocturnal fantasies, before she got in his car. Brian said, 'I'll give you a bell later,' and then he slid into the driver's seat and left. Even as they drove out of the car park, I'd swear I could hear muffled arguing. I looked at Nell expecting a similar argument, but she'd mellowed since storming out. My wife only shrugged and said, 'Sometimes old friendships are best left in the past.'

SEVENTEEN

Helen Drover

K eeping a business afloat on the high street was becoming more difficult for Johnny Wilson's partner, Helen. Half the other stores in town had closed, including some of the larger units once occupied by household name brands. Where some of the businesses had closed down the shops had been retrofitted to serve the new cafe culture deemed the saviour of city centres. Or cheaper-end shops had moved in, taking advantage of short-term leases. On one side Helen Drover's boutique store was sandwiched in by a tatty window display filled with replica mobile phones and fake covers. On the other side a shop selling cheap greetings cards and over-stocked paperback books at three for a fiver. Drover's sold expensive clothing designed for the discerning woman about town, or country lady. Helen wouldn't normally welcome the types of customers that shopped at either of her closest neighbours, but had been forced to lower her expectations these past four or five years.

She hated that she must deal directly with the hoi polloi these days, but there was nothing for it if she hoped to stay open under the current trading climate. Sadly, it meant she was inundated with time wasters. Women who had no intention of purchasing her expensive lines would often enter with a view to eyeing up the stock, to then go home and order something similar looking but costing quarter the price online. Other times she had to contend with fraud-sters and shoplifters. When she noted the mumbling, unkempt woman plucking at the dresses artfully arranged on a display, Helen caught the eye of her assistant, and Monica understood without a word passing between them. Monica moved in, offering assistance in a breezy tone. Usually, thieves would be rattled by Monica's attentiveness and leave empty-handed, other times Helen must intervene when a would-be thief knew they'd been rumbled and saw through Monica's cheerful, friendly act and turned things nasty.

Monica was in her thirties. A pleasant, round-faced woman, with hair dyed pale lavender, and a body used as a living clothes horse for some of Helen's less popular lines. An employee of Helen's since she was a fifteen-year-old 'Saturday Girl', Monica's stake in the shop's ongoing success was almost as important to her as it was to Helen. She did her best to catch the mumbling woman's attention, but was thoroughly ignored. Backing up, she folded her arms under her breasts and whispered to Helen out the side of her mouth. 'She's constantly whispering something to herself, over and over. I think she's high on something.'

Several of their most determined shoplifters tended to be users of hard drugs. It wasn't unusual for them to enter the shop so high that they could barely stand or string a sentence together. On those occasions, Helen didn't see any value in trying to keep the peace, and would simply muscle the junkie out the door and chase them on their way.

Before she could move in, the woman selected a dress off one of Helen's displays. She fingered the dress, scrunched the material several times, and Helen wondered if it was to check if it would easily crease. The dress slipped off one end of its hanger and trailed along the floor. Helen exhaled sharply at the inconsiderate treatment of her stock. She coughed sharply, hoping it was enough to dissuade any further rough handling of her merchandise. The woman turned and shambled towards her. Helen backed up, setting a serving counter and till between them.

Up close, the woman seemed mildly familiar. But try as she might, Helen couldn't dredge up a name to fit the face. There was nothing of recognition in the slack features that peered back either, so they weren't mutually acquainted somehow. Eyes as limpid as dishwater peered back at Helen. The mouth was wide, the lips rubbery, and the teeth could have done with the attention of a dental hygienist. An unpleasant medicinal aroma drifted from the woman, almost like that old-fashioned pink ointment that Helen's mother used to daub on her scraped knees when she'd been a clumsy little girl. There was something else too, a faint smell of decay, as if somebody had quickly opened and closed the lid on a festering bin on a hot summer's day. Helen made a quick sweep of the woman's clothing: she wore nothing that Helen recognized as branded, if anything her clothing was practically anonymous it was so plain.

'Here,' said Helen and outstretched her hand. 'Let me help you with that.'

The woman mumbled something, but didn't hand over the dress

as requested. Instead, she leaned towards Helen and her thick lips writhed, and words were uttered, barely discernible to anyone except Helen: 'I hear Johnny's been very bad.'

'Pardon? What did you say?' Helen demanded.

The woman didn't answer, only held out the dress.

Practically snatching it off her, Helen inspected the dress for damage, and also for dirt or mud, because it had immediately dawned on her who this scruffy wretch was, but was surprised to find none.

'Are you . . .' before Helen could confirm her suspicions about the woman's identity, the woman again leaned forward, this time close enough that Helen shrank back, balling the dress against her belly. 'I hear Johnny's been very baaaad . . . ' she repeated.

Her brittle voice crackled on the final word, and a cough broke out, spraying Helen with spittle.

Helen screwed her face in disgust.

The woman coughed again, and then again.

Tiny globules of saliva hung in the air, dancing on an up draught. So recently following a global pandemic, the shifting motes sent a qualm through Helen and she cried out and slapped a hand over her mouth and nostrils.

Monica protested and tried to move the woman so that she wasn't coughing spume all over her employer. The woman snapped around, facing her and Monica practically withered under her deathly glare. A cough sprayed droplets over Monica, and she turned aside with a cry, swiping at the droplets on her cheeks and hair.

'Go on,' Helen instructed her assistant, and indicated for Monica to get out of the way. She had grabbed a spray bottle of sanitiser. 'Let me deal with . . .'

The woman bent at the waist, slapping down both hands on the counter top. Helen jerked back, even as the woman reared up and a sound of abject horror issued from her. It was as if she couldn't draw in a breath because her throat was sealed closed.

She was choking!

Dying, right there before Helen.

In Helen's boutique shop.

Helen imagined the newspaper headlines. It was difficult enough stalling the downward spiral of Drover's, and a customer's death in her shop would only quicken its ruination. She dropped the spray bottle and lunged, intent on helping the woman.

The choking woman had a different idea.

Throwing up her head, she faced Helen directly, then she fed in one hand, pushing her fingers deep between her lips to fish in the opening to her throat. Helen gave a tiny bleat of horror as she watched the hand slide almost to the wrist into the woman's elongated mouth. Then the hand retracted and caught in between two long fingernails was some kind of green tendril. The woman tugged and yanked and more of the green thing spooled out. It was as thick as a boot lace, but the more she pulled, the more she disgorged, and the tendril grew fatter and it sprouted teardrop-shaped leaves that bristled with tiny white hairs. Gagging almost as loudly as the woman, Helen threw her wrist over her mouth and she backed away until halted by a wall. There were items hanging on a rail, clothing returned or handed over by customers unable to justify parting with the asking price, and Helen got caught in them. She pawed some aside, while her eyes grew wider, as more of the green 'weed' was spewed on to the counter.

Monica called out in dismay, and Helen searched for her assistant. She had backed away to a far corner, as disbelieving as Helen at the woman's horrifying magic trick: it had to be some kind of chicanery, some sleight of hand, an illusion because, surely, normal human beings were incapable of vomiting ropes of plant matter several metres long.

The woman finally made a retching sound, and the final few centimetres of greenery plopped from her open mouth on to the counter. She straightened, and after shoving back loose locks of her straggly hair, she wiped the back of her sleeve across her drooling lips, almost in mockery of Helen's actions of a moment ago. She eyed Helen for a few protracted seconds, and Helen held her breath, both her hands now domed over her own mouth.

The woman turned her back and walked calmly away.

Helen watched her wordless retreat.

Then she peered back to where Monica practically crouched between two displays, using the hanging garments as shields, her gaze questioning if somehow they'd both fallen asleep and tripped headlong into the other person's nightmare. She hadn't heard the exit door open, or the bell over it chime, and from where she stood there was no place for the woman to hide inside the shop. Her attention was off her for no more than a handful of seconds, but when she looked again, she was gone. Disappeared. Dissolved.

Helen and Monica stared at each other in complete disbelief.

'What did we just witness?' croaked Monica.

Helen had no sensible reply. She turned and looked at the slimy mound of plant matter lying in a coil on her service counter, and saw that it had exuded filthy water that dripped off the counter's edge on to the laminated floor at Helen's side – which could easily be cleaned – and also on the expensive carpet where she had stood.

As insane as the past minute or so had been, Helen still had the reputation of Drover's to protect. She held up her right hand, distractedly clicking thumb and middle finger, and Monica responded to the unspoken command and rushed to fetch a mop and bucket from the cleaning closet. The smell was horrid, reminiscent of that time she'd cleaned her fish tank out after some of the rotting food matter had blocked the air pump. Helen had no intention of touching any of the foul weeds or the smelly water, it was for times just like this that she was blessed with an assistant.

EIGHTEEN

Johnny Wilson

Johnny glanced at his mobile phone screen, and saw that he had missed several calls while his ringer had been turned off. He couldn't answer immediately, although there must be some urgency, as he was currently involved in fulfilling a customer's order with several different boxed items. As he scoured the shelves in the warehouse, he allowed his mind to roam and it was cast back decades.

He had entered the small ring of friends with Andy and the others via his association with Gavin Hill. They'd been friends at junior school. When they moved up to their secondary school they'd stuck together, and when Gavin began mucking around with Brian and Andy, Johnny had been drawn into their orbit too. Carl had tagged on to their group at some point, despite any of them truly liking him, and once he did, Johnny felt he'd been pushed down the pecking order somehow, almost to the level where he became the butt of most pranks and even some blatant bullying. To the others it was probably 'just a laugh', and to maintain friendships, Johnny had gone along with their behaviour towards him, while sometimes secretly seething in anger, or genuinely saddened by his treatment. Yesterday, in the toilet at the Manor House, Andrew had seemed genuinely shocked when he'd brought up the time they'd 'waterboarded' him: it might seem funny in a comedy movie where someone's head was pushed down the bowl, but to Johnny it had been a horrible, traumatic experience. Repeatedly the flush had been pushed, and he was convinced he was drowning, about to die; the more he'd howled and spluttered for mercy the harder he was punished. Whether or not Andrew had actively held him down, or had pushed the flush lever, it didn't matter, because as Johnny pointed out yesterday, he hadn't tried to stop the others either.

It was the same when he'd been forced into grassing up Ian to the police. Johnny's testimony wasn't required, not when four of them were already willing witnesses, but he'd been pressed into it, and again Andrew had done nothing to save him. Johnny had always looked up to Andy as some kind of inspiration. Though Andy had never thought of himself in the term, he'd been their gang's unofficial leader. Gavin was a follower, the same as Johnny was. Carl would have sworn the others followed him, while Brian would have made it his personal mission to show Carl how wrong he was but, when it really mattered, it was usually Andy that they looked to for the final answer or direction. Andy didn't tell them what to do, he just had a calm authority about him that the others respected. It was why Carl – insecure bully that he was – often tried to physically control Andy, because there was no possible way for him to do so intellectually. Johnny even felt that he'd checked with Andrew yesterday, ensuring that he was the one to decide on their next move as they'd prepared to leave the crematorium; deliberately Johnny had forced the initiative as they left the Manor House by taking his girlfriend Helen's hand and leading her to his car before any of the others could change his plans for him. Briefly, Gavin had paused, showing the others the damage to his car, but Johnny had ensured that Gavin didn't dally any longer by urging him to leave. That simple act of power lingered with Johnny more than twenty-four hours later, and he'd be a liar if he said he wasn't pleased.

Customer served, Johnny took out his mobile and brought up the list of missed calls. His girlfriend was Helen Drover, a divorcee, a full fifteen years Johnny's junior. She holidayed with him, socialized with him, had a sexual relationship with him, but beyond those, she was her own person. She was the owner-manager of a boutique store in town selling high-end women's fashion. Johnny worked at a chain hardware store he cynically called Screw-it, from a unit on one of the industrial estates on the east side of town. Usually, their days never intruded on each other's. And yet she'd called him a number of times in the past hour. Johnny had worked his way up to shift manager and he didn't require permission to make a call, yet he still looked around guiltily, ensuring his co-workers didn't spot him slink to a corner of the warehouse and hit the return call button.

'Johnny? Thank you, God.' Helen's voice sounded hoarse when she answered.

'Is there something the matter?'

'That woman,' she croaked, 'the one that Gav was talking about, she's been in my shop today.'

'What woman?'

'You know fine well who I mean.'

'The one that left the hand prints on his car?'

'Yes. That "Poppy" woman.'

Although neither Johnny or Helen had hung around while Gavin told the entire story to their friends, he had later related it to them in detail while they'd eaten lunch together.

'What do you think she wants, Johnny?'

'I dunno. Maybe nothing. Maybe she's just returned to live here.'

'Don't you think it's a bit coincidental?'

'How?'

'Your old friend was murdered, the same time another old friend shows up out of the blue.'

'Are you suggesting she's the killer?'

'No, just . . .'

'Good. Because there's no way I'm pointing the finger at *anyone* again.' His relationship with Helen was tight enough that he'd unburdened himself concerning what had happened to his cousin, after he helped send Ian to the Castle, and ultimately to his suicide. She must understand his reluctance to blame anyone for anything ever again.

'She's . . . extremely weird.'

'It doesn't make her a murderer, Hel.'

'I know that. It's just . . .'

'From how Gavin described her behaviour, it sounds as if she has mental health issues. Don't forget, she was assaulted and beaten unconscious with a claw hammer, it was bound to do irreparable damage to her brain.'

'She came up to me at the till carrying a dress. I didn't recognize her at first, not even from Gav's description, it was what she said that convinced me it was her.'

He stayed silent.

Helen said, and croaked the words so they were more impactful: 'I hear Johnny's been very bad.'

'Hey! What? She mentioned me by name?'

'Yes. And I'll tell you something else, Johnny. The second I heard her say it, I knew who she was, and remembered what she'd done to Gav's car. I took the dress off her, checked it . . .'

'It had muddy handprints on it?'

'No. Not a single mark,' she said, 'but here's where it got seriously weird; she leaned forward and said it again, that you've been very bad, and then started coughing and choking. I thought I was going to have to give her first aid, but she stuck her fingers in her mouth and grabbed something and began drawing it out. It was sick, Johnny, like one of those magicians pulling out a never-ending ribbon, except it was slimy and she kept on ripping it out and dropping it on the counter. Finally, she wiped her mouth with her sleeve, then, without another word, she turned her back and walked away. When I looked down, expecting only the slimy weed, the counter was soaked with dirty water.'

'You've got to be joking?'

'I'm not, Johnny. I'm freaking out!'

'Is she still hanging around?'

'I don't know. I haven't looked. Don't ask me to look, Johnny.'

'I won't. Look, it's obvious that she has some sort of problem with us lads. Gavin saw her, and by what they said, there was something weird about mud going on with Brian and Andrew too, so that probably means she deliberately came into your shop to spit out that stuff to get at me.'

'Why come here?'

'Bit easier than trailing all the way up here to the industrial estate, isn't it?'

'How would she know about me and you?'

'I . . . I don't know.'

'I don't like this, Johnny.'

'Don't worry too much. Maybe now she's done her little regurgitation act she'll leave things at that.'

'It was disgusting, frightening.'

'I bet it was.'

'She spoke to me immediately before coughing it up,' Helen went on, truly shaken, 'which means she must've swallowed that horrible stuff before coming into my shop. She must be a bloody loony.'

'Are you certain it wasn't some kind of salad leaves or . . .'

'What? You think she just got a coughing fit and accidentally puked up her pub lunch?' Helen laughed at the absurdity, but then must have realized that her next words sounded more insane. 'It's like she ate the contents of a bloody fish pond.'

'I can't think of any pond, or anything similar for that matter, anywhere near to your shop, Hel. Probably it was just something she puked and it looked like weeds and dirt.'

'Do you want Monica to keep the contents of her mop bucket to show you?' Helen demanded. 'Because it's beginning to sound like you don't believe me, Johnny.'

'No. Of course not. I do believe something weird happened.' Johnny thrived on the weird and uncanny, and for several years had investigated paranormal phenomena, but always with a sceptical mind. 'It just might have a plausible explanation.'

'It was weird, all right. Weird, disgusting and scary.'

'Do you feel threatened?'

'Not personally. But I think she was threatening you.'

'Why would she wish me harm? I never did anything to hurt her; in fact, I went against my own bloody family to help her.'

'Who could rightly say what goes on in a mad woman's head?'

'Not me. I'm going to have to talk with the lads, and warn them to be on the lookout for her. Who knows what she's capable of or what she'll do next.'

'You know that you said there's no way you'll point the finger at *anyone* again? If you're worried about what she's capable of, well, maybe you're going to have to.'

NINETEEN

Andrew Miller

I thought that more than a couple of days would pass before I saw either Gavin or Johnny again. When Johnny had left the Manor House the other day, I'd got the impression that he had done what was necessary but was then keen to leave the past exactly where it was, in his rear-view mirror.

Gavin's tale of Poppy Bishop branding her palm prints on the bonnet of his car had shaken me. Obviously, it had worked its insidious way into Johnny's brain too, because he showed up at my house a bit wild-eyed and jabbering about another incident involving Poppy. This one, from what I gathered from his rapid-fire delivery, involved third parties, including his partner Helen, and somebody called Monica.

'You're going to have to slow down, Johnny. You've lost me here.'

'She was at Helen's shop and . . .'

'Yeah, you said: she threw up.'

'No. That wasn't it, Andrew. She didn't *just* throw up.'

'Look, c'mon inside. We'll have a brew and you can tell me all about it.'

'Is Nell home?'

Why was that always a question asked of me before any of my friends would enter my house? I frowned a little, and Johnny clarified. 'She needs to hear this too, so she'll be on her guard.'

'She's out. Nell thinks we're all a bunch of delusional nutters. To be fair, some of the tales we've told lately verge on madness.'

'They're bloody weird, I'll grant you that. But being weird doesn't make them untrue.'

I led Johnny down the same hall to the same kitchen as I had Brian when he'd come calling with his story about Melanie invading his dream. We sat on the same stools at the breakfast counter. By comparison, Brian's erotic dream had probably been the least incredulous thing to happen compared to the rest of us.

'Coffee?' I offered.

'Got a beer?'

'No, mate, sorry, I . . .'

'Then, coffee it is,' he said, to stop me from blustering.

I had my usual pot on the hot plate, so I poured us a mug apiece. Johnny declined milk and sugar. 'I don't have beer,' I said, 'but if you wanted something stronger than black coffee, I'm sure Nell's got half a bottle of brandy left over from last Christmas.'

'Maybe you can put a splash of it in there,' Johnny said, and pushed his mug towards me.

I retrieved the brandy from a cupboard in the lounge. It was nearer empty than I remembered, but there was still enough to give both our coffees a boost.

'So, tell me. Start at the beginning, and slow down this time, eh?'

Johnny related a story of a woman that Helen believed to be Poppy Bishop visiting her shop, and making a strange threat of sorts towards Johnny, before vomiting up the contents of a pond.

'When Helen phoned me, I thought she was exaggerating but, by fuck! she wasn't. I made an excuse to leave work early and went downtown to her shop . . . y'know Drover's in the town centre?'

I nodded. It wasn't a store I'd been inside often, but had been towed behind Nell on several shopping trips over the years where Drover's had been on her official retail therapy itinerary. Before now I hadn't been aware that Helen Drover, whose name was kind of well known in our small city, and Johnny's partner were one and the same. Hers was one of those faces that often turned up in our local newspaper or TV channel. A scratch at the back of my memory told me that Helen had financially done all right out of a divorce, so Johnny had fallen on his feet when he jumped in with her.

'Monica kept the evidence to show me. I wouldn't have believed it if I hadn't seen it with my own eyes,' he said, cliché be damned. 'I'm not kidding you, Andrew . . . I've seen nothing like it, and I've seen some mind-boggling stuff in my time.'

'And she'd sicked up some sort of plants?'

'Plant. A single tendril. Y'know what it looked like; that duckweed shit that you get growing on still water. But this also looked like it might sting you if you touched it, covered in all these tiny white filaments, and I'd swear they were oozing sap or something.'

I must have looked incredulous.

'Do you think I'm talking crap? I'm not. I'd bet that this tendril thing was about ten or twelve feet long . . .'

'She can't have spewed it up, not that much; she must have been tricking Helen somehow?'

Johnny shook his head, adamant. He turned to his coffee and gulped it down, grimacing when the strong brandy hit his throat. I added the dregs from the bottle to his mug, then gestured with the empty bottle to continue. 'I asked the same,' he admitted, 'but Helen and Monica both watched her reach into her mouth and start spooling it out like a frigging fire hose. Helen said that she almost had her entire hand down her throat to get a hold of it, it wasn't any kind of magic trick.'

I turned side on, placed my fist alongside my open mouth and then moved my hand back by increments.

'Believe it, don't believe it,' Johnny huffed. 'But I believe Helen and Monica saw exactly what they said they saw, I mean, where was Poppy holding all of the weed and the dirty water if not in her stomach?'

I thought about hidden bladders or sacks, the kinds of things that street magicians must rely on when they are performing sleight of hand tricks involving liquids. But I kept my peace. However Poppy had performed the illusion, it was grotesque and disgusting and it was little wonder that Johnny was shaken, even after only witnessing the aftermath.

'Listen,' he went on, 'it wasn't only the stunt with her throwing up, it was the fact that she knew where to go and to use my name.'

'Yeah. What was it she said again?'

'That I'd been naughty or something like that.'

'I hear Johnny's been very bad?' I ventured.

'Andy, man, come to think of it, those were her exact words. How'd you . . .'

'She said almost the same thing to Gavin, didn't she?'

As I recalled she'd said, "*I hear you've been very bad,*" but that was directly to Gavin in some supercharged whisper, with Helen she would have to be specific and use Johnny's name.

Johnny's eyebrows practically knitted in a frown. 'What am I supposed to have done?'

'Unless there's something you'd like to get off your chest,' I said, opening both hands. I was kidding, trying to lighten the situation, but Johnny wasn't easily consoled.

'I haven't done a fucking thing wrong!' he snapped, and thrust up out of the stool.

'OK, calm down, Johnny,' I said, knowing full well that the last thing you asked an irate person to do was to calm down.

He stomped a few paces as if he was going to leave, but then turned back abruptly and pointed a finger at my chest. 'That fucking bitch has got Helen wondering if I had something to do with Carl's murder. Does "*I hear Johnny's been very bad*",' he parroted, 'sound like "*I hear Johnny smashed in his pal's skull*" to you?'

'Don't be daft, man,' I said. 'Helen won't believe that for a second.'

'Why not? Somebody murdered Carl. Why not me, eh?'

'Was it you?'

'No. No, it fucking wasn't, you arsehole.'

'I know it isn't in you to hurt a soul,' I said, trying to soothe him. 'I bet Helen knows you inside out by now, too.'

He exhaled. I was right and he knew it. 'You've got to admit though, it does make me sound as if I've something to hide.'

'Could be worse,' I said, 'Helen could suspect that you're having an affair, and that Poppy knows about it.'

'Bloody hell. I didn't think of that.' He chuckled at the irony. 'Maybe by being thought of as a murderer, I've got off lightly. If Helen as much as suspected I was cheating on her she'd have my bollocks in a sling.'

'Welcome to Brian's world,' I said and we both laughed.

After a moment, Johnny returned and sat down. He toyed with his now empty mug. 'What are we going to do about this, Andrew?'

'What do you mean?'

'Helen wanted to go to the police and make a complaint about Poppy. We could probably get some sympathy from the police if we all claimed she's harassing us.'

'Not like you to suggest this, Johnny,' I said.

'I'm suggesting nothing, it was Helen's plan. I'm hoping that you have a better idea.'

'Perhaps our best move is to do nothing, just wait things out.'

'Until when? Maybe now that she's said her bit Poppy will drop things.'

'Well, that's a good thing, surely?'

'Yeah, but what if things escalate?'

'If it happens, then we will be forced to do something,' I said. 'Let's not dwell on it until the time comes, eh?'

TWENTY

I t was noon the following day when I received a telephone call from Johnny. My administrative job meant that I was usually sequestered in my office, alone, and able to take personal calls without my employer's knowledge. But when my mobile rang, I happened to be standing in my boss's office, just about to hand over a sheaf of papers containing sales data I'd collated that morning. My boss, Norman Heatley, sat there with his palm up, but made no attempt to meet me halfway as I leaned in to hand over the paper-work. He could hear my phone, knew that it wasn't the ringtone set on the work's mobiles and deliberately kept me waiting. I was salaried; ergo, while I was at work, lunch hours and breaks included, I was on his pound sterling, and he didn't expect to have to pay for me to take personal calls. He sat there, with his big square head, boxer's flattened nose, and sickly sweet cloud of aftershave and stared at me. He didn't extend his fingertips an inch. I had to step further into his office and place the papers directly on his open hand.

'Are you still dealing with this bereavement thingee?' he asked.

His question surprised me, because I'd automatically jumped to the defensive. I mustn't forget that he had allowed me some time off following Carl's murder, or that he'd given me the day off to attend his cremation.

'I'm dealing with it,' I answered noncommittally.

He grunted and began flicking through the stack of data I'd handed over. 'You must be receiving lots of personal calls?'

'Eh? Uh, no, not really.' From my pocket my phone continued to ring, calling me a liar.

'If you need any more time off . . .'

'No, no. Thanks, Norman. As I said, I'm dealing fine with it.'

'I could give you more time off, but I'd have to deduct it from your salary. I try to be a sympathetic employer, but I don't have bottomless pockets when it comes to wages.'

'I . . . I'm not spending loads of time on personal phone calls if that's what's worrying you, boss,' I said, which was actually true but made me sound like a complete Pinocchio. Other than taking those calls from the police, this was the first time I'd been called by anyone connected with Carl since his death.

'They sound as if they need to speak with you quite urgently,' Norman pointed out, as my mobile continued to trill.

'Tell you what,' I said, 'I'm about to eat lunch, I'll deduct however long this call takes off my hour, OK?'

'You're salaried. Makes no difference.'

'I'll be back at my desk sooner than normal,' I replied.

He nodded, and placed down the stack of data. 'Your choice,' he said then coughed out a laugh. 'You've made me sound greedy.'

'Wasn't my intention, boss.'

'Nor mine to sound it.'

I backed out of his office, tempted to tug my forelock. My mobile never stopped ringing.

Turning my back on Heatley's office, I pulled out my phone and saw 'Unknown Caller' on the screen. I was certain this wasn't a cold caller or scammer trying to hook me in, and besides, I'd given my number to both Gavin and Johnny once we'd reconnected, so assumed it would be one or the other. Also, I saw that the depicted number was preceded by the area code for our town.

'Hello?' I asked . . . and for a second a flutter went through my innards as I waited for a croaky female voice to tell me they'd heard I'd been bad.

Instead, Johnny said, 'Andy, Andrew, mate! You aren't gonna believe me.'

'To be fair, yesterday's tale was a bit hard to swallow,' I said.

'Is that you trying to be funny, like "hard to swallow" when Poppy was actually doing the opposite?'

'It wasn't,' I said, 'but I wish I had been that witty.'

'Nah, you're not funny at all, mate.'

'Fair enough. Listen, I'm just going in my office and closing the door, if you lose me or anything I'll call you right back. I've got your number on my screen . . .'

'Isn't my number,' Johnny corrected me. 'I'm at Drover's, y'know, Helen's shop?'

'Oh, you've gone back there?' I had to juggle the phone from one hand to the other while I tugged my office door over a hump in the carpet, then closed it; for good measure I threw a small bolt, to ensure complete privacy. As I sat at my desk, I returned the mobile to my ear and said, 'It's all right, I'm still here.'

'Like I said, you probably aren't going to believe me.'

'You're going to have to give me some kind of clue before I can make up my mind.'

'Facetious git,' he called me. Back in the day it would have gone right over my head, but as an adult it stung.

'I'm only trying to lighten things up a bit, Johnny.'

'Yeah, OK, so listen,' he said, not giving a damn about lightening the situation: he apparently wanted things dark and mysterious. 'That stuff I told you about with Poppy yesterday, well it played on my mind all bloody night. I couldn't abide myself and had to see again what she'd regurgitated, so I dropped in at Helen's shop.'

'Don't tell me they kept it in the mop bucket?'

'Yeah. If you recall, we'd decided on talking with you before we did anything else, so Helen kept the evidence in case we decided on calling the police.'

'Bloody hell, man, don't tell me that it has festered and grown into some amorphous swamp monster.'

'Don't be ridiculous,' he said, and even over the phone I could tell it was with a straight face. 'Quite the opposite, in fact. The stuff has disappeared; the plant, the slime, the dirty water, the lot.'

'Helen must have tipped it out.'

'She didn't. Nobody did.'

'Her assistant, then. Monica, wasn't it? She must have emptied the bucket.'

'You're not listening to me, Andrew. It *disappeared*.'

'Can't have.'

'It dis . . . appeared.' When I didn't answer, he reiterated it again. 'It was left in the bucket as evidence. But it has gone. *Pouf*, just like that! Believe me, Andrew, I found it difficult to believe at first, but I've gone blue in the face asking Helen and Monica and they're adamant that neither of them touched it. Before you ask, the bucket was locked in a storeroom only Helen and Monica have access to.'

'So no early morning cleaners have . . .'

'Helen can't afford a cleaner, not under the current climate. Monica does the cleaning, and Helen covers for Monica when she's off work either sick or on leave.'

'I don't know what to suggest then, mate.' I had to think of an appropriate expression, and settled on 'You've confounded me.'

'This is some weird shit,' he said.

'It is.'

'How do you feel about finding out where Poppy lives and going round and getting some answers out of her?'

'What? Me go around?'

'You, me, maybe take one or the other of our missus so it doesn't feel as if we're ganging up on her.'

'Nell won't be on with that idea,' I said.

'Hmmm, come to think of it, I doubt Helen wants anything to do with Poppy again. She really did shake up Helen with yesterday's antics. Today has only made things ten times worse. Helen's got it into her head that there's something wrong with Poppy.'

'Maybe she never fully recovered from her beating,' I suggested.

'There's that to consider. But when I say "something wrong", I actually mean that something's not right, as in seriously off, as in "unnatural".'

'Now who's being ridiculous?' I chided.

Ignoring my scepticism, he posed another question. 'What do you know about ectoplasm?'

'Not much.'

'Wait till you get a load of these then. I'm going to text you over some photos, I'll use my own phone. Have a look at them, I'll be in touch with you again later once you've had time to give them some thought.'

TWENTY-ONE

S omebody hammered on my office door, snapping me back to reality.

'Hello?' I queried, hoping it wasn't Norman, my boss, ensuring I hadn't gone a second over my allotted lunch hour.

'It's Gemma,' replied a familiar voice. 'Just checking you're OK, Mr Miller. Are you feeling unwell?'

'I'm fine.'

'Are you sure? It's not like you to lock yourself in your office.'

'Honestly, I'm fine. Just dealing with a little *personal* problem.'

'Oh . . . oh, right, sorry . . . I'll leave you to it,' Gemma replied, taking the hint. I couldn't have shouted GO AWAY any louder if I tried.

Gemma Barker was a good kid, and for some reason she had taken to me, though I was twenty plus years her senior – or perhaps it was because I was much older and sexually less threatening than our younger male colleagues that she had befriended me – and I felt bad for sending her running. I resolved to apologize later, and let her know I appreciated her concern for me. But just then I was up to my neck in trying to make sense of what was going on in my life.

True to his word, Johnny had sent over a gallery of photographs contained in a PDF, as well as several different articles on the subject of ectoplasm, that I'd since emailed across to my computer, and it had got me wondering if indeed it explained Poppy's disgusting party trick and the subsequent dissolving of the evidence.

I wasn't totally ignorant of the stuff: I saw *Ghostbusters* at the cinema when it first came out in the early 1980s, and had watched it and subsequent sequels in the following years. I knew what it meant to get slimed by a ghost, and it had nothing to do with Brian flicking green bogies freshly picked from his nose at us, but had never given any credence to it being genuine phenomena. Most of the photographs that Johnny had shared with me didn't do anything to sway my opinion. Dated between the 1850s, through the height of the spiritualism movement, until the end of the First World War, the photos looked ridiculously fake. They supposedly depicted spiritualist mediums manifesting spirits cloaked in ectoplasm. To me it looked more like cotton wool or tissue paper, and usually steam that shrouded the corny looking spirit manifestations. In many photos the 'ectoplasm' originated either from the medium's nostrils or mouth, looking like poorly executed illusions. It was obvious to even the most casual modern observer that the photos were composites or that they were deliberate double exposures. I was about to write off the phenomena, but thought I'd give Johnny the benefit of the doubt and look at the actual articles.

They explained that – beyond actual biological terms where ectoplasm or exoplasm is the outer layer of certain types of cells – in occultism and spiritualism it is a vaporous or viscous substance said to exude from a medium during a séance to give form to a supernatural entity.

The articles were mostly sceptical to the point of debunking the phenomena entirely. I read about one famous medium noted for producing an ectoplasmic hand during her séances, only for the hand to be exposed by biologists as a piece of carved animal liver. Another well-known Scottish 'materialization' medium was shown to be a fraud when flash photographs revealed her 'spirits' and guide called Peggy to be nothing more than poorly constructed papier-mâché dolls draped in sheets while the ectoplasm was later discovered to be cheesecloth. However, as thin on the ground for proof those articles were, I wasn't blind or stupid. They were written from a critical viewpoint, and no evidence supporting the material-ization of ectoplasm would have been enough for the authors. Had he more time to research, and followed other pathways, I'd bet Johnny could have found more convincing arguments for its exist-ence.

What he hadn't found was any evidence, debunked or otherwise, of any medium claiming to summon a three metres-long tendril of stinging weed from the 'other side', which, to be fair, wasn't helpful either way.

Magician or medium?

If I'd to lay money on it, I'd lean towards Poppy having learned some kind of trick, where she appeared to throw up the plant matter and liquids, I just couldn't understand to what end she'd do it.

My car, my front door, Gavin's car bonnet, and now Helen's boutique had all been subjected to something to do with a pond

or, more likely, the canal beside which Carl was beaten to death.
Was Poppy trying to tell us something important about what had
happened to Carl and we were all missing it in our misguided and
self-centred belief it was all about us. What was it she'd said?
Although the exact words weren't repeated to Helen, the message
was basically the same; she'd heard that Gavin and Johnny had
been bad. Neither of the lads had any clue as to what she was
referring, and adamant that they were innocent in any wrongdoing.
I believed them.

Maybe Johnny's suggestion of directly confronting Poppy wasn't
a bad idea, but I was concerned that she might kick up a fuss. I
didn't want to be seen as the bad guy, and feared that by turning
up at her front door I might be seen that way. For all I'd be polite
and calm, it would only take her to start screaming and God help
me. Judging by her behaviour up until now, I suspected that there
was something seriously wrong with her brain, and maybe she
wouldn't or couldn't react rationally if I tried pressing her for
answers. I could go to the police and tell them about her, and let
them decide whether or not she had anything important to reveal
about Carl's murder. Of one thing I was certain, I wouldn't be
reporting to them that she had vomited up pondweed that had
subsequently done a magic trick of its own and disappeared.
According to Johnny and Helen it had happened, but I was yet to
experience the miraculous and for now wasn't ready to accept any
supernatural explanation for what had occurred. Sure, there were
those odd incidents I'd experienced, the sense of being stalked, the
song blaring from the radio, the weird scratching and squealing
sounds from my car, the subsequent appearance of mud at my house,
and how my shins and shoes had been soaked through, but any
detective worth their salt would explain those as a collection of
coincidences, and absent-mindedness on my part, and logically I'd
have to agree with them.

Closing down the files on my computer, I switched back to the
boring sales reports I'd been working on before. Reaching for a
notepad, I knocked over the small mug that contained a selection
of chewed pencils and biro pens I kept handy. Swearing at my
clumsiness, I gathered up the spilled implements and slapped them
back in the cup.

A knock at the door was more timid than before.

'Uh, hello?' I answered.

'Mr Miller,' Gemma Barker said, barely higher than a whisper. She knocked a knuckle against the door again, a soft rap.

I scrambled over and slid aside the bolt, hoping she didn't hear me, then quickly returned to my desk. 'Gemma, the door's open. Come in,' I announced.

She had to shove the door over the humped carpet. It opened only so far, but allowed her to poke her head inside. I hadn't sat down, making it look instead as if I was beavering away with the stack of envelopes and papers from my in-tray. Blinking at me from behind huge circular lenses, Gemma reminded me of an inquisitive owl. She stood barely over five feet in her flat work shoes, and carried more kilos than some men liked: I found her looks appealing though, and a complete opposite to the sharp edges, visible ribs and jutting hip-bones Nell had gained through the strain of losing our daughter. My interest in Gemma was purely platonic, I told myself, even if I can't swear the same in reverse.

She looked me up and down.

I was tidy, but for the open button at my collar and the way I'd tugged down my tie. Perhaps I looked fresher than she'd expected.

'Sorry if I sounded sharp earlier,' I began by way of an apology, but I never got to finish.

She flapped a bejewelled hand at me. Bracelets on her wrist tinkled. 'I was just concerned that you'd taken sick,' she said. 'You looked awfully pale before you went inside and bolted the door.'

'I . . . uh, didn't bolt the door,' I lied unconvincingly.

She looked at me for a protracted second or two. Then her eyebrows popped above the rims of her glasses. 'I hope you don't think I'm interfering, but Mr Heatley's been on the warpath lately about timekeeping and . . .'

'Yeah,' I said, my turn to halt the direction of conversation. 'I told Norman I had something to deal with, but that I'd work back the time, and take it off my lunch hour.'

'Oh,' she said.

I waited for her to expound.

'It's why I knocked again just now,' she said. 'With you looking so pale before, I was beginning to worry that you'd passed out.'

'I didn't pass out,' I said, and grinned to convince her.

'Oh, so did you fall asleep or something?'

'What? No . . .'

'It's just that you've been locked in your office for almost two hours.'

'What are you talking about?'

'Some of the team are waiting to go for their break but couldn't until you were back on duty,' she said.

'You must be mistaken, I can't have been here more than half an hour.' I took a quick glance at the time on my mobile phone to confirm my estimation. 'Look, it's only been twenty-five minutes.'

Gemma pushed inside a little more, speaking sotto voce so Norman Heatley didn't overhear.

'Mr Miller, uh, Andrew,' she said with concern brimming in her huge eyes. 'It was noon when I knocked last, it's now twenty-five past two.'

TWENTY-TWO

'Nell, are you home yet?'

I called out distractedly, my mind still on what had happened at work. I have been taking daytime micro-naps lately. Not deliberately. What with Carl's murder and all the weird incidents afterwards, my brain had been working on overdrive. At night I could barely sleep longer than an hour before my eyes popped wide, and a turbo fired up my thoughts, and it would be hours again before I was reasonably settled enough to sleep, only for the process to repeat itself soon after. My nights had similarly been disturbed after my daughter drowned, and back then I'd also found myself so exhausted during the day that my eyelids would involuntarily close, sometimes at the most inconvenient times, and I'd sleep. Sometimes the periods of sleep would last no more than a few seconds, but there'd been other times when I'd lost a couple of hours: on the latter occasions it was usually when sitting in an easy chair in front of the TV, and despite Nell snapping at me for snoring, they did no harm. If there was anything medically wrong with me, it had gone undiagnosed for the entirety of my life because I'd experienced periods of fugue since childhood. In recent years I'd worried that I was suffering from narcolepsy, or some other neurological disorder, but was told by my doctor that my naps were probably symptoms of fatigue and depression from the grieving process. It hadn't occurred to me that Carl's death would have a similar effect on me as Becky's drowning had.

While ruminating over Johnny's photos, and the articles, I must have nodded off. If not for Gemma's intervention there's no saying how long I might have sat there in my office, possibly so long that I would've had no way of explaining my lack of productivity to Norman Heatley. Heaven help me if it had been my boss that had come looking for me rather than Gemma otherwise I might have faced disciplinary action. I didn't tell Gemma about my sleepiness. I thanked her for saving my job, but made out that I'd just become engrossed in the private stuff I was dealing with and lost track of time, and she was polite enough not to push for more. Before she'd left my office, I'd largely convinced myself that the subject of ectoplasm had held my attention longer than I thought, and that, this time, I hadn't succumbed to exhaustion.

I followed her to the canteen, where I chugged down several cups of scalding hot coffee from the vending machine. It tasted like hot dirty water, which made me think about murky canals, but I desperately needed the caffeine. Back to work again, I ensured I knuckled down so astutely I completed my day's workload, plus a little more from the pile I'd set aside for the following morning: Heatley would have no idea I'd been snoozing on the job unless Gemma grassed me up.

Arriving home that evening, I pulled my car on to the drive at the side of the house, then ensured that the double gates were latched. I locked the car then made a check of it, walking a complete circle around it, crouching where necessary to see under the lower curve of the sills and into the wheel wells. The car was a few years old and had picked up some little scratches and scuffs, which I was familiar with, and I was happy to see that there had been no fresh scratches added to it. I'd been micro-napping of late; had I also been vividly dreaming the incidents that had spooked me so much?

No, was the short answer.

Because, unless I shared Poppy's uncanny ability to manifest pond water and mud from the ether, a dream, even a vivid one, couldn't explain my soaked shoes and jeans, or the filth plastered on the car, front door and throughout my house.

Letting myself in with my key, I'd called out for Nell.

She didn't answer.

The house was warm, and there was a faint aroma as if something had been heated in the oven hours earlier. No lights were on though. It wasn't dark outside, but enough gloom had invaded the house that Nell would've lit a few rooms had she been home.

'Nell?' I called out again, not trusting my senses. 'Are you here?'

Again, there was no answer.

OK. The reality was that I hadn't expected her to be back yet, I just wanted to be certain that I had the house to myself. There were times when I would remind myself that I loved her, and that Nell loved me, and that it was the wedge that Becky's death had driven between us that was continuously being hammered in, pushing us further apart. I didn't hold Nell responsible for the widening distance any more than I believed that she blamed me. It was just something that we had to contend with and hope that the gulf didn't widen too far for us to pull it back together. I'd found that, rather than clinging to her, it was best to give Nell the space she needed to heal. She went out regularly, and made use of all the new cafes and coffee shops springing up in the town centre and I put no constraints on her.

I've mentioned before that my father wasn't the bravest of souls. He avoided conflict, and that had included arguing with my mother, even when it was on my behalf. I always thought I took after my mother. Well, perhaps the apple didn't fall far from the tree in my father's respect, because I had no intention of scrapping things out with Nell again, not when I could give her free rein to come to terms with what had happened, and it also gave me time to do some of the things I personally enjoyed.

After changing out of my work clothes, I hit the kitchen and made a fresh pot of coffee. As soon as it was ready I filled a pint-sized mug to the brim. Carrying it with me I visited our American-style fridge-freezer, an item too big to fit among the other integrated white goods in our kitchen. The huge brushed steel mono-lith was nigh-on two metres tall, and one and a half wide. Yet when I opened the doors and peered into the bowels of first the fridge and then the freezer compartments, I could see nothing to eat. Both sides of it were packed with enough grub to keep an army marching for several days, but none of it appetizing enough to select it for dinner: I resolved to wait until Nell's return and then send out for pizzas or Chinese food.

Abandoning my idea to get dinner started, I wandered down the hall and into the lounge. Already I'd downed most of my pint of coffee, and knew that a return to the kitchen was imminent, but I went into the lounge anyway and dropped wearily on to the settee. I set down my mug, reached for the TV remote and brought up the evening news.

Shrill ringing brought me out of the settee, and I stumbled over to where we kept a push button landline phone, a habit of our generation we were yet to shake. I was halfway across the room before I realized how dark it had grown since I'd sat down only moments ago: a quick glance at the clock showed it was early evening still, but a full hour had passed since I'd got home. The news had segued into one of the long-running soap operas that dominate evening TV viewing. If Nell was calling, she was running later than usual.

'Hullo?' I asked.

'What did you make of the stuff I sent you?'

It took a moment for me to blink the sleep out of my eyes and shake the fog from between my ears. 'That you Johnny?'

'Who else?'

'I thought you were Nell.'

'Isn't she home?'

'No. Why would I expect her to be calling if she were home?'

'Fair point,' he said. 'I said earlier I'd be in touch once you'd had a look through the stuff I sent you . . . I tried your mobile, but you didn't answer.'

'I was napping and had the ringer turned down. Uhm, what was it you wanted?'

'The weird stuff I sent you?'

'Oh, aye. All of that supernatural nonsense.'

'That's your opinion made up then?'

'Do you genuinely believe that Poppy Bishop is some kind of "materialization medium"? Jesus, Johnny, if you'd read the articles you'd have seen that every last picture in those files was debunked, and even Harry Houdini made it his mission to expose the supposed psychics as money-grabbing fraudsters.'

'I have this problem with professional sceptics,' Johnny said, 'because they're going to do everything in their power to debunk and throw ridicule at a subject, and they'll deliberately avoid it when actual evidence presents itself so that they aren't forced to re-evaluate their world view or their bank balance. They call the mediums fakes, when they're a bunch of fakers and money-grabbers too.'

'Wasn't it Carl Sagan that said extraordinary claims require extraordinary evidence?'

'Yeah, and what a load of semantic bollocks that is. There are plenty of people sent to prison on the basis of eyewitness testimony alone, and by all accounts human testimony is the frailest of all evidence. Sometimes we can be mistaken but our word's still strong enough in a court of law to send an innocent man to jail. Where's the extraordinary in that?'

I knew who he was referring to without him even mentioning his cousin.

He said, 'To a sceptic no proof is possible, to a believer no proof is necessary. I've been studying this weird stuff for years. I kind of sit between the two extremes, and though I remain sceptical I have an open mind. I always thought you were similarly open-minded, Andrew.'

'I was more open to that stuff when I was thirteen,' I admitted, 'but then I grew up.'

'No, mate. Then you grew cynical.'

'You're right. I stopped believing in Santa Claus too. And I stopped believing in UFOs and little green men, and fucking ghosts and poltergeists too.' Without warning, tears flooded from me, and I screwed my face tightly as I almost spat into the phone. 'Then my daughter Becky died and I begged and prayed to a God I didn't believe in before, that He'd let me see and speak to her one last time, so that I can say how sorry I am for not being there and protecting her the way her father should have and . . .' I was raving, and went on to shout and swear and curse the unheeding God, but I didn't care, and from the way in which Johnny had lapsed into silence, he was acting like a good friend and allowing me to expel my grief in the torrent aimed at him.

Barely able to breathe, I held the receiver away from me, while my chest heaved in and out.

In control again, I said, 'You didn't hang up did you?'

'If I had, then who are you aiming your question at?'

Often we batted those silly questions back and forth . . . correction, we had done when we were kids. We'd fallen back into our old habits very easily.

His daft retort was to give me a little more time to gather myself. Before I spoke again, Johnny decided to get in with an apology.

'Andrew, mate, I'm sorry. It didn't occur to me that all of this craziness might bring up what happened to Rebecca. I know I wasn't really around when she, uh, passed, and I'm sorry I wasn't there to support you. When Brian got in touch with me about Carl's murder, he kind of brought me up to speed on the past few years and mentioned that your little girl had drowned. I can't think of anything worse than losing one of your children.'

'I never asked,' I said, my throat feeling scratchy with grief, 'if you have kids.'

'No, mate. I was never blessed with them.'

'Brian neither,' I said.

'Same for Gavin,' Johnny said.

'And Carl. Unless he has a few illegitimate mini-Carls running around, because he had quite a reputation for shagging around.'

'Strange, eh?'

'Nah, just the way that things worked out. Besides, it isn't too late for any of you to become fathers.'

Johnny laughed. 'I meant it was strange that Carl was some kind of ladies' man, I mean, he wasn't exactly Brad Pitt.'

'It baffles me,' I admitted.

We laughed again, this time together, and it was good because we'd got past the awkward moment and back on track.

I said, 'Gavin mentioned that he'd looked for Poppy, and spoken with her adoptive parents, the Bishops. I was wondering if perhaps we should go speak with them again before directly approaching Poppy.'

Johnny appeared surprised, and I recalled that Gavin had related this as we left the Manor House after Johnny and Helen had already got in their car.

I quickly explained.

'The Bishops might be a dead end,' Johnny replied. 'From what you just said, this was years ago and Poppy left them when she was sixteen.'

'Yeah, but I'm assuming that since she returned to town, she has maybe reconnected with them. Even if she isn't close to them anymore, I'd bet they know where she lives, and more importantly, what frame of mind she's in. Her actions up until now can't really be described as sane.'

'You can say that again. If she isn't off her head, then the bloody rest of us are.'

TWENTY-THREE

Kylie Hambly

S tanding partially undressed in the window gave Kylie Hambly a little thrill. From below she could be observed, and she ensured that she displayed her most curvaceous assets as she posed – without really posing – for her unseen audience. She held up her mobile phone and snapped off several selfie photos, pouting fish-like and sticking out her backside. The thrill wore thin rather soon, because there was no hint of a passerby at this late hour. She wandered away from the window, setting her phone to video her progress, intending gathering worthy footage to post to her social media accounts. Aged in her mid-thirties, she believed she could still compete for attention with all the little Ticky-Tocky tarts out there that were half her age. Once she posted these photos and videos, she'd show who got the likes and who didn't, and she'd bet it wouldn't be some narrow-hipped urchin filtered so much they looked alien.

Kylie enjoyed the attention of admirers.

Therefore, playing second fiddle to a dead girl was not Kylie's idea of a relationship. She'd been thinking of copping out on any future dates with Gavin Hill ever since his idea of a romantic outing was spending time with a bunch of old farts reminiscing about corpses. She wasn't totally callous; she understood that Gavin needed to pay his respects and attend his friend's service but, once they were done at the crematorium, she'd fully expected him to drop his old school mates and take her somewhere nice. That she'd had to endure another hour or whatever at that smelly old manor house and two more hours pushing some almost inedible peri peri chicken around her plate while Gavin and Johnny talked about the good old days, had almost finished them then. Only the fact that she'd grown a bit tipsy on wine and Gavin had taken her back to his empty apartment had their relationship endured: admittedly, for an older man he was better in bed than some of the younger supposed studs she'd hooked up with before. She'd heard that sex following a funeral was often excellent, because the participants were intent on living life to the full so they are at their most passionate and vigorous.

Since then, she could only claim that the sex had been decent at best. If it came to enjoying an interesting outing, visiting somewhere nice and expensive, she could forget about it! She should have known that Gavin was a bit of a penny pincher when he'd made such a fuss over the damage to his car's bonnet. A few hundred quid would sort it. Come to think of it, the damage was probably covered by his insurance policy, but the miserly bugger had already complained that claiming would affect his no claims bonuses and make next year's policy more expensive. She'd been tempted to chuck a couple of hundred pounds at him and tell him to get over himself, but hadn't: why should she pay him, it was the guys who paid, wasn't it?

Rather, she'd decided on saying *sayonara*, and moving on to somebody that would truly appreciate her and treat her in a manner more befitting her expectations. Kylie would be the first to admit that she wasn't looking for true love, all she wanted was financial support towards a lifestyle beyond her personal means, and appreciation for what she would give in return. Gavin had shown that he neither had the wealth to keep her the way in which she desired nor the sense to compliment her when satisfying his baser needs.

Unlike him, she remained unsatisfied.

She contemplated posting some of her photos on one of the hook-up sites and see if she got a response. Post-coital, Gavin was sleeping soundly, snoring as loud as somebody sawing logs, and she doubted he'd wake even if she did it right there in his apartment with another man.

She padded across the floor, returning to the large window. She posted herself at one corner, peering down at the street, and the narrow stream that paralleled it. She had no concept of the history of the building she was in, other than what Gavin had told her in passing, that it had once been some kind of factory, and the stream outside had once fed its steam-powered machines. He'd said that the stream was part of a network that tied into the canal and to the trio of rivers that the city was originally erected between. Fascinating! Fascinatingly boring, more like! These days the stream was more of a runoff for rainwater, better described, she thought, as a ditch. Iron railings stopped anyone from stumbling from the path into the pewter-coloured water. They stood shoulder height to a regular-sized man, and were topped with blunted spearheads.

Yet somebody had managed to clamber the railings and stood on the bank of the stream nearest the road. Kylie could barely make out the figure. At first she thought it was some bloke, who'd taken up a better position to ogle her from, but no, this was something different. For starters the figure was female. She verged on skeletal, with wild hair that fell in ragged coils below her slim shoulders. In the darkness, her clothing was shapeless, colourless even. Knee-high weeds on the embankment clutched at the person's skinny legs.

Homeless person, Kylie decided.

Maybe the ragged-looking woman lived under the cover of the bushes that grew on both sides of the stream, and used the stream as her personal bathroom. There was nowhere in Kylie's sight where she could access the stream through the railings, so she could only assume that the homeless woman entered elsewhere, and made her way to this section where she perhaps felt safer.

For no other reason than that the urge took her, Kylie turned around her phone and aimed its camera at the homeless woman and began filming her. Hopefully the old bitch would stumble and fall, and get soaked in the stream. That should make a funny reel to post to her monetized accounts: even the antics of the dregs of society could be used to bolster Kylie's earnings.

Kylie watched, silently commanding the woman to trip and fall by the force of her will. Nothing happened. In fact the woman barely moved at all: maybe there was the slightest ruffling of her hair but everything else was static. Kylie looked from the woman to the view on her camera.

She couldn't define the figure from the bushes beyond her.

'Shit,' she said under her breath, and zoomed in and out, trying to bring the figure into clarity.

'What's going on?' she wondered aloud.

The woman couldn't be seen on camera.

'Where are you?' Kylie demanded and looked directly at the woman once more. There she was, still standing where Kylie last saw her, unmoving but decidedly a female form. No, wait! She had moved, because now her head had tilted up marginally, pulling up her ratty hair so that it now sat around her collar bones. The faintest impression of eyes peered back at Kylie from under the tangled locks.

Kylie yelped and jerked back from the window.

Gavin rolled on to his side in the bed. The divan squeaked beneath him, but didn't wake him. Neither had Kylie's exclamation. She observed him for a few seconds, then once she was certain that his breathing had fallen into a sleeping rhythm once more, she eased past him to the opposite side of the window and peeked around the frame, trying to spot the woman. At the same time. she tried scrolling through the short video she'd just made, again trying to spot any sign of the homeless woman. She couldn't see her in the vid, nor in real life. She moved closer to the window and craned, turning her head from side to side so one eye took precedence over the other, but still couldn't spot her. Kylie wondered why she was hiding, and in her next breath wondered why she, Kylie, was hiding as well. She'd no reason to hide. So what if the old bag saw her filming her? She shouldn't be lurking about in the bushes like some sort of wild animal.

Kylie stepped past the bed to where she'd originally set up, and again ensured that anyone passing outside, glancing fortuitously up at the first floor, would be able to see up the front of her unbuttoned shirt. Again, she felt excited by the prospect of being watched by a voyeur, and wondered why she hadn't cottoned on to this particular kink before. From what she'd previously posted on her social media accounts she should've recognized that she was an exhibitionist. Outside the window there was a narrow ledge, and a set of ornate railings. There was no space to walk on the tiniest of Juliette balconies, but with the windows open she could at least use the railings so she could hang further outside and display her wares to her audience.

She opened one window, and heard a squeal of unoiled hinges.

Gavin mumbled, and turned on his side. One arm was flung haphazardly over the edge of the mattress and his long hair draped over his face.

The temperature had fallen as darkness crept in, and it was a cool breeze that invaded the apartment. Gavin grumbled, but turned back the other way, dragging the duvet around him. He was asleep the entire time. Kylie felt the play of cold air, and her skin prickled in response. She shivered, but leaned outside. The breeze was strong enough to pluck at her sweat-dampened hair. She squinted a moment then turned her face out of the wind.

The woman loomed before her.

Kylie cried out and stumbled backwards.

How was it possible? How could the scrawny old woman have got from the stream to the Juliette balcony in such a short space of time. Never mind how fast she'd performed the feat, how had she scaled the outside of the building? There was no fire escape, not even a drainpipe she could have clambered up. Had she dug her fingernails into the seams in the brick wall itself?

So many questions tumbled through Kylie's mind that she had no answer for any of them. She threw the inside of her left elbow across her face, croaking in horror as the woman swung round to face her directly. The scrawny wretch stood poised on the balcony railing, like some great scavenger bird at roost. Her hair hung in coils and it wasn't the breeze that moved them, but some unearthly force of their own. Her arms were like sticks under shapeless sleeves, but her hands were huge. Fingers twice the length of a normal finger pulsated from fist to claw, and were tipped with long, ragged nails. The feet gripped the railing, almost simian-like, and the nails upon the biggest toe were as long and ragged as her fingernails. Insanely, water dripped from her as if she crouched under constant rain. Bits of green weed and slithering things dropped off her to squirm on the balcony.

All this Kylie saw and absorbed even as the strength drained from her own knees and she sat down hard on her rump on the floor.

The woman – no, this was no ordinary human, *it* was a *creature* – rose up and balanced on the railing, even as its upper body craned forward and its long, twig-like arms reached for Kylie.

Kylie was unaware of pointing her camera phone at the creature. It was more of a defensive move to place something between them. She croaked and cried out, but couldn't find the ear-rending shriek she hoped for. She backpedalled on her bum, bare heels rubbed raw on the floorboards as she scrambled. Finally, free from the sweep of the creature's arms she bounded up, and still barely dressed, she fled. Throwing open the door she hurried down the internal stairs, feet slapping on the cold linoleum. Twice she slipped and fell, but in her urgency she didn't feel pain, only terror. She crashed out of the exit door, setting off an alarm, and ran, gasping and bleating into the night. She had no immediate destination in mind, as long as it was in the opposite direction to the stream from where the creature had originated.

Left behind, forgotten, was Gavin, and her phone, which she'd dropped in her haste to escape.

Still sleeping, but somehow sensing the uncanniness of the thing approaching, Gavin rolled on to his back, and pushed aside the duvet. He was still naked after his recent bout of lovemaking. The creature bent over him, and droplets fell, spattering him with filthy water and squirmy little bugs dredged up from the slime. His hands formed fists and his feet spasmed as the creature loomed over him. It dragged its long fingernails down his bare chest none too gently. Gavin squirmed in mild pain yet didn't wake up. Lifting one leg, she – it – straddled him. Its legs were inordinately long and thin, and its clawed feet rested flat upon the floor either side of the bed. It lowered itself on to him, sitting atop his pelvis, even as it lowered its face and placed its narrow lips alongside his right ear. Its hair and the stuff growing through it covered Gavin's head and neck entirely, and yet he still lay unconscious. Like a nightmarish succubus given form, the creature writhed upon him, and his gasps of pain turned to those of passion.

In gurgling syllables, the creature whispered, 'Ga . . . vin . . . I hear you've been . . . very bad.'

TWENTY-FOUR

1988

When Melanie Bishop was laid to rest the town almost came to a standstill. The funeral cortege stretched to so many vehicles that the tail of it was several streets behind the hearse and family limousines. People lined the pavements to watch its progress, some of them weeping openly. Children threw small bunches of flowers on the cars as they passed. Adults dipped their heads in respect, while others kissed fingertips and tapped them on the roof of the hearse as it drove sedately past.

Andy, Carl, Gavin, Johnny and Brian stood in a bunch at the junction of a major crossroads that sat roughly at the geographical centre of their neighbourhood. Nearby was the park where they'd recently huddled together under the bridge. Nearer still was a huge church erected to serve the estate when it was built following the Second World War. Outwardly, the church looked uninviting, a hunk of rendered breeze blocks the same colour as slushy melted snow. Its bell tower was almost hidden by the overgrown boughs of yew trees. Inside though was an entirely different story, decorated beautifully, and resplendent with religious icons and imagery. Stained glass windows that couldn't be seen from the front, and hidden by the gigantic yew trees at the back, were impressive and awe inspiring when viewed from within. There were enough pews to seat hundreds. The boys would not get inside for the ceremony, but they intended to pay their respects from the street corner. Dozens of their neighbours had the same idea.

The hearse approached and a hush fell over everyone.

Andy's eyes watered as the hearse passed by and he batted at them with the sleeve of his jumper. The coffin inside was white with chrome fixtures, and wreaths and other tributes had been laid atop it and along each side. Written in flowers, one wreath said DAUGHTER, another read MEL. There was a framed photograph of a smiling Melanie. Andy didn't dare look at any of his friends, but he could hear them sniffing and grunting and their shoes scuffing the ground.

Her parents got out of the first limousine. Her dad supported her mum to walk. They looked small, so fragile that they might crumble and float away on the warm breeze. At Andy's side, Johnny made a sound in his chest that Andy had never heard before: it was a whine that emanated directly from his friend's broken soul. Andy reached and placed a comforting hand on Johnny's shoulder. Under his fingers, he could feel the boy's slight frame trembling. Andy also trembled, and his gut felt as if it was turning over like a wet rag in a tumble dryer.

Other family members all clustered around the hearse, and friends and other mourners moved closer. It was difficult to see beyond them, but Andy spotted the funeral director's top hat as he moved to open the back door of the hearse. Pallbearers gathered and the coffin was lifted out and placed on their shoulders and could be seen above the mourners. Slowly the pallbearers advanced and the church doors opened to them. Her parents followed Mel inside, followed by other close family members and friends, and then other general mourners trudged in. The crowd kept moving until there wasn't any standing room left inside, and then they gathered at the open door and around the parked cars.

The service would last a while, Andy thought, so maybe now would be a good time for him and his pals to head for the cemetery and be there in good time before the cortege arrived. If they waited until the church ceremony ended and the coffin was returned to the hearse, they'd be forced into sprinting across two housing estates to reach the town's main cemetery, and he wasn't confident they'd make it in time to witness the interment. He'd already made the suggestion to his friends, and they were only waiting on the prompt to get moving – Andy was unaware that it was his prompt that would set them off – so he looked to Carl on one side, and then to Johnny on the other. Brian had interjected himself between Johnny and Andy, but only so that he could face the older boys standing directly behind them. There were three lads that Andy knew, if not by name, by boorish reputation. Caught up in watching the coffin enter the church, he'd missed that the atmosphere of melancholy had changed to simmering anger.

One of the three lads towered a head taller than Brian, who was the biggest in their gang, and the other two weren't much smaller. They obviously thought their trio outmatched five smaller and younger kids. The tallest lad had a self-inflicted haircut, shaved almost to the bone with a tuft at the front, while his mixed-race pals had trendier high-top fades so alike they probably got a two for the price of one offer. They all wore baggy jeans and shiny tracksuit tops, and a load of fake gold. Andy couldn't decide if they were supposed to be a hip-hop dance troupe or what? The tallest one jabbed Brian's shoulder, but Andy's best friend wasn't the actual target of his aggression.

'You've some fuckin' cheek showing your face round here, Wilson.'

'What's it got to do with you, Sammo?' Brian demanded. 'You in charge of the guest list or something?'

Sammo – or more rightly, Jason Samson – ignored Brian's retort. He craned forward, jutting out his chin and screwing up his nose. 'Have you got no fucking shame, Wilson?'

'What're you going on about?' Andy demanded.

'*Him.*' Sammo jabbed a finger at Johnny. 'Showing his face round here after what his cousin did.'

'Whatever Divvy Nixon did has nothing to do with Johnny,' Brian said.

'Yeah, it does. They're family. What's Mr and Mrs Bishop going to think if they see his face when they come out of the church?'

'What're the chances when there's all these people around them? There's more chance of your stupid faces sticking out in the crowd.'

Brian's words had the result of dropping a hand grenade among them.

Sammo barked and lunged, and Brian grappled with him. The high-fade twins started throwing punches, and Andy caught a knuckle under his right eye before he began trading punches with them. Gavin got stuck in, and so did Johnny. Carl though, the supposed hard man, kept his distance, watching with a feverish grin painted on his face as the boys jostled back and forward. Some of the nearest adults shouted in annoyance, and some of them interjected, grabbing and forcing the scuffling boys apart, and the next thing that Andy knew was that they were running, and the three bigger lads were in pursuit. Now that the race was on, Carl was in his element, goading Sammo and his friends to chase them, running backwards at times with his tongue rolled in his bottom lip and making monkey noises.

The pursuit didn't last long. Once beyond sight of the gathered mourners, Sammo and his pals lost interest. They had wanted an audience while accusing Johnny of bad form by proxy, and once nobody could hear and agree or urge them on, they wanted nothing to do with chasing the bunch of scrawny youngsters. Carl tried encouraging them with a few thrown stones, and Brian was seething, having come to blows with Sammo but dragged apart before he could prove he wasn't to be messed with. Of their gang, poor misguided Carl was not the leader – that role fell to Andy – nor the toughest in a scrap, because Brian was easily the braver and harder fighter.

They ran on, with Andy rubbing a swelling under his eye with the back of his hand. Tears ran from the affected eye, and the bone under the socket was painful to the touch. The last thing Andy had expected when they'd agreed to pay their respects to their murdered school friend was to get fisted in the face. Apparently, none of his pals got hurt during the brief scrap: Johnny appeared bright-eyed, on the verge of tears, but there was also a skip in his step, and Andy thought he was quietly pleased that his friends had stood up for him in the face of Sammo's accusation. Gavin and Brian were more sombre, while Carl appeared pleased with himself, miming punches and kicks never actually thrown by him during the scuffle.

They left their estate and entered the neighbouring one: often they would scout the estates around theirs on the hunt for mischief or to chat to girls, so they knew the shortcuts and back alleys of this one as well as their own stomping ground. They cut along various pathways, and across a junior school field and found themselves at the gates of the town's cemetery before the funeral cortege arrived. Already some people were in situ, waiting to pay their respects. As they entered the cemetery they saw that there were vans from national, and local, TV and radio stations. It had occurred that the burial of the murdered girl would bring out the reporters but none of the boys had expected this much attention. Of course, news as horrible as a teenage girl beaten to death with a hammer had travelled nationwide by then. The boys disdained the tarmac path that ran east to west from an arched gatehouse, instead cutting at an oblique angle through the cemetery. Most of the cemetery was filled with bygone burials and memorials, some nearing two centuries old. They had to jump a beck, and then duck under the low boughs of topiary trees, and then approached the section of the cemetery currently being used for burials. While they'd proceeded through the grounds, the cortege had caught up and was approaching another crowd of mourners gathered by an open grave. Dozens of floral tributes were arranged in preparation, some used to cover the fake grass on the mound of earth recently dug from the grave. The boys arranged themselves in front of the mound, close enough to see, far enough back to give respectful space to Melanie's nearest and dearest. More people gathered around, though Sammo and his friends hadn't followed from the church.

The hearse arrived to a shuffling of feet and dipped heads. The vicar's robes seemed to flutter in their own breeze. He went and stood at the grave as pallbearers carried the coffin and laid it on trestles across the open grave. Melanie's family and closest friends gathered. Andy closed his eyes, clasped his hands. Anyone watching him might think he was praying, but he wasn't, he tried picturing the girl inside the coffin, first cold and clay-like, next alive and vibrant again. He shivered and opened his eyes and was surprised to find the committal almost over. Melanie's parents had each been handed a rose. They dropped them into the grave, on top of the now lowered coffin, and then they accepted dirt from a bowl offered by one of the funeral attendants. They sprinkled earth in the grave, then moved aside, hugging each other, Mrs Bishop openly wailing. Mr Bishop was as pale as the white rose he'd dropped into the grave a moment ago, his eyes flat. Others moved to dip their fingers in the bowl and sprinkle earth on to the coffin. As the crowd thinned out, Andy moved with his friends to also sprinkle earth on the coffin. Andy looked down, and wished he hadn't when the coffin looked a thousand yards below him: he swayed and almost toppled into the grave until Brian's hand on his shoulder dragged him back from the precipice.

There was a wake, but the boys had not been invited.

After leaving the cemetery, they had nowhere to go. Out of respect to the Bishop family, their school had closed for the day, allowing teachers as well as pupils to pay their respects, so they had the rest of the day off. Ordinarily the boys would've been delighted at the unexpected holiday, but they were too maudlin and soon separated, making their way home in smaller groups. Carl and Johnny were the first to drift away, leaving Andy, Brian and Gavin to walk home together.

Brian, the moneyed one of their gang, handed out Marathon bars. They were soft and bendy in their brown wrappers, having been carried around in the heat for hours. 'Sorry for holding out until now. Didn't have enough dosh to buy five bars,' he explained.

They wandered on, munching on the sweet treats.

Around a mouthful of chocolate and peanuts, it was Gavin that finally asked, 'Did any of you see Poppy today?'

TWENTY-FIVE

Andrew Miller – Present Day

'I swear I saw Poppy again last night,' said Gavin.

Taking a leaf from Nell's playbook, I'd gone into town having agreed to have a coffee with my old friend. We had taken seats outside a chain coffee shop, at a vantage where we could see the entire way up the town's main shopping street. There were about a dozen other cafes we could have chosen, but this one had existed for decades under the old town hall clock, a sort of fixture that even us older guys were comfortable with.

'She seems to be getting about.' My coffee was extra strong, and in a cup so large that it could have doubled as a wash basin, another reason for choosing that particular coffee shop. 'According to Johnny,' I said after a hearty slurp of Americano, 'she turned up at his missus' shop the other day. The boutique up there. Drover's.'

'Really?'

'He didn't tell you about it?'

'I haven't seen him since we had lunch the other day.'

'Oh, right. He came to see me, concerned by what happened.'

'How do you mean?'

I told him the story of Poppy and her 'ectoplasmic' trickery.

Gavin frowned. 'You really believe it happened the way they say?'

'I've no reason to doubt them. Johnny's Johnny and I barely know Helen, but they both seem adamant that Poppy sicked up some weird shit that subsequently disappeared.'

'Kylie buggered off and left me last night,' he said, and for a second I thought it was an abrupt segue from the subject of Poppy, but no, it was to enforce whatever he was about to say. 'She called me earlier today, and to be honest I thought she was high on something, or had bloody lost her mind.'

'How come?' I prompted.

He scratched his hipster beard. Looking up, he blinked at me from behind his glasses. His eyes looked large and clear, guileless.

'She claimed she was frightened from my apartment by an old hag that scaled the wall and climbed inside through an open window.'

'An old lady climbed up to your flat?'

He rocked his head.

'That's what she claimed. When I woke up the window was open, and there were some scuff marks on the railings of my Juliette balcony. I can't say an old woman made them but . . . well, according to Kylie she did. Kylie more or less crapped herself and ran away only half dressed.'

'Oh, aye?'

He smiled briefly, more of a grimace, and I understood what they'd probably been up to beforehand for Kylie to be in a state of undress. *Good luck to them*, I thought, *it isn't all of us that have to be involuntarily celibate.*

'She's using what happened as an excuse to dump me,' Gavin said. 'Says she's too frightened to come back, even though she sneaked back to grab her phone. What a load of bollocks, eh?'

'Was your relationship in trouble before this?'

He grimaced again.

'I only ask because it seems to have become a bit of a theme since . . . well, since me and Nell started having problems.'

'You guys lost your daughter,' Gavin pointed out. 'It's not surprising that you've struggled to continue the way you had been before. With me and Kylie, well, it was different. You probably guessed that she's a lot younger than me, and was only using me for what she could get.' He rubbed the tips of his fingers and thumb together, the universal gesture meaning 'money'. 'To be fair to her, I was also using her for . . .' this time he winked lasciviously, then checked he wasn't being overheard by other alfresco customers, 'you know what. It was only a matter of time before she upped and left when she realized I'm not actually as well off as I hinted at when we met.'

This close up, I could tell that his Rolex wrist watch was not actually a Rolex, but a clever copy, and some of the gold plating had rubbed off in places.

He scratched in his jacket pocket and pulled out his phone. He snorted. 'She sent me this video. It's supposed to be proof of – in her words – *the witch.*'

He started the video playing then handed it across. I took it, and fumbled up the sound. I could hear snoring, the muffled creaks of somebody moving in bed. I saw right up the front of Kylie's unbuttoned shirt. 'Jesus, Gav, you sure you want me to look at this?'

'You aren't the first man to see Kylie Hambly naked on their phone, I'd bet.' He nodded at me to carry on.

I looked.

The camera briefly swept the room, and I caught sight of Gavin sprawled face down, the covers only partly concealing him.

'Have many men ogled your bare arse on their phone before?' I asked.

He grunted in laughter. But then he eyed me firmly, and said, 'Watch.'

I watched.

Kylie pouted and wiggled her shapelier bum.

She wasn't a bad-looking woman, to some she might be described as hot, but her antics were too slutty and did nothing for me.

She obviously thought she looked foxy; more like desperate.

The picture snapped to a view outside. At first I couldn't tell what I was looking at, because there was reflection on a window that washed out the darkness. Kylie moved closer to the glass, aiming the camera and it focused on some bushes next to a run-off stream adjacent to Gavin's apartment.

'Shit . . .' Kylie whispered.

'What's going on?' she wondered louder. 'Where are you?'

I watched, expecting to see somebody, *something*. I saw nothing. Kylie must've, because she jerked back with an audible yelp and the picture went crazy as she darted around the room. I got the impression she had moved to the opposite side of the window because the picture again settled on the bushes beside the stream but from a wider angle, before sweeping back and forth as Kylie searched for a target. She obviously believed she'd seen something, but to me there was nothing of interest. Nada. I caught a flash of her bare arm, and then a squeal of hinges as a window opened. Behind Kylie Gavin muttered but didn't surface. She didn't bother checking on him, she immediately turned the camera to the open window and stumbled back with a shriek. She must have gone all the way to the floor, because the next images were of a rug and the bottom of the bed, a pair of discarded boxer shorts. The camera snapped up again.

'D'you see her?' Gavin asked. 'The old hag?'

Despite the trembling of Kylie's hand, causing a momentary

distortion in the picture, I saw only an open window. I shook my head.

'Me neither,' he confirmed.

Kylie saw something that had totally terrified her. She thrust the camera out towards the open window, even as she backed away, and then scrambled to her feet. She dropped the phone, and maybe it landed on some discarded item of clothing or something else, because it stayed partially propped up. The next images were accompanied by chaotic sounds as she fled the apartment and down the stairs. She ran a fair distance away with the camera still recording, and I could hear the panic in her bleating cries. The video rolled on for several minutes, and I fast forwarded it until Kylie returned, snatched it up and ran, gasping and crying a second time. The video ended.

I looked at Gavin.

'That's proof?' I asked.

'Proof she was on strong drugs,' he said. 'Or was having a waking nightmare or something.'

'I didn't see anything,' I repeated. 'Certainly not an old hag, a witch, or whatever the hell Kylie thinks she saw. If there was something there, it was only in her mind.'

'And there I was, sleeping through it, happy as a sandboy,' he said.

'Wait a minute,' I said. 'Didn't you swear you'd seen Poppy though?'

'Aye, but that was after. When I woke up half frozen. It was before dawn, and it was bitterly cold. I got up, and more or less knew that Kylie had buggered off in the night. You know when you can tell there's no other living presence in a place? I saw she'd opened the window, and for a second or two was concerned she'd leaned too far out and fell over the balcony. I checked, and of course she hadn't. But guess who was standing outside, looking up at me from next to the drainage stream?'

I didn't have to say her name.

'I, uh, waved,' he said, 'but she didn't respond. Just stood there staring, and little wonder.'

'You were bare-arsed naked,' I stated.

He grunted in laughter. 'I know what you're thinking: no wonder she was staring, she was getting an eyeful.'

'She probably hasn't seen one as small as that before,' I joked.

He chuckled, then reached and took his phone out of my hand. 'I turned to quickly grab my jeans and pulled them on. When next I looked, she'd gone.'

A couple of teenage girls took seats at the next table to ours. They had huge paper cups with paper straws, and all sorts of gunk on top of their coffees. They didn't even acknowledge that we existed, and immediately pulled out their phones and began scrolling. One showed the other her screen and they giggled, then vice versa. We were safe from them eavesdropping on our conversation, but I still lowered my voice. 'You believe that Poppy's stalking you?'

'I thought that her turning up on Duke's Heart Road was probably a coincidence, but I'm sure I've seen her in other places too. Just for a second or two, in passing, and like Brian told you about thinking he'd spotted Melanie, when I looked for Poppy she'd disappeared. It was the same again this time, there one second gone the next. I mean, what are the odds of her being the one standing outside my apartment before dawn, looking up at the very instant I wake up and look out the window?'

'The odds are probably astronomical,' I kind of agreed. 'Unless she's deliberately following you, so they'll diminish quite a lot.'

'That day at the Manor House, you suggested that we might be being stalked, and I disagreed. I have to say, I've since changed my mind. What you said about Poppy turning up at Helen's shop, that sounds deliberate and pre-planned. As was turning up at my apartment this morning. Here, take a gander at these . . .'

Gavin arched away from me, pulling up the tail of his sweatshirt to bare his side.

'What are they?'

'What do they look like?' he countered.

'Claw marks.'

Up his ribs and extending on to his abdomen were obvious scratches. He hadn't pulled his sweatshirt high enough to see clearly, but I could tell there were more gouges on his chest. They must have been red raw and stinging when they were made, but had since knitted together and scabbed over. My first thought was that Kylie Hambly was as demanding in bed as she was for attention out of it. Gavin pre-empted my theory.

'They weren't done by Kylie. They didn't exist even when I woke from sleep and spotted Poppy outside. They appeared afterwards, maybe an hour after I asked to meet you here. That stuff

Johnny went on about, ectoplasm? Well, isn't there something in the paranormal lore about phantom scratches appearing on people?'

'Gavin. Come on. We're back to poltergeists and shit again?'

'Unless it's some kind of psychosomatic reaction. If you've a better explanation, I'm all ears.'

The trouble being, I had none.

TWENTY-SIX

We went to see the Bishops. Of our remaining group, only Brian was absent, despite him initially agreeing to come with us to speak with Melanie's mam and dad. I felt odd now thinking of them as Poppy's adoptive parents, when she had spent so few years living with them and many more apart under a different name. Brian had agreed to meet us, but as we'd converged at the pub we'd decided on as our meeting point, my phone rang and he made his excuses for letting us down. I'd asked him if Joyce was still being awkward about Melanie, but he shut me down too quickly without a straight answer and ended the call.

Maybe it was best that only three of us turned up at their door, otherwise the Bishops might feel ganged up on and intimidated. Looking at Gavin, who resembled a university professor, and Johnny, whose dark wavy hair and darker eyes gave him the stereotypical aspect of a waiter in a pizzeria, I couldn't believe anyone would find them intimidating. For my part, I was bigger and stockily built, but apparently I also had an amiability about me that most people found soothing. I'd been told I was the cuddly teddy bear type; aye, well they should see me before I've downed my morning coffee.

Deciding it wouldn't be a good idea to take Gavin's car to their house, with Poppy's muddy handprints seared into the bonnet, the choice was between mine and Johnny's. Johnny's car was a smaller model, so we took mine, and left theirs in the pub's car park. Gavin sat alongside me and Johnny, in the back, leaned between the two front seats, hands on his spread knees. Never as older teenagers had we sat together in a car to cruise around our patch, because by the time we had driving licences we'd already drifted apart. Yet I still felt a sense of nostalgia, as if we should have. I imagined songs playing on the radio and us singing along with them – I was a Shakin' Stevens and Matchbox fan back then, but it didn't mean I was oblivious to the other chart toppers of the time. I pictured the three of us headbanging and hollering along to a Bon Jovi or Guns N' Roses hard rock anthem, instead of travelling sedately as we did.

For a reason unknown to me, I took the long way round to the Bishops' house, driving down Duke's Heart Road. We passed our old favourite chippy, and I swear I could still smell hot frying oil, and noticed how both my old friends fell silent as we crawled past. I could easily imagine that memories of our youth played across their internal screens, not adverts for e-cigarettes and vaping paraphernalia. I wondered if Mr and Mrs Giovannini were still alive, because they'd been well into middle-age back then; they would be old now, or gone.

The car bumped over a hump in the road, the steering wheel almost snatched out my grasp.

'Bloody hell!' I snapped.

'Warned you about those sleeping policemen, didn't I?' said Gavin.

He had, when telling us about his run-in with Poppy. There were speed calming measures all over the estate, but these were particularly severe. I slalomed my way down the hill, even as I began searching the gaps between parked vehicles, anticipating Poppy lunging out and slamming her handprints into my bonnet.

She didn't, and we continued through the estate.

'You've visited before,' I said to Gavin. 'Point out the right house to me, will you?'

'Yeah. It was years ago, mind you, just after I came back from college so . . . hang on, wait, that's it there. The house with the blue door.'

'You're certain?'

'The one with the blue door,' he reiterated. 'The hedge has been ripped out, and a drive put in, but I recognize the door. It's one of the few private houses on the street with its own door.' The door was unique, most of the others on the street were white PVC, stock fittings used by the housing association.

I stopped adjacent to the drive, blocking in an older model Nissan Qashqai. It didn't look as if the car was used very often these days, not judging by the weeds growing under its tyres.

'Maybe I shouldn't have come,' Johnny elected from behind us.

'The other day you wanted me to go and challenge Poppy with you?' I reminded him.

'This isn't Poppy's house, it's Mel's parents' place.'

'You aren't chickening out on us, matey,' said Gavin.

'It's not about bottling things,' Johnny responded, 'just that I'm not sure they're going to want to see me. Not the cousin of their daughter's murderer.'

'What are the chances they'll remember you? In fact, what are the chances they have even heard your name before?'

'They'll have heard it during the hearings.'

Because of Ian Nixon's suicide, both an inquest and hearing took place, where he was posthumously investigated. He was deemed responsible for his self-inflicted death, but due to insufficient evidence, the court never found Ian guilty of Melanie's murder, or of the assault on Poppy.

'Only as the name of a witness,' I reminded him. 'You were on their side so why should they not wish to see you now?'

Johnny's face drained of blood. His normally dark complexion had a green tinge. 'I wasn't on *their* side,' he whispered under his breath, as if hoping his denial would appease the family members that had turned against him in the following years. Despite the courts not finding him guilty, he wasn't exonerated either, and Ian Nixon's name had gone down in the town's collective memory as a foul, child-molesting murderer, and him barely more than a child himself at the time.

'Do you think they're home?' Gavin wondered.

'Their car's here.'

'Their car looks as if it never moves. Maybe they get the bus. They'll be pensioners by now, won't they, with bus passes?'

I didn't bother doing the sums with any exactness. We were in our late forties, even if they'd been young parents when Melanie was born, they'd now be in their mid-to-late sixties at least. Wondering about their age, if they were home or not, or out adventuring on a pensioner's bus pass, was a stalling tactic, because each of us had suddenly grown cold feet about speaking with the Bishops.

'There aren't any lights on inside,' said Johnny.

'It's daytime, who needs lights?' I countered.

'It's Sunday, maybe they've walked over to church,' Gavin suggested.

'Who do you know that actually goes to Sunday morning services any more?' I asked.

'Maybe the parents of dead children do,' said Johnny, and immediately caught himself, recalling Becky's demise. 'Uh, Jesus, Andrew. I didn't mean you should . . .'

'It's all right. I know what you meant and I'm not upset. I'm an atheist now. Maybe losing Becky gives me something in common with them.'

'Go on then,' Johnny prompted.

'Me?' I asked.

'Yeah. Go and knock. Tell them who we are and why we're here, and if they respond OK you can wave us in.'

'Why me?'

'Because you're our leader,' said Johnny.

'Since when?' I scoffed.

It was Gavin that said, 'Since for ever, Andy.'

We sat in contemplation for a moment. I switched off the engine, unclipped my belt and got out. 'I'll give you lads a nod if all's going well.'

Approaching the door, I could feel my breakfast churning as if my stomach performed a continuous flip. I rehearsed what I'd say in my head, and immediately discarded the idea. I sounded as if I was trying to sell them something they wouldn't like . . . which I suppose was exactly what I was about to do.

At the door I paused. I tried casting my mind back to when the girls were full of life and fun, imagining them letting themselves in through that door, pushing and giggling to be first inside. I put my hand flat on the wood, and tried sensing their youthful presence, but I felt only cold wood, and old blue paint cracking and flaking under my touch. Drawing back my hand, I surreptitiously wiped it on my jeans, even as I reached for the doorbell and depressed it. I didn't hear a corresponding chime, so balled my fist and rapped on the door. Looking over my shoulder, I saw my friends watching me with intent. Their faces were filled with dread.

Hearing nothing from within, I guessed I'd been rewarded with a get-out clause: except my own bloody inquisitiveness got the better of me. I pressed the doorbell again, judging if it was working or not, and when I heard nothing, I kept it depressed again for probably a few seconds longer than appropriate.

'All right, I hear you, I hear you,' came the muffled grumble from behind the door. 'Who the bloody hell is it?'

'Uh, Mrs Bishop?' I asked, while tilting my mouth to the letter slot. 'Can you hear me OK? My name's Andrew Miller. I was a friend of your daughter and . . .'

'I don't have a daughter. Now bugger off.'

'Uh, Mrs Bishop . . .'

'And that's another thing. I haven't been *Mrs-frigging-Bishop* for twenty-odd bloody years, not since that stinking two-timing rat ran off with his bloody floozy!'

I cringed at her words. Could I expect mine and Nell's relationship to devolve to a point where one or the other of us spoke in such horrible terms of the person we'd once loved, had a baby with, and then suffered its loss together?

'Mrs . . . uh, Bishop, I'm sorry, I don't know what else to call you.'

The door was dragged open and a small, fierce-eyed woman with nicotine coloured hair striped with white, and wearing a green zip-up jogging suit stared up at me. 'You can call me Margaret. And you can take your finger off that buzzer unless you want me to bloody well chop it off.'

I snatched my finger away. 'Sorry.'

'What do you want?'

At that moment I wasn't sure what I wanted: confirmation that her adopted daughter was some kind of street magician? How would she know if she had not had any interaction with Poppy since she left home.

'I don't know if you heard about the death of Carl Butler, it was all over the news and radio?'

'That's the bloke beaten to death down by the old canal?' she said, surprising me.

'Uh, yes. That's him.'

'What's it got to do with me?'

'You didn't recognize his name from before?'

'Should I have?'

'He was one of the boys that led the police to arrest Ian Nixon for the attack on your daughters.'

'Daughter,' she corrected me, but didn't expound on why things had gone sour with Poppy. 'And little good it did when that crazy bastard took his own life before he was tried.'

I touched my chest with a fingertip. 'I'm Andrew, Andy Miller.' I allowed the name to sink in a few seconds before carrying on. 'My friends in the car are Gav Hill and Johnny Wilson. We've another friend that was unable to join us today called Brian Petrie. We were the group of boys that last saw Melanie and Poppy that day, and who saw Ian Nixon nearby with a hammer. It was us who informed the police and led to his capture.'

'So what is it you're after? My thanks?'

'No. Not at all. It's just . . . '

'Hang on a minute.' She pushed me aside, jutting her torso out from the door frame without leaving the house. She studied my friends. I could tell Johnny was horrified by the prospect of engaging with her. She ignored him though. 'Him with the specs and the beard,' she said, 'didn't he come here once before?'

'Yes. That's Gavin. He visited you after returning from college, several years after Melanie was killed.'

'That's right. The nosy bugger thought he'd nowt better to do than dig into what had become of Poppy. Well, we told him then that we didn't want anything to do with her.'

'That's a shame, Margaret, because it was Poppy we hoped to ask you about now.'

She shook her head, flapped a hand at me, and began to withdraw. Before she could slam the door in my face, I stuck out my hand and wrapped my fingers around the door jamb. 'Please, Margaret,' I said, 'if you can just give us a few minutes of your time.'

'No, you've kept me from my TV programme for long enough,' she snapped, and began closing the door. I quickly shifted so that my thigh would stop it shutting all the way and chopping off my fingers.

'Margaret, Mrs Bishop, please. We just need to know if you've heard that Poppy is back in town and that she's . . . '

'Eh? What are you blathering on about? Poppy's back in town, is she? Don't be so bloody stupid and hurtful. And get your bloody fingers out of the way or I will bloody well cut them off.'

I didn't doubt her. Mention of her adopted daughter had set a fire inside her, she was literally flaming mad. And maybe not a little mad-mad, as in out of her head, because her reaction went far beyond that expected of a rational mind. She began screeching as she threw her weight against the door, attempting to physically outpower me. I stood a head and shoulders taller and probably outweighed her by forty kilograms, yet there could be only one victor in our tussle with the door. It was never our intention to terrorize the old woman. I jerked back quickly, throwing up both hands in surrender, and she fell forward, shoving the door with her shoulder. The slamming door echoed the length of the street.

I checked on my friends. Neither had deemed it wise to come to my assistance, which was a good thing in hindsight. I backpedalled down the garden path, listening as the screaming continued indoors. It sounded as if Margaret Bishop was berating herself as much as she did me. Some smaller items crashed and tinkled, and I couldn't say if she'd blundered into them or deliberately thrown them. She made it to the living room, and for a second she glared out at me from between the drapes, before grabbing them and snapping them closed. I turned and marched double-time to my car and got in.

'Well,' said Gavin, 'that went well.'

Without replying, I started the engine and pulled away from the kerb. As I drove from the house, I felt Johnny's hand on my shoulder. I was shivering with adrenalin, and more than confused by her outburst.

'You all right there, Andrew?' he asked.

'I honestly don't know what to say,' I replied.

'Pull over,' Gavin instructed me. 'It's not as if she's chasing us up the road.'

'I wouldn't put it past her,' I replied and slowed the car. Conscientious, I parked avoiding the dropped kerbs into private driveways. 'Sad to say, but Margaret Bishop has lost the plot.'

'What did you say to set her off?' Gavin asked.

'Nothing bad,' I explained. 'She remembers you asking about Poppy all those years ago, and telling you they wanted nothing more to do with her. It wasn't that which sent her nuts, it was when I asked if she was aware Poppy was back in town. She accused me of being stupid and hurtful. I mean . . . what the fuck? What's more hurtful than denying your own kid?'

Johnny said, 'You know more than most that grief is a funny thing. Different people handle it in different ways. Maybe every time she thinks of Poppy it brings back the pain of losing Melanie.'

'Maybe she's just a vicious old trout,' I growled.

'Yeah, that's also an option,' said Johnny.

We laughed, but Gavin wasn't amused. 'What about speaking to Mr Bishop instead?'

'We'll have to find him first,' I replied. 'According to Margaret, he left her for another woman years ago. In fact, unless I'm mistaken, her exact words were "the stinking two-timing rat ran off with his floozy!" Correction, "bloody floozy".'

'Who knows where he's got to in the meantime,' Johnny lamented. 'He could still be in town, or moved elsewhere, or dead for all we know.'

'This doesn't have to be difficult,' said Gavin. 'You said she remembered me; maybe if I go back she won't be as mad with me as she got with you, Andrew.'

'You can try. It's your funeral,' I said.

TWENTY-SEVEN

We didn't return immediately. We allowed Margaret time to calm down, and for her TV programme to end. Neither did I park directly outside her house. Johnny and I got out of the car though and he stood just out of sight, close enough to hear without Margaret seeing. I joined Gavin reluctantly, my words ringing in my ears about it being his funeral. The ease with which she'd blown up before, I wouldn't put it past the fierce old woman to pick up something heavy and try beating us off her property with it. At first Gavin had planned on returning alone, but we decided it would help if Margaret had me as a target for her ire, should she grow enraged again, sparing Gavin to get the answers we sought. The old good cop, bad cop routine.

As we walked up the path, past the parked Nissan, she must've been watching between the drapes. The door was wrenched open, and she stood there, hands fisted on her hips this time.

'Do I need to call the police on yous lot?' she demanded.

'I can assure you there's no need,' said Gavin, sounding plummy-mouthed.

She aimed a finger at me. 'I just told this one to sling his bloody hook,' she said 'What makes you think I'm going to say anything different to you?'

'Hopefully I won't give you a reason to send me packing,' said Gavin, and I think he must have smiled disarmingly. Margaret's features quivered, but I could see that Gavin had struck a light in her eyes that hadn't been there before.

She said, 'It's a long time ago, but I remember you coming here and asking about Poppy. You were respectful and polite, a nice young man.'

I thought I'd been respectful and polite. I mean, what exactly had I said to make her grow mad? I caught her peeking past Gavin at me, giving me a sour look, and playing my part, I only jerked up my chin. She snorted, and turned her attention back on Gavin.

'We genuinely have no intention of upsetting you, Mrs . . . Uh, my friend tells me you don't go by the name Bishop anymore?'

'I'm still Margaret Bishop, it's the *Mrs* bit that doesn't apply.'

'Ah, I see,' said Gavin, and he turned a withering look on me as if I was some sort of ignorant dolt that should have known better.

'It wasn't made clear to me,' I muttered, but made no further argument. The last we wanted was for a blazing row on her front step for the sake of semantics.

'Maybe I was a bit on the defensive,' Margaret said by concession.

'All's fine, I assure you,' said Gavin.

Margaret glanced over her shoulder, as if checking indoors.

'Do you have company?' Gavin asked. 'We don't wish to intrude and can come back when it's more suitable . . .'

'No, no, there's nobody else here.' By the sound of things, she didn't sound convinced. Perhaps she required a witness to assure her, the reason why she next changed her tune. 'You'd best come in then, rather than broadcast my business to every bugger in the bloody street.'

'Me too?' I wondered aloud.

'You too,' she confirmed, 'and tell your little mate hiding behind the hedge he'd better come in as well.'

'Oh, you know about him?' Gavin grinned, keeping her disarmed.

'I can hear him puffing and panting like he's run a bloody mile,' she said.

'Johnny, you may as well show yourself, mate,' I called, and a few seconds later, Johnny poked his head around her neighbour's huge privet hedge and blinked at us. He had a cigarette in his hand and must have been pulling on it quite hard; he'd already taken it almost down to the filter. Margaret had probably spotted the smoke, not merely heard him as she'd claimed. He chucked his smouldering stump into the road, then walked towards us, trepidation in his approach.

'I'm not going to eat you,' Margaret said, and laughed as if it was the funniest thing ever. 'Come in, and close the door behind you.'

We trooped into her house. It reminded me of the home I'd lived in with my parents prior to marrying Nell, only two streets away. Many of the families on the estate from back then had fragmented, the younger generations moving further afield, but many of the older folks had put down roots too deep to pick up and move. There were concessions made to modernity in the house, like a flat screen TV, satellite TV receiver, and even a digital personal assistant sitting on

the front window sill, but otherwise, stepping into Margaret Bishop's
living room was akin to a hop back in time. Maybe not as far back
as my memories had been wandering of late, but perhaps to the turn
of the millennium. VHS video tapes were stacked on shelves, a
cordless phone on a side table, cheap ornaments displayed in a cut
glass corner cabinet, music CDs were stored in a wire tower, alongside one of those old home entertainment centres: a cabinet complete
with combined CD, radio and cassette player. It was not unlike my
parents' home now. I assumed that the museum state of her home
probably coincided with the same year that her husband abandoned
her for another woman, while the status of my parents' house was
down to me leaving home.

She indicated to us to sit down. There was an easy chair and a
small settee. She commandeered the chair, giving us no other option
than to squeeze shoulder-to-shoulder on the settee. We ensured that
Gavin was closest to Margaret, while I was farthest away. She shot
me occasional glances that told me I was not fully forgiven for my
brash intrusion into her busy life. I was still unclear on what I'd
said to upset her, but couldn't help noticing that the picture on her
TV had been paused; so I'd had no part in her missing the end of
her programme, as she'd lied.

'I don't have any milk, so can't offer you tea,' she said to Gavin.

I was happier she hadn't offered us a drink. Even if she had
coffee, I'd have declined for fear she'd have spat in my cup.

'It's OK, we're fine. We don't intend to keep you or put you to
any trouble . . .'

'Call me Margaret,' she said, and smiled at Gavin. She'd taken
a shine to our professorial-looking friend.

'Of course,' he said. 'We're Gavin, Johnny and Andrew.'

'Aye,' she said, and eyed me spuriously. 'So he said. And you've
a pal called Brian, and one dead called Carl, and together you were
like the Famous-bloody-Five, running to the coppers with the name
of the murderer. I'm getting on, I might be a bit white-haired but
there's no cotton wool between my ears. I'm fully compos mentis,
and my memory is sharp.' She pointed two straight fingers at me,
and I squirmed as if I was the recipient of a curse. 'I remember
you from when you were a boy. You were Glenda and Henry's lad;
they used to call your family the Windy Millers.'

Did they? If it had been a nickname for us back then I was
unaware, but I wouldn't put it past our neighbours to have an alter-

nate name for us; it was a common practice round where we lived, especially where distinction was required between different families with similar surnames. I knew the name Windy Miller for an animated character in a children's cartoon regularly aired on TV when I was a child. Maybe she was talking rubbish, because had I had a nickname Brian or Carl would have delighted in using it.

'You,' Margaret aimed her fingers at Johnny. 'It was your cousin that attacked my daughter.'

'Allegedly,' said Johnny.

'Allegedly? So alleged that he took his own life out of guilt,' she snarled.

Gavin quickly interjected before she could lose control of her mood.

'We did the right thing in telling the police about him. Johnny also.'

She leaned forward. 'I bet you were popular afterwards, eh? Nobody likes grassers around here, especially not one grassing up their own folk.'

'Would you rather we hadn't come forward?' Johnny replied. He didn't appear as disturbed as I'd have been under her direct attack.

'You did a good thing, I'll grant you. All you boys did.'

I hear you've been very bad.

Those words, or very similar, had been repeated to me on several occasions now, and although they were almost the opposite to what Margaret said, I felt they were connected.

Maybe her words also resonated with Gavin, reminding him why we were there, because he said, 'We are only sorry we couldn't help Melanie before she died, or before Poppy was injured.'

'Only one could have helped Melanie was the sicko that attacked her,' she said.

'It was fortunate that the weather was warm at the time, or poor Poppy could have perished before she was found,' Gavin said.

'Poor Poppy,' Margaret grunted, 'Poor Melanie more like. It should've been the other way around, it should've been my daughter that survived, not that wicked little orphan girl.'

None of us said a word in agreement. How could we? It was one thing for a mother choosing her flesh and blood daughter over a stranger's child, but we couldn't.

Margaret's chin dropped, and she entwined her hands. 'I must sound awful. But that girl was never mine. She behaved badly towards me, did anything she could to annoy me. She never accepted me as her mother, and never once said thanks for taking her in or . . . well, it doesn't matter. I suppose it's all water under the bridge now.'

'You told me years ago that she left home as soon as she was old enough, and that she reverted to her birth name.'

She looked up at Gavin. 'That's what I told you?'

'Yes. You said she'd changed her name back to Jennifer Seeley.'

A sneer ghosted across Margaret's features. 'I'm happy to hear the story has stood until now.'

'Story? What do you mean?'

'Poppy . . . no, Jenny, never recovered from the attack. She was in a coma, bed-ridden, fed with a tube, and pissed into a bag. After losing my daughter, there was no way that I was going to be that ungrateful wretch's nurse twenty-four-seven, not when she wouldn't accept me as her mother before. I mean . . . why should I?'

Again, none of us answered. Acidic bile fizzed in my throat.

'They took her away, and put her in a care home, changing her name back to Jenny Seeley to protect her from any media intrusion. As far as I know she's still there and good riddance.'

'She isn't,' said Gavin. 'She's back in town.'

She shook her head in denial. 'Nope.'

'I've seen her personally,' he said. 'So has Johnny's partner and we think Brian has seen her too, but mistook her for . . .' Mentioning Brian seeing a grown-up Melanie, and subsequently having erotic dreams involving her, would not do '. . . another woman. Andrew . . .'

'I haven't seen her,' I said quickly. And it was true. I hadn't seen Poppy, albeit I was beginning to believe that she and the twigs and rags creature I'd glimpsed that day I'd parked at the lonning might be indelibly connected. 'But I believe the others have.'

'Nah,' said Margaret and shook her head again. 'She was very badly injured. That monster cracked open their skulls like they were soft boiled eggs and Poppy's brain got all mushed up. She couldn't even breathe without help, let alone get up and move around. Believe me, at best that girl is still lying in a hospital bed somewhere, being spoon fed and having her backside wiped for her.'

I'd heard enough. I stood up sharply. 'I think we've heard all we need to for now,' I announced.

She jutted her chin at me, and I am certain I spotted the pooling of venom behind her eyes. She said, 'You asked, I'm only telling you the way it is.'

'Frankly,' I said, reflecting back on how my mother despised and mistreated me and how so alike Margaret was towards Poppy, 'I think you're a horrible person and didn't deserve children, especially not an adopted child.'

'Yeah, well, we're not all perfect are we?' she snapped. 'Feel free to fuck off.'

'I'm leaving,' I confirmed.

Johnny began to stand too.

'You OK, Andrew?' he whispered. 'It's not like you to talk to anyone like that.'

'I'm fine. I just can't stand to listen to her bile any longer.'

Lastly, Gavin pushed to his feet. Margaret didn't stir, only sat with her jaw locked to one side as she glared up at us.

'We'll let ourselves out,' said Gavin, still keeping a reasonable tone.

'Door's unlocked,' Margaret grunted. 'Make sure you pull it shut behind you. If she is up and about, I don't want wicked Jenny letting herself in. Huh! Wicked Jenny. That's a good name for that little bitch, isn't it?'

We'd already begun to leave. I was in the tiny hallway by the time she named Poppy Wicked Jenny, and had pulled open the front door by the time she went on to slander her more. I set off up the path, Johnny tight on my heels while Gavin was the last to leave. Margaret, for several minutes lucid, had degenerated to the muttering, swearing, horrible bitch that was true to her nature. It was no wonder young Poppy had hated her.

TWENTY-EIGHT

Brian Petrie

B rian stood up to his ankles in chilly mud. Raindrops dotted his shoulders and hair, but were yet to fall with any great volume. His hands were fisted in his pockets, and his jaw lowered, breathing sharply through his nostrils. Anyone observing him might think he was angry, but he wasn't; challenged to explain his emotions, he might say he was confused, or frightened. Or he was confused because he couldn't put a finger directly on why he was afraid. Brian had never been one to be afraid and could be reckless because of it. It wasn't that he was overly brave, more that he didn't grasp the concept of danger the way others might do. The old adage about looking before leaping was lost on Brian, he was more the type to close his eyes, run blind at a cliff and then leap, and be surprised by whatever cushioned his fall, be it water, soft rags or a bundle of barbed wire: he knew each of these from past childhood experience and still had not learned a lesson from the latter.

He had lied to Andrew earlier, telling his friend that something personal had come up that he must deal with, so couldn't join the gang at the Bishop house. Andrew had immediately assumed his problems with Joyce had intensified, and he'd ended the call rather than go deeper down that rabbit hole. Yes, his relationship with Joyce was on the rockiest, slipperiest slope, and most likely coils of rusty barbed wire waited for him at the bottom, but he didn't want to go over things again with Andrew. At another time? Sure, but first there was something else he must deal with, something that had been pulling at him for days, drawing him like a sliver of iron to a magnet.

He hadn't told anyone where he was going. Not Andrew or the other lads. Certainly not Joyce, who wouldn't understand the relevance anyway and who would surely kick up a fuss if he tried explaining. In fact, he was unsure if the location still existed the way it did in his memory, because it had been decades since he was last there, and the sprawling city had grown into some of the wilder spaces he'd played in as a boy. He had driven so far, and been forced to abandon his car at the head of what had once been a lonning, and was now at the front of a gated community. Access was still allowed, but only on foot. He entered the gated area, and cut quickly past the cluster of red brick houses and more parked cars than seemed necessary for the residents. A narrow cut, a single tarmac strip between tall wire fences, allowed access back to the old lonning mid-way down. Brian recalled sports pitches on one side and a joiner's yard on the other, terminating at an unofficial rubbish dump. Beyond the dump, where there seemed to be constant smoking fires, was where there used to be a railway marshalling yard, demolished before he was born, but the mounds of rubble had been left to rot under the elements for years. All were now gone. The sports pitches had been built on, so too the joiner's yard. The rubbish tip had been bulldozed over and the rubble mountains removed. Clusters of bushes had been planted, and had now grown wild and dense, and narrow paths had been laid out with small signs indicating each as either nature trails, public footpaths or bicycle paths. If he went straight on, he could access the largest of three rivers that once formed the boundary to the medieval walled town before it sprawled into modern times, but he turned left and paralleled the river. He found old pathways he'd used as a child, and before long came upon where he was certain that Ian Nixon had built his den under spreading branches. There was no hint of the furniture he'd dragged there, the tarpaulin roof or pictures of nudes pinned to the branches, but if he inspected closer he thought he would find spots where Nixon's hammer had knocked chunks out of the tree trunks.

He continued on, and distractedly understood that the stiles had been removed, and the gravel path he followed had been given more substance: probably it had been designated as a public footpath leading to the ring road that had since encircled that end of town. The multi-million-pound by-pass had been built a dozen years or more ago, redirecting the traffic from ploughing through the town centre, but at the expense of some green spaces and part of a nature reserve. While it was being built, some demonstrators had staged noisy protests, sitting in front of bulldozers and chaining themselves to trees, and at the time Brian had scoffed at them as tree hugging loonies. Now, seeing the ugly swath of concrete and tarmac that cut through the landscape, formed a bridge over the river and stretched to each side, he thought perhaps he should have joined them in noisy protest. This was the treasured landscape of his youth and it had been ripped in half. A hundred metres to his left was where the five-bar gate once slowed access to the decommissioned railway line. It had disappeared, as had most of the trees that originally shaded it. As he trudged across to where the gate used to be the ground grew boggy, until he sloshed through mud and kicked up water with each step. Finally, he reached his destination and stood there, fists in his pockets, breathing sharply through his nose as he brooded over why the scene before him caused such trepidation, such fear.

The frog ponds didn't exist.

Not as they had before.

The narrow valley formed of railway embankments and single gauge rail track now only had one shoulder. The embankment to his left remained, but it formed the sloping edge to a field, and was topped by a low wire fence, the only thing separating it from an industrial estate that had sprung up in the intervening years. The ponds must have been drained, and the right-hand embankment bulldozed and ploughed to form the field. It formed a fallow area, a large half circle that abutted the new by-pass route. Where the frog ponds used to stretch into infinity, the raised by-pass chopped off its head like a massive guillotine.

Tears stung Brian's eyes.

His youth had somehow been violated, and it hurt.

Worse. This was the place where Melanie Bishop had died, and it felt as if her grave had been vandalized. No, it had been desecrated.

'Is this why you are haunting me?' he asked, barely above a whisper.

There was no answer.

He stared, misty-eyed, and at the base of the surviving embankment he could make out several depressions where the ground was still as boggy as it was where he was standing. However, the scrubby grass that covered the field also extended up the embankment, replacing the reeds and duck weed he recalled from when he was a boy.

Almost robotic, he moved forward, his fists now extended from his sides to aid balance. He walked through the bog, mud sucking at his shoes with every footstep.

He had no way of pinpointing where the girls had been attacked. Recalling conversations with his friends, and other kids at school, they had added their own impressions to each telling of the attack. Some had it that Melanie and Poppy were assaulted on the right-hand embankment – now gone – and then dragged deeper into the bushes. Others said they were left lying face down in the water, as if something had tried dragging them down into the murky depths beneath the ponds. Yet others were adamant that the girls had fled their attacker, and he'd brought them down separately, then dragged the senseless Poppy and laid her near Melanie so he could have his wicked way with the prettier girl, while not having to worry about the other escaping unobserved. It was all speculation and downright fabrication.

Brian tried recounting the events of the day, when his little gang of mates had teased the girls – or immaturely flirted with them, as he now believed they were doing – until Carl's nastiness towards them had sent them scurrying up the embankment with their timid dog. He attempted to place them in the area where they'd hunkered after Carl threw armfuls of pond weed at them. Jesus, in hindsight, Brian was responsible for setting Carl off, teasing the girls that Ginny Greenteeth would get them if they lingered too near to the water. Brian tried convincing himself that he was only joking, and had been simply acting his usual daft-self, making cackling noises like an old witch.

'Ginny comes for the naughtiest boys and girls . . .' he'd claimed.

Well, despite Carl accusing them of being slags, a complete untruth, the sisters should have been safe from the clutching talons of Ginny Greenteeth, the local name for the evil water sprite said to lure wayward children to their watery deaths. All the girls were guilty of being were the targets for immature boys overflowing with raging hormones.

Andy, playing the diplomat, had tried to convince the girls that everything was done in jest, but Carl had to be Carl, and started chucking the pond weed at them.

'Git before ol' Ginny drags you underwater,' Carl had shouted, or at least words similar to those to which Poppy had answered that they were all a bunch of horrible little shits.

She had been right, because what Brian said then about the colouration of her pubic hair was embarrassing to the adult that he'd become. His proclamation that Poppy should be named 'Copper

Pubes' was the breaking point that had sent the boys running, laughing, hooting and catcalling until stumbling across Ian Nixon's lair and into the terrible situation that had defined them for years to come. That stupid name was even having an impact in Brian's current life, and if what he'd learned from his pals was true, his earlier words were being turned on them too.

'Ginny comes for the naughtiest boys and girls,' he'd quoted, 'and from what I hear you've both been very, very bad.'

'. . . you've been very bad.'

He turned sharply.

Whose voice was that?

There was nobody in sight, but he was certain that he had heard his words echoed back to him, though subtly changed.

'Who's there?' he demanded.

A trio of birds broke from the trees on his left, their wings clattering through denuded branches.

He turned and watched them flee, then his gaze dropped, seeking what had disturbed them.

He raised his clenched fists. 'Whoever's there, you'd better show yourself or we are going to have a problem.'

There was nobody there. The tree trunks were too narrow to hide anyone fatter than one of Brian's legs. Fleetingly he wondered if the speaker was lying just beyond the curve of the surviving embankment. He started towards it, then halted. Perhaps he'd heard a voice carrying from the industrial estate; except this was late Sunday morning and it was unlikely that anyone would be at work on the site. Besides, the voice had been too sharp and too clear, and had originated from in front of him.

Brian had never laid much stock in the supernatural before.

Not that he didn't believe that miracles were possible, or that there was high strangeness at work in the world, only that his thought processes rarely jumped to paranormal explanations when something more rational was available.

To him it was more likely that he'd heard a distant voice, carried somehow and amplified by the nature of the land around him. Case in point, the cars whizzing past on the ring road sounded super loud one second and then barely audible the next. Maybe what he'd heard was a snatch of music blaring from the lowered window of a car as it shot past. Likely it had not said *you've been very bad*, but something similar and his brain had twisted the words to fit what was in his mind.

'So why ask why you're being haunted?' he challenged himself for an answer.

'You've been very bad.'

The voice croaked in his ear, as if somebody stood directly behind, their mouth almost touching his skin.

Brian cried out, and swung with an elbow.

He staggered, seeking and failing to find the source of the voice.

'Who are you?' he cried out. 'Where are you?'

He ran several steps, feet splashing water high in dirty crescents. He halted, spun around and stood, chin jutting, neck straining. 'You need to stay the fuck away from me!'

'Ol' Ginny drags you underwater,' the voice said, again from inches behind him.

Brian spun around, swiping with his forearm, but again found no resistance.

'I don't believe in you,' he shouted. 'You aren't real. You have to stay the hell away, do you hear me?'

No answer was forthcoming.

He completed several full circles, the mud sucking at his shoes, soaking his socks and invading his trousers.

'This is a load of bull . . .'

He stormed away, hands slashing at the air, as if it would assist him to move through the boggy field.

He halted and turned back.

From this vantage he didn't recognize the scene as the frog ponds where he'd played as a child. Over the tops of the trees, he could see the roofs of warehouses. Those voices had to have originated there, and his overactive imagination was making more of them than they deserved.

That was the rational explanation.

So why was he fearful?

What was it about that voice that sent cold shivers down his back, drove daggers in under his ribcage and sought to bury their tips in his heart?

He turned and jogged across the field, his breathing ragged. Pressure behind his eyes made them bulge from their sockets. His teeth were clamped so tightly that his jaws ached.

Again, reaching the gravel path, it was as if he'd reached a safety zone, beyond the reach of ghosts and sprites. He crouched there, one hand grasping a tuft of long grass at the edge of the path. He stared back across the field, almost expecting something shadowy and uncanny to detach from the spindly trees beyond the boggy margin and begin an ungainly, yet insidious crawl towards him.

He stared, mouth hanging open, hands clutching at his chest, but nothing came.

'Bloody hell, Joyce,' he groaned. 'You were right, love. I'm losing my bloody mind!'

Joyce had counselled him over the past couple of weeks, warning him that he was growing fascinated with Melanie Bishop, and unless he gave himself a mental shake, he was going to fall victim to obsession, a surefire route to madness in her opinion. Well, without fail, he'd dreamed of Melanie every night. Not all his dreams had been erotic like the time when he'd gone to Andrew, seeking his best pal's advice on how to handle things with Joyce after he'd cried out the dead girl's name during orgasm. Most of his dreams had been mundane, and barely recalled after, except that Melanie had inhabited them. Sometimes she was the middle-aged woman he'd first dreamed of, sometimes she was a young teenager as when he'd first seen her. On those occasions when she was the younger incarnation, so had Brian been his younger self in his dream. Nothing sleazy had ever happened between current Brian and teenage Mel for which he could only be thankful.

His relationship with Joyce had always been solid, despite her being the second love in his life. She'd accepted that his previous wife, Trisha, came first in his affection, and had settled into second place. Theirs was almost like a polygamist marriage, but she sure as shit wasn't prepared to slip further back in line for the sake of another dead girl. She'd warned him: 'Get yourself together, Bri, or I'm out of here.'

His reason for visiting the scene of Mel's murder was so he could lay the past to rest. It hadn't seemed a bad idea when he set off, but now he realized that, if anything, he'd dug a burr deeper into his skin and it would take a lot of scratching out before he was done dreaming of Melanie. It was partially through his stupid antics that they'd ended up teasing Mel and Poppy, then running away like the bunch of immature juveniles they were, and into Ian Nixon's sights. And yes, Brian had joined in the baiting of the big nutter with the claw hammer, and possibly set him off on his murderous rampage. He had come to the frog ponds to say sorry to Mel, rather than visit her grave. The grave held nothing of the girl's vitality: if there were such things as spirits, or an everlasting consciousness as some of the New Agers preached, he doubted that Mel would hang about where her bones had been left to moulder in her grave. If she'd been parted from her carnal body at the point of her murder, then perhaps she did return there to the ponds, or could be summoned to the place by his will, and he could apologize.

He was sorry.

Carl's murder under similar circumstances had brought his feelings to the surface. He had never been religious, but since Carl's murder, and his connection to Melanie Bishop's shade had ignited, he had certainly grown spiritual. Sadly, that spiritual awakening wasn't through enlightenment, nor peaceful acceptance, his attachment to the murdered girl was defined purely by soul-devouring guilt.

Being sorry he hoped to tell her so, and through the act of contrition maybe she would leave him be. But it had only taken coming to the frog ponds and experiencing those disembodied voices to understand that any apology he made would fall on deaf ears. There was no forgiveness forthcoming, not from whatever haunted him. He knew now, too, that it was not Melanie. Aye it was her face and body that invaded his dreams, but the image was a sham, and something else entirely lurked behind the facade. He had tried denying the truth, but it hit him now; the originator of that voice and the creature determined to destroy the little happiness he had in life was one and the same.

He swore aloud.

Threw his hands in the air. Swore again.

Immediately he felt foolish. What if he was wrong, and it was as he'd initially asserted, that he didn't believe in spirits, ghosts or sprites? Who exactly was he shouting and swearing at if the target of his ire didn't exist? He thought of some of the homeless people in town, those that screamed and raged at the heavens, whether or not they had an audience. Their ruination was through alcohol and drugs, but had probably begun with something else entirely; maybe even guilt. He didn't want to end up like one of those pitiful people, with a damaged mind and a host of imaginary listeners to berate.

He shut his mouth, and stood there feeling the blood tingling in his cheeks. His vision grew a little foggy and momentarily he swayed, as if about to fall down. He reached out behind him, and his fingers found the topmost wire on the fence that separated the cinder path from the river's steep and wooded embankment. The wire was rough, and a loose metallic thread dug into his palm. Hissing in pain, he sucked at his hand, fearing that the thread had broken off and was embedded in his skin. He tasted blood. Spat it out.

A shadow invaded his vision.

Somebody was standing behind his shoulder blocking the sunlight. Somebody bigger than him.

He had not seen their approach, and was confident that they hadn't arrived via the cinder path from either direction. They must have stepped out of the woods on the riverbank behind him. He hadn't heard their approach, and they must've taken care not to break a twig underfoot, or knock loose a stray pebble.

Sneaking about as they had, they must mean no good.

'What's your game?' Brian spun, even as he thrust out with his elbow, then forearm. Making space he brought up his balled right fist and swung it in a clubbing blow.

His fist swept through space, and he almost wrenched the muscle in his shoulder with the miss.

Swearing, he adjusted, expecting to find his stalker had dodged or crouched or . . .

Where the hell were they?

There was nobody there.

He completed a circle, checking the field and path, and then leaned over the fence to check that somebody hadn't climbed the riverbank to lurk at his shoulder, then dropped back into a hiding place when he struck at them. He knew beyond doubt that there was nobody there, and yet he forced himself to check. To do nothing was to accept that he was going insane.

'Only one . . .' a voice croaked.

Never the type to fear before, reckless by nature, he was suddenly terrified. This was an emotion he'd never suffered from, and it debilitated him. He stood a moment, knees threatening to give out beneath him, his bladder on the verge of emptying, as much at the terror of the unknown as it was the thought he could be losing his mind.

Brian turned and ran, bleating loudly, his arms and legs wind-milling as if he'd lost control of them. Had any of his friends witnessed his retreat they might not have immediately recognized him, because this ungainly figure was nothing like the Brian Petrie who'd always been the first into battle whenever they were threatened. He ran, staggered, his loose limbs jerking spasmodically. He barely made it more than ten metres before his legs failed completely, and his arms clutched at his body. Crushing pain sucked his left arm to his side. He pinwheeled off the cinder path and back on to the couch grass, again finding a boggy spot.

He crashed face down.

Filthy water splashed, then fell in droplets.

But for the popping of bubbles released from his settling form, there was no other sound or motion and then . . .

The rain that had only threatened before arrived in a downpour that hissed in the grass and on Brian's back and legs.

It didn't rouse him.

He did not rise again.

TWENTY-NINE

I learned afterwards that by an ironic case of coincidence, another group of young boys was drawn into the current situation when they discovered Brian Petrie's body. Using the wooded riverbank as an adventure playground they'd scrambled their way, using low branches and tree trunks for handholds, traversing almost half a mile along the embankment before the concrete bridge carrying the ring road over the river foiled any further progress. There they'd been forced back on to the cinder path and turned back towards home. Within minutes they had found Brian lying face down in the boggy grass, in water barely two fingers deep. He was saturated, with broken blades of grass and weed adhering to his clothing and hair. He had obviously lain there for hours, since before the heavy rainfall had petered off before noon. The boys, both sickened and astonished by equal amounts, chose to roll him on his back, claiming afterwards that they thought they were doing the right thing in clearing his mouth from the water. Seeing the stricken look contorting his features, they'd panicked and rolled him back over again rather than continue witnessing the agony – or was that terror? – on his face. His hands had formed rictus twin claws, wrists and elbows bent, and had somehow become trapped beneath him when he collapsed. They could see where he'd thrashed a path off the cinders and into the field, with deep gouges cutting through the sodden turf where his feet had ploughed through it.

In a twist that differentiated these boys from my gang back in the 1980s, there was no need for them to run for help, or to seek out a coin-operated telephone box: each boy among them carried their own personal mobile phone. I've no way of knowing which of them was elected their spokesperson, but I could imagine a lad of a similar nature to mine informing the authorities about their horrific find.

The police arrived, and shortly after them the coroner attended. Parked closer to the field on the ring road, the emergency vehicles caused quite a stir, and soon after an air ambulance helicopter was drafted in to help recover Brian's body. He was flown to the local infirmary and placed in the morgue, awaiting an autopsy to establish a cause of death. It was already accepted that there was no sign of foul play, and that Brian had probably died from a cardiac arrest. Having identified him from the contents of his wallet, a police officer was dispatched to inform his next of kin and that was how Joyce learned of Brian's passing. I heard that my oldest friend was dead during a tearful telephone call from her, where she was full of self-recrimination and guilt, feeling that she might have helped Brian to his premature death through stress.

Unlike the time when hearing of Carl Butler's murder, I was alone, so didn't experience the same dynamic involving Nell, and instead of wailing, gnashing my teeth and pulling out clumps of my hair, as might be expected when losing my best friend, I took the news with a deep melancholy and very little reaction. Maybe Joyce expected more from me, or perhaps she understood that this time the shock was enough to knock me sideways, and she ended the call with a promise that she'd ring back once she knew more. In hindsight, she was perhaps seeking somebody to hold her hand and walk with her through the process of identifying her common law spouse, and beginning the funeral arrangements. Hell, I didn't know until days after, that Brian's car had been abandoned at the head of the lonning, and Joyce had no immediate form of transportation and was probably hoping I'd offer to take her to the hospital. I would have, of course, except that I was stunned and found it difficult ordering my thoughts. The rest of my evening was spent talking on the phone with Johnny and then Gavin, and totally out of character for me – because Brian and I had previously polished off the brandy – downing a bottle of vodka also left over from a previous Christmas. I fell asleep, drunk and melancholic, in an easy chair in the living room, and when I awoke, the house was cool and silent. Still half-cut I staggered upstairs, and found Nell soaking in the bathtub. I stared at her for long seconds, wondering if the act of trying to explain the latest tragedy while drunk would make matters worse, so I backed out of the bathroom and closed the door and returned to my place in the living room. I didn't want to upset the current status quo. I simply had no energy for more tears, nor to go over Brian's death with her, and decided to wait until morning. Besides, there were still a couple of glugs of vodka left in the bottle and I'd no desire to share.

In darkness, I supped, and as the drunken fog descended over me once more, I welcomed the oblivion.

THIRTY

'You shouldn't be here,' Gemma Barker told me, the next morning.

'Why not? It's my office.' I smiled at my weak joke.

'You should be home, dealing with this with your loved ones.'

She stood in the doorway, with one hand on her hip, the other resting on the door handle. She had dyed her hair since last I'd seen her, now it had a reddish tint, and a feathery blonde slash that tapered towards the crown of her head. Her glasses reflected my overhead light, concealing her eyes behind the glare. For a moment I thought how maternal she could be at times, but then recalled that I was old enough to be her father.

'I'm not sure Heatley would authorize me any more time off,' I said.

'Your best friend just died! He'd have to be heartless to deny you compassionate leave.'

I shrugged noncommittally.

'Didn't you even ask him for time off, Mr Miller?'

'Nope. And, please, call me Andrew, eh? Calling me Mr Miller makes me sound as old as my dad.' I was pretty certain I'd used that old duck egg on her more than once, but she would persist in calling me by my title and surname, at least she did if there was a possibility of being overheard.

'Are you certain you're OK? I mean, you've been dealing with quite a lot lately and . . .'

'I'm OK,' I cut her off. 'Dealing with my friend's death is different this time. First time with Carl, well, that was through his murder, and it was harder to accept than Brian having a heart attack. It's sad that he died, but it happens. In fact, I've been thinking about having my cholesterol checked and getting a course of statins prescribed by my doctor, I mean, look at this . . .' Without standing, I pinched a roll of fat at my waistline.

Gemma shook her head. 'If you don't want to go home, then maybe you should speak with somebody. Perhaps making an appointment to see your doctor isn't a bad idea.'

'Yeah, I will. It's just that I've too much work to do at the present.'

'It can wait, surely.'

'No, it has to be done.' I tapped a few keys on my computer. 'Norman was good to me, allowing me time off last time and I don't intend to take any liberties with his generosity.'

Gemma performed a double-take. She then checked over her shoulder, ensuring she wasn't overheard. 'That's a laugh. Generosity and Norman are two words that don't work in one sentence. He's a greedy sod.'

'The man's got a business to run,' I countered.

'You've got your mental health to take care of,' she answered quickly.

Trying to bring light to the situation I said, 'Are you calling me nuts, Gemma?'

She was horrified by the question. 'Absolutely not. I'm concerned that you are bottling up your emotions and sooner or later you'll explode. You must take the time to grieve properly otherwise . . .'

'Gemma,' I said, and smiled sadly. 'I've been in a constant state of grief since my daughter died.'

A single tear ran down her cheek, and she dashed it away with the back of her wrist. 'I know that. Then your friend Carl was murdered, and now another friend has died. How are you able to carry on without . . .'

Again, I cut her off. 'Compartmentalization. And lots of vodka.'

I only meant the latter as a joke, but she took it seriously; after all, it was blatant to anyone with eyes or a nose that I'd enjoyed a heavy drinking session the previous night.

'Maybe it's too obvious?' I ventured.

She nodded. Stepping further into my office, she said, 'Mr Miller, I'm only saying this for your sake, but . . .'

'I know I look a mess. I was up most of the night, thinking and drinking. Then this morning I had to break the news to Nell and . . .'

This time she butted in. 'How did Nell take it? You were all close friends, yeah? She must be finding things tough too. More's the reason why you should be at home, to be together.'

'Do you mind coming in and closing the door? Things are getting a bit personal.'

'Uh, yeah, of course. I'm sorry if I'm overstepping the mark, it's just that I'm concerned about you.'

She shut the door, and I stood up and did a sideways dance

around my desk. There was not much room for the two of us in front of my desk, considering one side of the room was stuffed with a bulging filing cabinet, and a plug-in fan. I towered over Gemma, and she stood looking up at me, expectant, with her bottom lip nipped between her teeth.

Wringing my hands, I said, 'Nell and I aren't getting on too well at the moment. In fact, well, we are barely able to communicate civilly.'

'I'm sorry to hear that,' she said, and adjusted her spectacles. That close I saw how clear her eyes were, still sparkling from the tears of a moment ago. 'I don't know your wife that well, but she always comes across as a nice person.'

'She is. It's just that we are not in the nicest of situations just now, and haven't been for some time. We are more like . . .' I thought about it, '. . . cohabiters in the same space at the moment than we are man and wife.'

Gemma didn't reply. I could read the workings of her mind through her micro-expressions, and for a second I thought she'd make an excuse to leave. Things were already a bit tight in the office, without either of us getting hot under the collar.

'It must be very difficult for you both . . .'

'It is. Our only interactions are perfunctory at best, and outright shouting matches at the worst.'

'I'm really sorry to hear that, Mr Miller, uh, Andrew. You know that if you ever need somebody to talk to, I'm here, yeah?' She laid a hand gently on my forearm.

'I do. You've been nice to me, Gemma, and I really do appreciate your friendship.'

She paused for a moment, and it was understandable, then she moved in and we hugged, a bit rigid at first. If anyone were to enter my office and find us in such close proximity it would be bad enough, let alone in a position that could be misconstrued as compromising. But then she made this pitiful face, lips pursed and turned her head to one side and leaned in to me. I adopted a similar position, though my larger body kind of engulfed hers. I could smell my body odour, faint but with a sharper tang from the alcohol oozing from my pores, but Gemma's perfume was far headier. As I gently squeezed her, she squeezed back, and my breath shuddered as I inhaled her scent.

I should have released her then, but I held on a fraction longer, and Gemma nestled in a bit tighter. I allowed my hand around her lower back to slide, and gently caressed her backside. When she didn't slap me, I caressed it again, this time with a little more force, then allowed my hand to remain there, cupping the swell of her bottom. She looked up, blinking, her mouth open, and my mouth was so close that I exhaled into hers. And, there was a stirring of my loins, and perhaps I nudged her and she felt, and suddenly she pulled out of my grasp with a startled exhalation of her own.

I held up a palm, to forestall her. But before I could begin to explain my ardour, or to apologize for it, or whatever she expected from me, she grabbed at the door handle and began to drag the door open over the hump in the carpet. As the door finally wrenched free, she shot me a look. 'I really do think you should go home, Mr Miller, and try making things up with your wife.'

'Gemma,' I croaked. 'I'm sorry, I . . .'

She didn't hang around. She fled down the corridor towards the staff dining room. Or towards my boss's office. I collapsed in my seat, jammed my elbows on the desk and waited for her to return with Norman Heatley and an accusation of sexual harassment and assault.

'Silly little tease,' I moaned.

What the hell had she expected from me after asking for it?

THIRTY-ONE

I f Gemma complained about me, it was not directly to Norman Heatley. Maybe she sought the confidence of another of the girls and told them how I'd fondled her backside. Maybe said girlfriend had helped convince her that there was probably nothing salacious in my action, and that I had simply been returning the hug, my hands wandering without any conscious volition. Maybe they convinced Gemma that it was not in her interest to cause a fuss, when nothing would come of it other than Gemma perhaps losing her job, or at least stymieing any future hopes of promotion for her. Theirs was still a patriarchal company, where the top positions were all filled with men – in actuality, me and Norman – and it would come down to my word against hers, and who was the boss most likely to believe? And besides, I was suffering from grief, shock, and maybe still partially drunk, so was probably acting totally out of character. Yeah, I could just imagine how the conversation went. Maybe even Gemma had confided that when she closed my office door behind her she had kind of hoped I'd take the initiative because she'd been giving me the come-on for long enough; it was only after she felt my burgeoning erection throbbing against her that she thought things were moving too quickly. Maybe it wasn't in her plan for me to take her over my desk in a few frantic lustful seconds and she entertained designs of a more romantic 'first time' instead. Maybe she had ended up giggling with her pal, exchanging risqué jokes and plotting her next move.

I wasn't summoned to the boss's office. When I later went to the staff dining room and warmed my lunch in the microwave, a few of my junior colleagues sat at tables, eating and scrolling through their mobile phones, but there was no sign of Gemma. None of the girls in the room as much as glanced at me, and certainly didn't smile, or scowl, with secret knowledge having been brought into Gemma's confidence. Gemma wasn't around for afternoon break either, and again I was not the subject of scrutiny by a different set of colleagues in the dining room. The only time I saw Gemma again that day was as we left to go home, and she was ahead of me in the corridor leading to the exit. She 'clocked out', tapping her unique employee code into a keypad next to the door, even as I hurried to catch her.

'Gemma. Can I . . .'

Before I could stop her, she hit the press bar on the door and stepped out into a cloudburst. She hunched her shoulders against the rain, even as she dug for an umbrella in her bag. She deliberately avoided looking at me, and by the time I had reached the pad to tap myself out, she had darted away. I'd hoped to offer her a lift, talk things over, and try to reassure her that I wasn't some sort of creepy predator. How could I convince her that I'd been denied any affection from Nell, let alone intimacy, since we'd lost our Becky, and that I was simply a normal man with a normal man's needs? She shouldn't fear me, and in fact, if she still fancied me, we could perhaps try again and . . .

What the fucking hell are you *thinking?*

The train of my thoughts were derailed at that very point. They crashed and burned.

I staggered out through the exit, bewildered by my stupidity.

I loved Nell.

Usually there was nothing I'd do to deliberately hurt her.

Planning sexual trysts with a work colleague young enough to be our daughter was not the way to bring my wife back to me.

Gemma was ahead of me, fairly clipping along with her umbrella aimed into the driving rain. Perhaps her speed was more to do with getting out of the rain than it was giving me the brush off. Moments ago I might have scurried after her, and tried catching her before she could make it to her bus home, or taxi, or whatever she had in mind. But having come to my senses, I deliberately stalled. The rain plastered my hair to my forehead, and soaked through the shoulders of my jacket, and my shirt beneath. Water dribbled off the end of my nose, and hung in shivering droplets on my eyelashes. I waited until Gemma was out of sight and then began a slow walk to where I'd parked my car.

Driving home, I did so with a sense of guilt gnawing at me. Should I tell Nell about my near miss with Gemma? It might help, by reminding her that we were supposed to be a couple, one conjoined unit, that we should be doing what was necessary to ensure a modicum of happiness for both of us and that should include intimacy. Nell was doing her thing; I should be allowed to do mine. Right? But in that direction lay wrack and ruin. Unless it became common knowledge there was no need for Nell to learn what had happened with Gemma in my office. It was a moment of weakness, where the blood and good sense had drained from my brain into my genitals, that was all, and admitting to it couldn't help, and would in fact knock in further the wedge that already forced us apart. A secret was best kept, when divulging it would only hurt us. I could only hope that Gemma continued to be candid. She obviously hadn't told a soul about us yet, and hopefully things would continue like that.

The rain came down in torrents. Almost biblical in its intensity. Roads and gutters were awash. Pedestrians caught outside scrambled from one shelter to the next, in hopeless attempts at getting home dry and only achieved further soakings as they passed under teeming awnings. The traffic was slowed, and as I sat waiting to move ahead at some red lights, I felt the world going hazy at its edges, and something not unlike a thick rubber band tugged my forehead towards the dash.

Horns sounded behind me.

The traffic in front had moved on, the light now green. I'm unsure how long I was out of it, but it could only have been seconds. The drivers weren't as patient as to let the lights go through a full cycle before leaning on their horn to get me moving. Flustered, I worked the gear stick, while my feet padded up and down on the pedals. My car lurched and stalled. Another few seconds passed in frantic confusion before I got the engine started once more and my feet complied with the correct timing and pressure on the pedals. I pulled forward just as the green light went out and cycled back towards red. As I drove off the drivers behind me showed their appreciation with more extended beeps of their horns.

Minutes later, I pulled off the road on to my drive. The twin metal gates had been left open by me that morning. There was another car parked on the roadside adjacent to my garden gate. Through the battering rain I didn't immediately recognize it as Johnny's until my friend got out and jogged up the path towards my front door. I left my car and darted to join him, shielding my hair this time by an arm held above my head.

'Hope you don't mind me dropping by?' Johnny asked.

'You should've waited inside,' I said.

'I would've but nobody's home.'

'Nell isn't back yet?'

'If she is, she must be taking a shower or nap because I rang the bell and nobody answered.'

I shrugged. Nell came and went as she chose, and lately her times spent with me in the house had grown less than before. 'She's probably waiting out the rain before coming home,' I suggested.

'It's terrible this thing with Brian,' he said.

'It's bloody awful,' I emphasized. 'And totally unexpected.'

'If we keep on going at this rate there won't be any of us left by the end of the month.'

'Don't even joke about it,' I said.

'Sadly, I am not joking.'

I let us indoors, where I shook the rain off my jacket and then hung it on a hook behind the front door. Johnny wasn't as wet as me, but he still slipped out of his coat, conscious about dripping a path along the hallway carpet. His shoes were dotted with moisture, but not too badly: he'd only jogged from his car to the front door. By comparison my shoes and socks were soaked, as were my trousers and the shoulders of my damp shirt adhered to me like a second skin.

'Do you want to get a brew going while I go and get changed?' I asked. 'I'll only be a minute or two.'

I sent him towards the kitchen while I headed upstairs. On the landing I stopped and sniffed. A faint smell hung in the air, as if some soft fruit had been forgotten about in a bowl and had begun to rot. I checked the bathroom, the first spare room and then Becky's room – we'd kept it practically the way she'd left it, a mausoleum to her memory – and then I knocked on the door of the second spare room, where Nell had taken to sleeping these past few months. There was no hint of rotting fruit in there.

By the time I closed her door, went to our room and dug through wardrobes and drawers for a fresh set of dry clothes, I'd forgotten about the scent. As I descended again, all I could smell was the pot of coffee that Johnny had prepared.

'You remembered, eh?' I asked.

'Yeah, last time I was here you downed a bucketful of coffee. I also remembered that you have no beer in your fridge.' He hoisted up a mug into which he'd dropped a tea bag and boiling water. 'So I'll stick with this.'

I filled another mug with the coffee he'd prepared. Took a sip. It was good.

'I was telling somebody at work I might see my doctor and get some statins prescribed,' I said without preamble. 'I need to start looking after myself. Maybe he can help me get off so much of this stuff and on to decaf. This much caffeine can't be good for my heart and the last thing I want is to end up like our poor pal.'

'I'm not going to stand here and preach about your caffeine intake when I smoke twenty ciggies a day.'

'You aren't far behind Brian there,' I warned. I remembered how I'd given up smoking, but still yearned for a cigarette every time the subject came up. I thought about asking Johnny for one, and smoking it alongside him in the kitchen. Nell would give me hell if she knew what was on my mind; then again, it was a good job she couldn't read my mind or my secret involving groping Gemma wouldn't last long. 'You wouldn't happen to have one going spare, would you?'

'Of course,' he said, taking out a packet from his coat. The box was a cacky-brown to black with lurid images of cancerous lungs or something equally gross depicted upon it, and bold warnings about the harmful effects of cigarettes in blood red type. Johnny was oblivious, and I chose to zone them out as I plucked out a cigarette. Johnny paused. 'You sure you want to light up in here? We could go outside.'

'In this rain? No. You go ahead, Johnny, and I'll find you something for the ash. I might just keep mine for later . . . if that's OK?'

'Your house, your rules. Do what you want, mate.'

'Until Nell gets home,' I laughed.

'How are you guys?'

'Aah, you know . . .'

He didn't push the subject. He found his lighter and set a flame to the cigarette nipped between his teeth. His first inhalation was made with slitted eyes. 'You sure this is OK inside?'

I passed him a saucer. 'Go for it.'

'You're going to miss Bri more than the rest of us will. He's been your mate all these years, even after we kind of lost touch with you all.'

'Yeah, I've known and been friends with Brian as long as I can remember. I knew Carl equally long, even if we weren't friends at junior school. You and Gavin were late comers to our little gang

and unless I'm mistaken Carl started tagging along with us all about
the same time.'

'Long time ago, eh?'

'Feels like yesterday to me.'

'Yeah, me too.'

We sat in silent comradeship, thinking our own personal thoughts.
Johnny smoked. I wished that I had lit up with him, because I knew
that once he left the house and I cleaned up his ashes, I probably
wouldn't want to make more. As soon as he was gone I planned on
destroying the cigarette I'd begged off him in that moment of weakness. Jesus, two moments of weakness in one day: I was on a roll.

Johnny grew glassy eyed at one point, and he scrubbed at the
end of his nose with the back of his wrist.

'Are you going to be OK?' he asked me.

'Yeah. It's a tough time, but I'll get through it.'

'You don't think . . .'

'Think what?'

'That Brian's death had something to do with what's going on
with Poppy.'

'He suffered a massive cardiac arrest,' I pointed out. 'At least,
that's the preliminary thinking.'

'Yeah. I appreciate it wasn't like Carl getting mugged, but he's
dead all the same, and less than a stone's throw from where all that
trouble with Melanie and Poppy started.'

'I spoke to Joyce about that,' I said, but was elaborating on the
truth. 'She's under the impression he went back to the frog ponds
to lay his ghosts to rest. He'd still been dreaming about Melanie,
and thought that he was somehow suffering from guilt over her
death.'

'Brian did nothing to hurt her.'

'Didn't he?' I countered. 'It's a long time ago, but I recall that
day in detail. Maybe it's because of what later happened, and I've
gone over it so many times since then, but I can almost recite what
everyone said and did as if I'm watching a movie. It was Brian that
nicknamed Poppy "Copper Pubes", and who started all that nonsense
about "Melons Melanie" being the school bike and having the pox.
That was only Brian trying to be funny. I know that better than
anyone, but it must've hurt the girls to hear it.'

'Do you remember sticking up for them and getting punched by
Carl?'

'Yeah. He gave me a sore lip.'

Johnny snorted. 'You should have kicked his arse. You could have, you know, if you'd really wanted to.'

'I wish he was here now,' I admitted. 'I don't know if I'd hug him or kick his jacksie.'

'Same with Brian,' Johnny said and chuckled. 'I could strangle him for making me the butt of most of his jokes back then, but would give anything to have him back, taking the piss out of me, as usual.'

'He was good at taking the piss,' I acknowledged. 'It was him that started all that rubbish with the girls about Ginny Greenteeth getting them.'

'What was that?'

'Ginny Greenteeth. Remember, he told them if they got too close to the water she'd drag them in and Carl and you began tossing handfuls of pond weed at them.'

Johnny grew thoughtful. 'Bloody hell. I'd forgotten all about that. Ginny-bloody-Greenteeth. She was like some sort of witch that supposedly lured kids to their deaths. Or was it Jeannie, or Jenny Greenteeth, also known as Wicked Jenny by some people! Didn't Mrs Bishop call Poppy Wicked Jenny when we were at her house?'

I eyed him spuriously. 'Don't sit there and tell me you just drew all those names out of the back of your mind.'

'Nah. I've been looking into some weird stuff since the incident with Poppy at Helen's shop. Because I searched for myths involving weeds and stuff I was pulled down some weird rabbit holes, and several of them led me to the Ginny Greenteeth precautionary tale. I'd forgotten Brian mentioned it back then. You don't think that Poppy remembers what he said about Ginny, and is using it against us?'

At a loss for words, I just stared at him.

'I'm serious,' he said.

'What, like some kind of Scooby Doo bollocks? She's dressing up as an old witch and scaring the bejesus out of us?'

'Have you heard of an *egregore*?'

'No.'

He nodded, but didn't expound. 'I just can't figure out why she'd choose to punish us though,' he said. 'I mean, all we did was try to help catch their attacker.'

THIRTY-TWO

S peaking with Margaret Bishop hadn't proved too helpful, and despite attempts at finding her estranged husband, we were out of luck. Between them Gavin and Johnny had been talking things over, hypothesizing at what was going on, before presenting their conclusions to me. I think that they believed my scepticism had to be won over before they would act on their findings, and I was reminded that Johnny had claimed I'd always been our gang's unofficial leader. They really didn't need to seek my permission to do anything, certainly not to follow their initiatives, but when they began going down the route of a vengeful woman aiming to punish us, perhaps they thought my guidance couldn't go amiss.

Having worried that asking for any more time off work would prove difficult, I made it until mid-week before my two remaining pals talked me into joining them on a road trip. In a conversation with Norman Heatley, I asked for a few hours the following afternoon, and was surprised when he told me to take the day off, and get my head together. He knew I was waiting for the arrangements to be finalized before Brian's funeral could take place, and that I'd be requesting more time off, but I guessed he'd had enough of me moping around and the less that he saw of me for a day or two the better.

We drove across the country the following day, this time with Gavin at the wheel, then turned south and took the A1(M) down towards Leeds. His car's bonnet still carried the handprints as if they'd been branded into the paintwork. Johnny rode shotgun, while I had the back seat to myself. As we travelled, we spoke about the past, most of our stories top heavy with anecdotes about Brian or Carl, and we also got around to throwing back and forth a few more theories about what could be going on. As far as we'd heard, the police were not treating Brian's death as anything more than an unfit middle-aged smoker dropping dead while running to find cover from a sudden cloudburst. The investigation into Carl's mugging was ongoing, but there was very little momentum on it: an attack by a transient was still the overriding theory, but it was beginning to sound more like an excuse for the lack of a true suspect.

I lost track of our route when Gavin took us off the motorway and on to roads leading into the North York Moors National Park. The landscape was pretty and distracting at times. I chose the moment to confess to the lads that I'd visited the crime scene, and found where Carl had been beaten to death: I also told them about the detective slipping up with Brian and I and mentioning that a hammer had been used in the attack.

'Brian thought there was some significance in a hammer being used on Carl,' I added.

'If Poppy was involved,' said Johnny, 'it would make sense she'd use the same weapon that was used on her and Melanie.'

'Did she have a hammer when she was in Helen's shop?' I countered.

'No, but . . .'

'Did she exhibit any violent tendencies at all?'

'No. Just that weird shit where she regurgitated the plants and water.'

'Why go to Helen's shop?' Gavin wondered. 'She wasn't involved when we were kids, so why bring her into it?'

'She wanted me to hear her message loud and clear,' suggested Johnny. 'Doing what she did in Drover's was bound to make an impact.'

'Why not just approach you directly though,' Gavin asked, 'and say, hey Johnny, you've been a naughty boy?'

'Because it wouldn't have had the same impact?' I suggested. 'Like the way she approached you, Gavin, and left those handprints burned into the paint. If you ask me, that was done purely for lasting effect too.'

'I still can't figure out how she did it,' he said.

'Maybe she had gloves on, and they were lathered in paint remover or some other chemical . . .'

Even I didn't believe my theory, as having studied the handprints I knew they had nothing to do with the outer layer of paint being removed. The handprints were within the paint layers, beneath the lacquered surface. Johnny sat forward as if checking the prints were still embossed upon the bonnet. He sat back, exhaling loudly. I took it that they were.

He said, 'Margaret said Poppy's skull was very badly injured, cracked open like a soft-boiled egg. It kind of explains why she might be acting a bit weird, but not why she'd come after us all these years later and torment us like this.'

'Are you both certain that it was Poppy you saw?'

'I didn't see her, only Helen and her assistant Monica did,' Johnny confessed. 'There were times before and after when I thought I was being followed but, no, I didn't actually see Poppy.'

Gavin nodded. Without turning to me, he said, 'When she stepped out in front of my car, she looked like how I imagined Poppy might look, if you get my drift? And after Kylie did a bunk, and I spotted who I thought was Poppy from my apartment, it was just brief and from an awkward angle.'

'So, none of us has actually seen Poppy, not indisputably her?' I carried on. 'Don't forget what else Margaret said: Poppy couldn't breathe without help, and couldn't get up or move. Maybe we are blaming the wrong person altogether.'

'We'll find out soon enough.' Gavin indicated his satellite navigation system. We were swiftly approaching our destination. I sat up straighter and peered out of the side windows, seeking the place I'd agreed to accompany my friends to.

'Do you think that's it?' asked Johnny. There was a sprawling mansion perched on top of a nearby hill. It looked like something out of a gothic horror novel.

Gavin checked the directional arrows on his sat-nav, shook his head.

He took the next right turn, placing the mansion in his mirrors and followed a narrow lane towards the crest of another hill. Once over the peak we saw a cluster of buildings in the valley before us. The structures were modern, formed of steel and concrete and glass, and very utilitarian. Signs at the roadside welcomed us to the Ingrid Michaels Institute.

'Some of the stuff we've seen and heard, we'd best watch out or they're going to check us into some nice padded rooms of our own,' Johnny quipped.

The institute was not a mental health clinic, rather it was a residential home that specialized in the care of brain injured individuals. Gavin's digging into what he'd managed to learn from Margaret Bishop had led him to follow the name Jennifer Seeley, and it had brought him here. A respectful telephone call to the institute had confirmed that one of their long-term residents was known as Jenny Seeley, and we'd been given permission to visit, on the understanding that Seeley was not very communicative, and any of her specific medical or personal details would be kept strictly under lock and key.

We didn't need details, other than to convince us that we were completely off track in blaming Poppy Bishop for what had happened lately.

Gavin parked the car, and we walked across to what was obviously the main entrance to the small clinic. We were nervous, and at first Gavin and Johnny fell behind me, allowing me to take the lead.

'Uh, no,' I said, raising both hands in surrender. 'This isn't my gig. Come on, Gav, this is all on you, mate.'

I fell in behind with Johnny, and Gavin reluctantly pressed the door buzzer. We were possibly observed via CCTV cameras, because we were allowed in without question, the door making a loud click as the lock disengaged. We entered and stood in an empty foyer. There was a desk but no attendant. We waited, but nobody approached us. Finally, Gavin took the initiative and pushed through a second set of doors. We followed, and traversed an echoing corridor lined with windows until we came upon another door, and another buzzer. This time we could see human activity beyond the door. There were two women behind desks, both wearing royal blue jerkins and white trousers, and a third standing behind a counter who beckoned us to enter.

We entered, then stood there, milling about, like we were thirteen years old again and under the scrutiny of female-kind. Finally, I dug my knuckles into Gavin's hip and he practically jumped forward, a hand extended in greeting. The woman behind the counter didn't accept it. A bottle of hand sanitiser sat proudly on the counter, an indication that such physical greetings were frowned upon. I guessed that it was a practice adopted during the Covid-19 pandemic, yet to be relaxed.

'You're the gentlemen here to speak with Mr Choi?' the receptionist asked.

'We are,' said Gavin, and gave his name in return. Johnny and I were invited to give ours, and they were checked off against a pre-approved visitors' list.

We were asked to sign into a ledger, which we did, each passing the pen to the next: so much for pandemic avoidance practices, eh? Then we were escorted by one of the other two women to a room with comfy leather chairs and a small flat screen TV mounted on the wall. By that time the early morning magazine shows had been replaced with a panel of opinionated women. We sat there, knees spread, hands clasped, and got cricks in our necks from watching the screen above us.

We sat for the best part of ten minutes in my reckoning before a small, bespectacled Asian fellow appeared and gestured at us to follow. I thought this was the venerable Mr Choi, but not so; the first man seemed to be an assistant of Choi's. The actual Mr Choi waited for us in an office, and as we entered I was surprised when the little man excused himself and a much larger man stood up from behind a desk. He was of mixed race, African–Asian, I'd say at a guess, and shattered all my preconceived notions of what a clinician should look like. Choi had the good looks of a movie star, and was built ready for the boxing ring. I was deemed big next to my friends, but Mr Choi made me feel diminutive by comparison. He didn't follow the no handshake rule, coming out with a huge glossy palm extended. He pumped each of our hands in turn as we gave our names, and then waved at us to take seats. There was the obligatory chair facing his desk for consultations, and a couple more set against the nearest wall.

Over to you, Gavin, I thought, and took the furthest chair away. Johnny perched next to me with his hands clasped between his thighs. One of his knees bounced almost imperceptibly, and I could feel it through contact with his chair.

'From what I gathered from your earlier communications you've an interest in speaking to Miss Seeley,' he stated.

'That's right,' said Gavin, and I was impressed by his ability to lie with a straight face. 'We are old school friends, and recently got together to organize a bit of a school reunion do. Class of 1990,' he gave a sheepish grin, 'and while trying to track down our old school year we had some trouble finding Jennifer Seeley. I don't know if you're aware but she had a different name back then. It was . . .'

'I'm aware of Miss Seeley's failed adoption,' he cut in. 'Beyond that I can't say anything that might breach confidentiality.'

'You don't need to,' Gavin grinned, and threw up his hands as if tossing confetti at a wedding. 'By confirming you know about that, you've just confirmed to us that your Jennifer is our Poppy Bishop.'

He smiled. His eyes were flat. Not that he'd been caught out, more he was used to playing with rules and regulations to get where he wanted quickly. He was probably a busy man who had more on his mind than entertaining a bunch of liars, whose agendas had f-all to do with school reunions, but nothing he could determine as nefarious.

'I don't know what else you expect from coming here,' he said. 'Without any known next of kin, Jennifer is our ward, and therefore it's down to us whether or not to allow you visitation rights.'

'Can't Jennifer speak for herself?'

'She can,' he admitted, 'but she's unable to form cohesive responses beyond monosyllables. She isn't in a position to make judgements and requires assistance with even the most mundane and basic tasks.'

Gavin hung his head a moment, then more for mine and Johnny's sake, he said, 'We had heard that she had perhaps returned home and was once again living in our town, I take it from what you've said that she's a permanent resident here?'

'Let's just reiterate that she requires assistance with most tasks and I'll allow you to deduce from that what you will.'

'I understand,' said Gavin.

'In other words, as much as you'd have liked to enjoy her company at your class reunion, I'm afraid that Miss Seeley will be a pass.'

'Such a shame,' said Gavin, and genuinely sounded sincere. In fact, if this was our Poppy, and she had been permanently institutionalized, there was no reason to feel anything other than pity and regret for her. Margaret Bishop, in her uncouth manner, had determined that Jennifer Seeley was likely being spoon fed and having her backside wiped someplace, and she was right. This woman that required constant care and the one terrorizing us were not the same. How could she be?

'Can we still see her?' Gavin asked, and I wondered *why*? We didn't require further confirmation, so let's just leave while the going was good.

'A face to face can be arranged,' said Mr Choi, 'but it's not something I'd advise. Perhaps it would be best for you all to keep your memories of her as a young woman in mind, rather than what she has become.'

'Yes,' I piped up. 'For me I'd rather remember the girl than somebody who's obviously become a stranger to us now.'

Johnny looked at me and I could tell he was thinking along similar lines to me, but Gavin straightened up and said, 'I only need a minute. Not even as long as a minute. I only want to lay eyes on her one time, just so I can convey my best wishes to her.'

Choi wasn't a fool easily hoodwinked. He knew there was more to our visit than what we'd let on, and now for Gavin's reason for seeing her in the flesh, but what harm could come of him allowing it?

'We have a viewing room,' he said. 'Let me arrange for Miss Seeley to be moved there and you can have as much time as you like . . . within reason.'

'That will be great,' said Gavin, and in my nervous discomfort I felt my toes drumming inside my shoes quicker than a boogie-woogie pianist's fingers. Beside me, Johnny's knee now bounced visibly.

Choi pressed a button, and as if he'd been waiting outside the door to be summoned in an instant, the other little Asian man came in and asked us to follow him. We were taken back to the room where we'd waited before and the man left to arrange for Seeley to be moved. The panel show with the loose-lipped women was still playing on the flat screen. Thankfully, somebody had muted the volume while we'd been in Choi's presence.

'Why'd you ask to see her?' I hissed in a tight whisper. 'We know now that Poppy can't be the one who's tormenting us.'

'You're right,' Gavin said. 'But I need to see her, so I can tell if there's any resemblance between her and the woman I've seen.'

'And how will that help?'

'I'm not sure yet,' he said, 'but, well, let's just have a look at Poppy and take things from there, eh?'

'Jennifer Seeley,' said Johnny. 'This isn't Poppy, it's Jennifer Seeley. How can we be confident that it's the same person? We only have Margaret Bishop's word on it that she changed her name; what if this is another woman entirely and . . .'

We bickered back and forth for a few minutes more, always at a whisper, and I remained unconvinced that seeing the patient would help.

I grabbed Johnny's arm, hushing him.

The small Asian man was on his way back, only the faintest of rubber soles sucking on the linoleum announcing his return.

He probably picked up on the atmosphere when he entered the room. His smile flickered, before he set it in place once more. 'If you'd like to follow me, gentlemen?'

We trooped behind him like the three blind mice, almost stepping on each other's heels. I had no desire to see Poppy – or Jennifer Seeley – but had no option other than to follow. We were led along a corridor not unlike the first one we had walked, lined with windows and at the mid-way section, fire doors on each side. We continued, and were taken towards a third building on the site. This one stood several storeys tall, and unlike the others where the windows had slatted blinds, this building had the addition of curtains and flowers and plant pots on sills. As we entered, music filtered from a speaker system in the halls and several other TVs vied to be heard. I heard laughter and somebody singing. At a guess, I'd confidently say it was the residential block, and unlike any hospital I'd visited before.

We were let into a room, and I was instantly reminded of one of the worst days of my life. After Becky was recovered from the lake, she was initially identified by her belongings and by her friends, but before she could be repatriated home, I had to fly out to Austria and officially identify her remains, being her immediate next of kin. On that occasion I'd been in a stuffy little space, where a hatch opened and all that separated me from my child's corpse was a single pane of glass and a white sheet. Somebody out of my line of sight had the unenviable task of flicking back the sheet and exposing her face and shoulders, while I sobbed that it was her. Here the differences were that the window was larger, almost the length of the room, and the person on the far side was seated in a chair rather than lying on a gurney, and there was also a nurse in blue jerkin and white trousers in attendance.

'You may say hello,' said the little man, 'the glass is not sound-proofed. But don't try asking anything too taxing. When you are finished, please join me again in the corridor and I'll show you the way out.'

At our nods of assent, he smiled a final time then stepped out of the room. Beyond the glass, the nurse acted nonchalant, as if we didn't exist, and she wasn't being ogled alongside her patient like exhibits in a zoo. We couldn't help staring, and perhaps the nurse was used to this reaction from anyone on first seeing Jennifer Seeley.

There was something in the middle-aged woman that reminded me of the red-headed girl from our youth, but I can't quite put a finger on it. She had gained a lot of weight, and I supposed it was through inactivity and confinement to her wheelchair. She wore a black sweatshirt emblazoned with the name of an American Ivy

League university, and black leggings sheer enough you could see the colour of her skin through them. Her shoulders were rounded and slumped, and both hands lay on her thick thighs, palms up. Her hands were tiny by comparison, and almost bleached white, like lilies probing from the dark earth. Her mane of red hair was a distant memory. Now her hair was shorn almost to the scalp, and though there were darker red strands here and there, what remained of it was white stubble. As horrible as it is to point out, they had only two options with her hair: allow it to grow ridiculously huge so that it covered her injury from sight; or shave it off so that it didn't become problematic. The right-hand side of her skull was concave, seriously concave to the point it looked as if half her head was missing. Her right eye was sealed closed, and her right ear sat at an angle. Because of the horrid contortions to her features, the rest were pulled askew, so that she resembled a face drawn on a partly deflated balloon. I tasted bile the instant I looked at her, and in the next instant I had to turn aside.

I heard both Gavin's and Johnny's breathing quicken as they too eyeballed her. At least they had the grace not to turn away in disgust. I should have been ashamed of my reaction, but it was gut instinct first, and false emotion second, under the circumstances.

'Nyah, nyah, nyah, nyah,' I heard.

The sound was wet, as if Poppy spoke through a mouthful of syrup.

Her words, for what they were, sounded negative: No, no, no, no . . .

I turned and glanced back at her, trying not to dwell too long on her awful deformation, and her one good eye was snapped, laser tight on to me. In that single eye there was complete and utter condemnation.

'Nyah, nyah, nyah, nyaaaaah . . . .NYYYYAAAAAAAHHHHH!'

Poppy, or Jennifer, or whatever she'd become, thrashed back and forth in her wheelchair. The wheels had been locked into place, but her sheer bulk and frantic movements were enough to cause the chair to skid about. The nurse lunged, trying to grab at the push handles, and she laid her other hand comfortingly around her patient's shoulder, tapping gently on her upper chest as she crooned softly in her good ear.

There was no soothing her though and Poppy continued to grow more frantic, her screams ringing out throughout the building. The little man had been correct, that bloody window did nothing to soundproof the room. I guess our exclamations of surprise made quite a racket too. The door crashed inward and the little man appeared from where he'd been waiting in the hall.

'I'm sorry, gentlemen,' he called in his most authoritative voice, 'but I must ask you to leave immediately.'

I didn't need to be asked twice, I bounded for the door. Johnny was only seconds behind me, and then came Gavin. He had his hands steepled to his bottom lip, as if in prayer, and he kept blurting out, 'I'm sorry. I'm sorry,' and I couldn't tell if it was to the nurse struggling to calm down her charge, or to Poppy who we'd upset with our very presence.

THIRTY-THREE

Most of the journey back was completed in contemplative silence but not all. Occasionally, there were also some expletives and not a little disbelief at how things had transpired. I thought we could confidently write off Poppy Bishop as the weird woman who'd been tormenting us, unless Johnny's point about Jennifer Seeley being another woman altogether held any water – uh, pardon the pun. In my opinion, the institutionalized woman was definitely Poppy. It had been decades ago that I last saw her, and under totally different circumstances, but I recognized her, as clearly as she had registered us. Recognizing us must've thrown back her memories so abruptly to when she was attacked, that she'd replayed the trauma again and it set off her maniacal behaviour. Margaret Bishop had not picked any old name out of the ether for her estranged daughter. It would've been too far a stretch to think that another Jennifer Seeley, with a resemblance to Poppy, had suffered similar injuries, so I thought we could strike off Johnny's concern.

We took a break at a service station on Scotch Corner, a name I always found unusual in that part of the country: it was more than one hundred miles to Scotland if you stuck to the main road, and probably eighty or so if you cut across country towards the famous Gretna Green, the destination of eloping couples for several centuries. When we pulled in, the car park was heaving: where on earth so many people were en route to on a Thursday afternoon this late in October I never found out. We hoped to find a seat in the coffee shop, and take some time to gather our thoughts and for me to replenish my caffeine quota. A look through the window showed us we'd have more chance of winning the National Lottery than to find an empty table. Instead, we visited the loos, and bought take away coffees from a vending machine. Outside, we stood under uniform grey skies and drank our scalding hot drinks out of paper cups. Johnny sparked up, making the most of the break to smoke, having previously declined Gavin's offer to do so in his car. He checked with me once, not to ask permission to enjoy a cigarette, but if I wanted one. No, thanks. I didn't tell him that I'd destroyed the one I begged off him in my kitchen. For a second or two Gavin looked tempted but decided the coffee would have to do. Steam from his cup misted his glasses as he sipped from the tiny hole in the lid.

'What now?' I wondered for about the hundredth time.

'I think we're all in agreement that we can check off the Poppy Bishop box?' said Johnny.

'You don't think it's mistaken identity then?' I countered.

'No. That was before we saw her and she started screaming like a bloody banshee. That was Poppy, no doubt about it in my mind. So, who the fuck was it that spewed all over the counter in Helen's shop?'

Gavin exhaled, and looked down at his feet. He gently kicked at the concrete. 'I don't know how to tell you this, lads, but that woman back there *was* Poppy. I'm not going to dispute that. But the woman that I've seen twice now was also Poppy. I know before that I'd nothing to base identifying her on, except for the girl we barely knew from school, but now I've seen an adult version of Poppy I'm more convinced than ever.'

'Can you hear yourself?' I asked, somewhat caustically.

'I know it's nuts but . . .'

'It's more than bloody nuts,' I said, 'it's a bloody impossibility, man.'

'So is leaving your frigging handprints stamped in the bonnet of a car!'

Aye, that was a fair point.

'So, what do you think's happening? That poor Poppy back there is somehow being rejuvenated through a miracle drug, sticking on a wig and escaping that institute and travelling up to Cumbria to frighten the life out of us?'

'You don't have to get bolshy over it,' Gavin growled.

'I'm not trying to be,' I said. 'I just can't think how else she could do it. Which, by the fucking way, she can't.'

'I know. I know.' Gavin fell silent, scowling over his drink.

I chugged down several mouthfuls of mine. Then looked at Johnny, checking if he had any theories that weren't as ridiculous as mine and Gavin's.

'I've got nothing,' he admitted. 'To be fair on Gav, he's the only one of us to lay eyes on her for real, I've only Helen's assertion that it was Poppy.'

'Gavin's and your stalker are one and the same,' I said. 'The descriptions of them are the same, the hair's the same, and don't forget the phrases she used are almost identical.'

'So, what about you, Andy?' my friend asked as he drew in a couple of lungsful of smoke. 'Why is it that you haven't seen her?'

I shook my head, and then scratched at my temple with a fingernail. 'Remember I told you lads that I visited Carl's murder scene? Well, I might not have told you the full story. A couple of weird incidents happened, that I initially thought were coincidence, but were enough to spook me.' I told them about the sense of being watched, and followed back to my car, and how the radio had blasted out a song pertinent to Carl boasting about living forever when we were kids. 'I drove and ended up at the old engine lonning, same place where Brian left his car the day he died. While I was there, I heard these scratching noises and I'm sure there was drumming too but it wasn't clear enough to make out the beat. The scratching turned into like, I dunno, as if somebody wearing rubber gloves was running their fingers across my car. In my window I glimpsed *something . . .*'

'Her? Or else the woman that looks like Poppy?'

At first I didn't know what to say, then thought that the stuff they had experienced was equally crazy, so maybe I wouldn't sound too insane. 'I thought I saw a figure made of rags and branches with long weeds for hair.'

Johnny's eyeballs grew twice as large and the cigarette hung smouldering between his lips. 'Ginny Greenteeth,' he intoned.

Gavin also eyeballed me, and a smirk tugged at his lips. *Can you hear yourself?* he might have asked, if not for the description his slutty girlfriend had given for the hag she'd sworn climbed through Gavin's balcony window.

'It was for a second at most,' I said quickly, and slashed away my comments with my left hand. 'Then I realized I was only looking at the bare trees reflected in my windows. It wasn't really a hag like ol' Ginny, more likely it was my brain trying to make sense out of something and filling in the blanks.'

'Yeah, like it filled in the blanks when you got home and smeared crap all over your door and house, and soaked you through to the knees,' Gavin reminded me. I couldn't recall relating those details to him before, but I must have told one of them, or it had been Nell who'd brought it up, and the lads had talked.

'I think I must've got wet when I was down at the canal,' I argued weakly. 'I was sick – didn't I mention I actually threw up my guts? Maybe when I hurried to get back to my car I splashed through some muddy puddles . . .'

Neither of them bought my explanation. Neither did they challenge it again. We finished our drinks, binned the cups and Johnny's cigarette end, then got back in Gavin's car. It was another hour and a half of slow-moving traffic until my mates dropped me outside my house. They each turned down my offer to come inside for a cuppa and left, and I went inside, wondering if I should share some of my confusion and misgivings with Nell.

My wife was in the bath again, with the door shut.

We never used to keep doors closed between us, it was another facet of our failing relationship.

I abandoned the idea of seeking her opinion and went to the kitchen where I began pulling together the ingredients for our evening meal.

THIRTY-FOUR

A t work the following morning, Gemma returned to my office full of smiles and a happy greeting. I worried that she was trying to set me up and that while I'd been gone some covert cameras or audio recorders had been set up in my office space, there to trap me if I tried to grope her again. While surreptitiously checking the water sprinkler heads for hidden cameras, I returned her hello and invited her in. She entered my office, but didn't close the door this time. Maybe she'd thought things through and realized she had been as much to blame for my forwardness by the tilt of her behaviour, and decided I was worthy of a second chance at friendship. Whatever influenced her change of mood, she sat opposite me on the hard plastic chair that was usually pushed up to a wall and holding my folded coat and maybe a rolled newspaper if I'd bothered to grab one on my way in. Daily newspapers were fast becoming a thing of the past, and I was growing as guilty as everyone else for going first to the internet for the daily gossip. I bought the paper for the cartoons, the crossword and Sudoku puzzles. Gemma had placed my stuff on the floor in order to jostle around the chair.

We looked at each other for a long second or two. Then Gemma kind of crinkled her nose, which had the effect of physically lifting up her glasses and perching them higher. She had redyed the blonde slash in her hair, it was now bright orange. On another the style might look forced, too flamboyant, but on Gemma it was lovely.

Once we gathered our breath, I sat back a little and again eyed her. 'Was there something specific you wanted from me?'

'I just wanted to check on you,' she said.

'I'm OK.'

'You weren't in work yesterday, I wondered if . . .'

'I took some time off. There was something me and a couple of old pals had to do.'

'Was it to do with your other friend passing away?'

'In a roundabout manner.'

'That's good,' she said, to my astonishment. She smiled sheepishly. 'I don't mean good that your friend passed, I mean good that you took some advice and reached out to others to help you get through your grief. You said you'd speak with your doctor . . .'

'Yeah. I haven't got round to that yet, but I'd swear it did me good spending time with my pals again.'

'Did they know Brian?'

'Brian and Carl. We all messed around together when we were boys.'

'It's good to have a shoulder to lean on.'

'Listen,' I said, worrying where she was leading. 'About that hug we had the other day, if it was inappropriate and I overstepped the mark, well, please accept my apology. I never meant things to . . .'

'It's totally fine,' she said, her mouth pulled in a wide rictus smile, and shaking her head. The orange slash in her hair quivered in time.

'It's just that, well, I might have touched you.'

'On my bottom?'

I grimaced, waiting for an accusation of assault to be hurled at me, and for Norman Heatley and maybe even some detectives to come charging into my office.

'No big deal,' she said. 'In fact, there's a possibility that my hand was on your backside too. I, ahem, left in a hurry before things went too far. I like you Mr Miller, I do, but I know you're a married man and I'd never do anything to come between you and Nell. I'm sorry if I made you uncomfortable.'

'Oh.'

I'd been worried that I was going to be vilified as some kind of predatory pervert, and yet Gemma had returned in the hope of apologizing to me and putting the incident behind us. I should have accepted the apology, agreed to forget all about it, and get back to enjoying a mutually platonic relationship. I didn't.

'I, uh, like you too, Gemma. And you needn't worry about getting between me and Nell, as we aren't exactly a couple at this time. She is still my wife and I respect her, but we have drifted apart since the death of our daughter, and to be honest, I don't see how we can ever close the gap that has grown between us.'

Gemma's tongue darted across her bottom lip and she put one hand on my desk.

I reached across and laid my fingertips over the tops of hers and was gratified when she didn't withdraw.

'It's why I grew aroused when I was holding you,' I admitted. 'Holding you is the first female contact I've enjoyed in a long time.

I think you realized you were turning me on, and that's why you left the room. I believe what you just said; your morals wouldn't allow you to do anything to jeopardize my marriage, but you needn't worry. It's already over, finished, all but for the legal paperwork.'

'I'm sorry to hear that, Mr Miller.'

'Don't be. And please, call me Andrew, eh?'

'I will from now on.'

'Promise?'

'I promise.' Her cheeks bloomed with colour. 'Look at me, being all forward and stuff. I hope you don't think I'm dead pushy or anything but . . .'

'I'm glad we're being open with each other,' I said. 'How about we go for a drink after work and, well, see where it takes us?'

'I'm up for that,' she said, 'but won't Nell be expecting you home?'

'Like I said before, these days we cohabitate at best. I never know when to expect her, and it won't harm her to be the one left wondering for a change.'

'As long as I'm not going to cause you any bother.'

'Not at all. In fact, if you came home with me after, I'd be surprised if Nell even noticed.'

She smiled, dipping her chin. 'I think it's maybe a little soon for inviting me back to yours, Andrew, but . . .'

'It isn't too soon for me, Jenny,' I said huskily, sounding a little too desperate, but meaning every word.

'Gemma.'

I squinted at her. 'Huh?'

'Gemma. You just called me Jenny.'

'Did I?'

She didn't answer, and I thought for a second that I'd blown things with her before they'd even begun.

'Sorry. Slip of the tongue. Yesterday, me and my pals went looking to find an old schoolfriend called Jenny. She has been on my mind lately. Apologies.'

'No problem. Should I meet you at your car later?'

'It'd be best, rather than leaving work together. Maybe we should just keep things between the two of us for now, eh? Nobody else here knows we are . . . y'know, *friendly*.'

'None of them need to know,' she said with the tiniest hint of a wink.

THIRTY-FIVE

Johnny Wilson

I t had been an incredibly long day at work for Johnny at the hardware store. There had been a non-stop stream of customers, some of them buying the tiniest of items like screws and bolts, while others arrived to collect pre-ordered electrical generators, high pressure washers, extendable aluminium ladders, and others browsed first and then left with armfuls of snap purchases. Each customer required time and service, and Johnny had barely lifted his head to breathe after serving one before the next arrived. Several times he'd mucked up orders, and was forced to give himself a telling off, and a pep talk to get his head back in the game.

His thoughts, of course, had been filled with the revelations of the previous day, and what it could mean to him and his friends in the future. He was unsure what the others' expectations were, but he had prepared for finding Poppy Bishop, no, Jennifer Seeley, difficult to look at. People try to be nice around others with major deformities, and rightly so, and not show their emotions, but sometimes the deformities or injuries are so extreme that it's difficult not to be overcome. Johnny had tried holding in his pity, but it had spilled from him in an exclamation of disbelief on seeing her malformed skull and warped features. Back when he was a boy, and the attack was fresh in everyone's mind he'd tried picturing what Melanie might have looked like after his cousin allegedly struck her repeatedly with his claw hammer. As points of reference, he had only horror movies to pluck a description from, but it had been in the manner of ropey pre-1980s special effects. He'd never quite grasped how horribly disfigured the girl had been before Ian was finished with her. As for Poppy, he had believed she'd been struck on the head, he hadn't known that most of one side had caved in. Perhaps in these modern times more could have been done to rebuild her cranium, but those kinds of surgical procedures were still quite basic back then. He wondered why more had not been done to help Poppy as the years progressed and techniques grew more advanced. He'd heard of people with severe injuries who came out of a series of surgical procedures looking much as they had before sustaining their horrible injuries.

The Ingrid Michaels Institute had not been a medical hospital. As far as Johnny had discovered before the trip, Jennifer Seeley had spent many years living there receiving residential care. On his return home, after they dropped off Andrew, he had spent some more time with Gavin at his apartment. There they had scoured the internet for more information regarding the institute and also the resident consultant, Mr David Choi. Choi, they discovered, was a specialist in neurological problems and cognitive recovery; it was said, though only in unsubstantiated articles and chatter on forums, that Choi had pioneered techniques to help develop the under-used portions of the human brain. Rather than undergo painful surgeries to rebuild her broken skull, Poppy's rehabilitation most likely centred upon brain training exercises. Johnny had no template to go by, but he guessed that Poppy's trauma must have been beyond extreme when all that had been achieved in more than thirty years of rehab was to get her talking again in monosyllabic slurps or screaming at the top of her voice.

Jesus, that's so unkind, he thought, but he was only being truthful.

Last night in bed, Helen had asked what was wrong, and he would have told her but he didn't want to add to the weird dreams she'd been suffering lately: they didn't involve Poppy, nor Ginny Greenteeth, but he'd bet if he described Poppy's current appearance to her it would figure front and centre. Instead, he reassured her that he was OK, simply restless, and he'd struggled to contain himself until she drifted into another night of troubled sleep. He'd thought about Brian, and how sad and ironic it was to lose his old friend so soon after making contact again. Young Brian was as hard as nails, and Johnny found it difficult believing that something like a weak heart could bring him down. More so than thinking about Brian, he couldn't get Poppy's face out of his mind.

He had looked at her through the viewing window, and she had looked directly back at him. In her one good eye he'd watched her go from a blank stare to pinpointed clarity as his and Gavin's faces had struck chords with her, and then she'd spied Andy.

Seeing the three of them must have flipped her switch.

Something about them had.

Johnny would swear that her screams had followed them all the way along those corridors and back to where they'd left Gavin's car. Even as he drove away, heading back towards the motorway Johnny's ears still smarted to the high-pitched screeches and not until they'd pulled in at Scotch Corner and he'd finally been allowed to light up had he managed to get his mind in some semblance of order. While Gavin and Andy verbally sparred, throwing in theories and discarding them with the next breath, Johnny had smoked, and he'd thought. Finally, he'd asked, 'So what about you, Andy? Why is it that you haven't seen her?'

Andrew claimed he had experienced her, but in a different form to the one that had troubled Brian and Gavin, and who had pulled the stunt in Helen's shop, and Johnny had to admit that the thing of rags and sticks and weeds for hair trumped the normal-looking woman she'd appeared on other occasions. She? Who was *she*? Because they could all agree, that it absolutely, one hundred per cent, could not possibly be their initial suspect.

Or could it?

Johnny had always been open to subjects some people found whacky. He believed in UFOs back before the US Pentagon admitted that the phenomena was real and rebranded them UAPs. He believed in paranormal activity, and in his thirties had actively been involved in a ghost hunting team that had scoured castles and manor houses and abandoned prisons in search of evidence of the uncanny. He'd studied diverse subjects like remote viewing, telekinesis, poltergeist activity, the Loch Ness monster and Bigfoot, but hadn't come to any firm conclusions on them. Recently, due to the incident in Helen's shop, he had looked into ectoplasm as a phenomenon, but it had left him wanting. However, he'd thought there was some validity in NDEs, also known as near-death experiences, remote viewing and in astral projection, and it was through the latter that a hypothesis had begun forming in his mind.

The other day, at Andrew's house, he'd asked his friend the question in an off-hand manner: 'Have you heard of an egregore?'

Andrew had not.

At the time the idea was basically the tiniest of embers smouldering beneath a pile of damp tinder. The spark had not taken, but neither had it gone out completely. He had carried it, fanned it, blew ideas across it, testing it and studying reactions, and suddenly the spark had ignited. For now, it was a weak flame, but it was there all the same, and he'd been desperate to share his idea with somebody all day before it could gutter and go out.

Helen was intelligent, but she was too straight up and down to throw his idea by her. By now she had practically convinced herself that the woman in her shop had just been some random lunatic who'd sicked up her lunch, despite the weight of evidence against that scenario.

Any other time he would have gone directly to the leader of their little gang, but Andrew seemed to have made up his mind already not to accept the supernatural route, had even scoffed at Johnny for having the temerity of suggesting this had to do with the Ginny Greenteeth myth. He'd called it some kind of Scooby Doo bollocks, with persons unknown dressing up as an old witch to frighten them. No, he needed somebody open to talk the idea over with at least, and rather than bring in an outsider he had only one recourse.

He went to see Gavin.

THIRTY-SIX

Andrew Miller

Avoiding the busier town centre pubs, and anywhere usually associated with me or with Nell, I drove Gemma to a public house in one of the villages yet to be absorbed into the outskirts of town. I chose to avoid the western and northern suburbs because they were still too close to home, and chose instead a pub I'd heard of but never frequented just off one of the eastern routes. It was a quaint old place, with archaic dark wooden furniture and taxidermied pheasants and hares on shelves. A row of pewter trophies lined another shelf. The music on the jukebox was to my taste, unlike the inane modern music today's kids listened to.

Once seated in a quiet corner I felt reasonably discreet and unlikely to be discovered by anyone that knew me. It was one thing feeling an inkling of shame due to my behaviour, but it would be far worse if my planned tryst with Gemma was foiled before it even happened. We ordered food and drinks, and then sat in companionable conversation, our knees occasionally touching under the table; Gemma was as conscious of the contact as I was, and delighted in it, and began initiating it more and more. I wanted to reach under the table and touch her, but kept both hands on my cutlery and for the best part my attention on her face.

Meanwhile, I kept one eye on the door, ready for anyone I recognized entering and an excuse on my lips. Already I'd concocted a lie about meeting a potential client, should anyone question the reason I was dining with a woman half my age: nobody needed to know my job description as chief administration officer didn't extend to entertaining new clients. I'd have to use the lie out of Gemma's earshot, because she couldn't be expected to play along completely off the cuff.

As it turned out, the lie went unrequired. We had the pub to ourselves most of the early evening, and when other customers arrived, they were local working men and women, in from the fields or cow sheds for a swift pint or two before bed. None of them even

looked in our direction for longer than it took to decide we were
strangers and none of their business.

We had finished our desserts, and were on the last dregs of our
third or fourth drinks: Gemma was tipsy on white wine, while I'd
stuck to beer. I was probably over the drink drive limit by then, but
knowing so only added to the sense of danger, and the excitement.

I settled the bill at the bar, and then returning to Gemma I pulled
out my mobile phone.

'Oh,' I announced, 'I've missed a couple of calls.'

She was engaged in pulling into her jacket. Being the perfect
gentleman, I assisted her to find the sleeve opening then helped her
to settle the jacket around her. When I offered to button her up, she
playfully slapped my hand aside. I looked at my phone again, and
then leaned in to whisper. 'The calls were from Nell's phone; I
didn't hear because I had the ringer turned down.' Gemma didn't
respond to my explanation. I flashed the screen at her, so that she
could register the message box displayed on it. 'She has sent a text
instead. Want to know what it says?'

'If it's personal, I don't need to hear . . .'

'It's personal, but it's also . . . good news?'

'Oh? What did she say?'

'I'll tell you outside,' I whispered, and offered a conspiratorial
wink.

We left the pub and walked towards where I'd parked my car.
'She said she tried calling me, but I didn't answer, she does that,
puts the blame on me.'

'To be fair, you did just say you had your ringer turned off.'

'True.' I grinned, trying not to look like a madman. I ignored the
phone, and related the message from memory. 'She's not coming
home tonight. She needs some space so is going to stay with her
older sister for a couple of days.'

She didn't answer, and for a moment I feared I'd gone a little
too far too quickly.

'What do they warn about gift horses?' she finally asked. Then
she grinned, and winked drunkenly. 'Ride 'em, cowboy!'

She'd replaced her flat work shoes with a pair of high heels for
our impromptu date. She didn't feel as diminutive as I took her
elbow and steered her towards my car. My head was filled with her
perfume, and swimming with promise.

Once in the car, Gemma sat with her hands on her knees,

smoothing out the material of her trousers. She faced directly ahead, and while I turned on the engine I looked across at her profile. Her glasses were huge from this angle, and her nose was a little upturned button. Her trembling bottom lip was moist and eminently kissable. I darted a look at her reflection on the inner curve of the windscreen, and my stomach tweaked, as if I was about to vomit. She glanced at me.

'Something wrong?' she asked.

'All's great with the world,' I answered. I coughed to clear my throat, and then wiped my palm from my forehead to my chin.

Sneaking another look at the windscreen, I noted that it must have rained while we'd been inside the pub and any reflections or objects outside were warped and malformed because of the runnels of water. For a second, Gemma had positively not appeared to be a snaggle haired old hag with sackcloth clothing and twigs for arms!

No, she looked lovely, and I couldn't wait to get her back to my place and progress from knee touching to . . . well, wherever it took us was open to the outer limits, now that Nell had given us free rein for a couple of days.

'How about we go back to my place for a nightcap?' I asked.

'Won't we risk being spotted?'

I shrugged. 'I'm not expecting anyone else, and as far as my neighbours go, they can bugger off and whistle. Not one of them has ever come to the house to pay their condolences about Becky, so why would any of them come now? Besides, where I live, I can drive my car into my garden and it's out of any of my neighbours' lines of sight; we can smuggle you inside without anyone knowing you're there.'

'I don't know if I should feel excited or dirty about that,' she said, and bore down with her front teeth on her bottom lip.

I said, 'So dirty it's filthy.'

She chuckled.

Taking her laughter as permission, I reached across and caressed her nearest thigh, and when she didn't slap me away, playfully or otherwise, I allowed my hand to move incrementally towards the inner curve of her thigh. Her legs grew taut beneath my touch, and shivered and her backside squirmed on the seat. She hummed under her breath. I reversed out of the car park and took off out of the village at a rate well beyond the posted speed limit.

THIRTY-SEVEN

Johnny Wilson

'I thought you were the coppers doing a raid, the way you banged on my door,' Gavin laughed as he let Johnny in his apartment.

'Why'd I be raiding you if I was the cops?'

Gavin held up the end of a hand-rolled cigarette.

'Funny fag?'

Gavin grinned widely. Behind the lenses of his glasses his eyes looked odd, kind of sparkly.

'You don't smoke, unless it's having the occasional toke on a joint?'

'We all have our vices, Johnny-boy,' said Gavin. 'Kylie left some of her stuff lying around. After yesterday's outing, I just needed something to settle me.'

He offered his friend a draw on the joint.

'Nah, I don't touch the stuff.'

'Just nicotine, huh?'

'Nicotine, alcohol, caffeine, junk food and paracetamol. Oh, and hot women. Anything else? No thanks.'

Gavin shrugged, unmoved, and held the joint to his mouth with the tips of his fingers. He drew on the cannabis-laden smoke.

Behind Johnny the automatic lights on the interior stairway went off. A steady green light on a panel inside Gavin's apartment showed that the downstairs door had closed and locked. Gavin stood aside to let Johnny further in.

Johnny immediately headed across the open plan living space to the huge windows and Juliette balcony. Gavin had one of the windows open and a seat placed strategically so he could breathe out the smoke through the gap. He had likely sent most of the smoke outside, but his apartment still held the sour reek of his joint, or perhaps more than one.

Johnny looked around. Gavin had discarded some dirty laundry on the floor, and his bed was unmade. It was easy seeing that there was no woman currently residing with him: then again, from what

Johnny knew from previous visits, Kylie had never been one for cleaning, more likely she would be the one to leave her stuff lying all over the place.

'Do you want a brew?' Gavin asked. 'I've got coffee and maybe a mint tea.'

'No, I'm good. I came here to talk something over. I've been bursting to bring it up and now I'm here, well, it sounds a bit nutty, even to me.'

'I've been smoking weed,' Gavin told him. 'Trust me, anything nuts you bring up, I'll bet it doesn't surprise me.' He giggled.

'How high are you?'

'Oh, about yay high,' he said, and cut a line with the side of his hand from the front of his forehead.

'Jesus. Maybe I should make you a brew.'

'Yeah, and something to eat. I'm starving.'

'Any more clichés you can think of?'

'It isn't the drugs, Johnny, I'm genuinely starving. I haven't eaten today . . . haven't really had the appetite after what happened yesterday.'

'Do you have one of those apps on your phone to order a delivery?' Johnny asked.

'Nope. But if you check in the kitchen I've a drawer full of menus from all the nearest outlets.'

Gavin's kitchen was actually a compact range taking up one corner of the apartment. There was an oven, a hob, a microwave oven, and several standalone gadgets: none of them looked used. Johnny opened drawers until he found the one stuffed with a multitude of printed menus. 'Anything special you fancy?'

'Lobster thermidor, if you're paying?'

'You can have pizza and like it,' said Johnny.

'Smashing,' said Gavin. 'Any chance of a side of fries?'

Johnny found an outlet specializing in Italian take away food and rang through their order. He added a two-litre bottle of cola, just for good measure. The sugar would help stabilize Gavin, as he came down from his high. He hadn't come here for his friend to fall asleep on him.

While waiting for their food, Johnny again went to the windows. He peered down at the pedestrianized area adjacent to a stream. A metal fence and bushes practically concealed the beck, as the waterway was locally known: in truth it was some kind of man-made gulley, once used to direct water to and from the factories there-abouts. Johnny's grandma had once worked in the building now housing Gavin's and another nine apartments. Johnny recalled her talking about it before she died, how she'd loved working at the 'shirt factory' as she'd called the old textile mill. Johnny couldn't begin to guess the multiple-million buttons she'd sewn on to men's clothing over the decades she'd worked there.

'Is that where you saw Poppy?' He nodded down at the pavement running adjacent to the beck.

'Turns out it wasn't Poppy, just her less-messed-up doppelganger.'

'Yeah. My bad. We can agree to that now.'

'Don't mention her, for Christ's sake. One thought of that face again and you'll have to eat that pizza yourself.'

Johnny frowned at Gavin's horrible words. But to be honest, he couldn't think of Poppy's horrific deformity without a qualm of disgust, mostly self-disgust by then.

Gavin checked out the gap. He aimed the end of his joint at the very spot where the woman had stood, staring up at him. Then he flicked the joint, and it arched away towards the beck, trailing sparks. 'What the fuck is going on, Johnny? I can't figure this out at all and am sure I'm going to lose my mind.'

'That's the weed talking. Listen. I've some ideas. What do you know about astral projection?'

'I dabbled with harder drugs in college,' Gavin admitted, 'Tried LSD once; what a bloody trip that was.'

'I'm not talking about being out of your head,' Johnny said, 'I'm talking about being out of your body.'

'Trust me, Johnny-boy, I know exactly what you meant. LSD, the result of using it, it's called a trip for a reason. Have you heard of *ayahuasca*?'

Johnny shook his head.

'It's popular among Amero-Indian shamans, it's a kind of hallu-cinogenic tea that they brew and use in medicinal and religious rites. Lots of people are embracing it for the psychedelic dream state it induces and the sense of being out of body. Back in the 1960s the mind-expansion properties of LSD, DMT, psilocybin and *ayahuasca* were all studied, especially by the CIA and US military. Some of the recipients of the drugs experienced vivid hallucinations where they described leaving behind their physical shells and flying about the room and even further afield.'

'I'll bow to your greater knowledge on the subject of narcotics and their effects,' Johnny said. 'But what do you know of astral projection on a spiritual level?'

'You didn't quite get me just now, did you, Johnny? The drugs helped induce the spiritual level, allowing the projection of the astral body.'

'Oh, right. Then we're kind of on the same page.'

'I don't swear to believe that users actually shrug off their meat coats and go flying around the place, or if it's only a result of being shit-faced, but hey! What is it you want to throw by me?'

'Another angle has just come to me right now. Poppy's being treated by a doctor specializing in neurological problems and cognitive recovery; what if Mr Choi has been feeding her some of those drugs you mentioned and it has given her the ability to free her mind from her shattered body?'

'Bloody hell,' Gavin laughed. 'Are you sure you haven't been smoking your own shit on the way over here?'

Johnny grimaced. Yeah, the scenario was rather ridiculous when he thought about it. But what if, after all these years, the results of Choi's treatments were allowing Poppy to astrally project her image? It would explain how she'd been seen one second and been gone the next. However, there had to be more to it, because the stuff she'd yakked up in Helen's shop had existed longer than the fleeting image of the woman had, so too the mud showing up at Andrew's house and in his car, and there was still the matter of those handprints on Gavin's car bonnet.

'You heard of an egregore?' he punted the idea again.

'I've heard of a "head-the-ball",' Gavin said, and laughed harder than pertinent, as the term was local Carlisle slang meaning a stupid person and pronounced more along the lines of 'heed-the-baw'.

'You're a bloody head-the-ball,' Johnny told him, and Gavin laughed uproariously again. Those drugs must have been 'good shit' or his friend genuinely was losing his mind. 'Now listen up, and let me explain.'

Gavin held up his hands in surrender, though it took him a moment or two longer to control himself. He sat on the end of his bed, looking up at Johnny. 'Go on, mate.'

'Right. This is what I've learned, and yeah, it's to do with the paranormal, but studies conducted at a university in Canada more or less proved it to be a genuine phenomenon when they manifested phenomena related to a fictional character they called "Philip". It's to do with the collective consciousness. Imagine all these people, all at the same time, believing in the same thing, and through the strength of their beliefs they give life to an actual being. Through some kind of psychic projection they actually bring their belief to life, giving it solidity and purpose. You've heard of the Slim Dude entity, haven't you? It started off as a fictional being originating as a creepypasta meme on the internet, but people began believing in him, and soon after he began showing up all over the place. He was connected to a near fatal stabbing of a girl in the US, when her friends swore they had to kill her to stop him from snatching them.'

'I heard of that, yeah. But what has it to do with us?'

'What if we collectively brought to life our own egregore, our own thought form?' Johnny waited. When Gavin continued in silence, he said, 'After Carl was murdered, we all were thinking about him, and about the catalyzing point of our youths together, when Melanie was murdered. What if we each had our own beliefs, and the strength of them brought to life this amalgamation of Poppy and Ginny Greenteeth and gave it purpose in tormenting us. I mean, think about it, even Margaret Bishop recently gave it a name of its own: Wicked Jenny. If Jenny is part of each of us, it would explain why she appears differently as we each have our own memories of that day, and our present thoughts would be formed by them. Brian thought of her as a resurrected Melanie and was having dreams about her, you saw an adult version of the girl you pitied for being brushed aside, my version I sent to fuck with me by proxy of my partner Helen, while Andrew has seen something more like a creature out of a dark fairy tale. Jenny looks different, but is the same collective thought form, the same egregore . . .'

'How long is that pizza gonna be?' Gavin asked.

'Seriously?'

'Huh? I'm starving.'

'Did you zone out or something?'

'I dunno. Heard the bit about the skinny fella stabbing a girl . . .'

'Can I see your phone?'

'Why? There's stuff on there I'd rather keep personal.'

'I'm not interested in your drug dealer's phone number, or any dick pics you sent to Kylie. But I was hoping to get a look at that video that Kylie sent you, the night she ran for it.'

'There's nothing to see. Just her being a nut job.'

'I'd still like to see it.'

Gavin pointed out where his mobile was currently charging on a lead plugged into a socket beside his bed.

Johnny fetched it, but handed it over to Gavin to find the right video segment. He took it back and watched Kylie's amateurish attempt at becoming a social media star and then being engulfed by panic. He tried pausing and restarting to see better what the camera caught while she was thrashing about on the floor and then jumping up and fleeing.

'Any chance we can mirror this on to your TV?' Johnny asked after being frustrated for several minutes.

'I know about drugs and stuff, you're the paranormal and tech guy. What do you even mean by mirroring it on my TV?'

'Don't you know you can cast stuff from your smartphone to a compatible smart TV?'

'D'you mean I've been wasting time watching porn on my phone when I could've been watching HD films on my widescreen?'

Unsure if Gavin was joking or not, Johnny didn't reply. He found the TV remote and switched on the power and brought up the necessary app. Within a short time, Kylie's exit video was playing on Gavin's sixty-inch screen TV mounted on the wall opposite his bed.

'You told Andrew that you had scratches on you the morning after Kylie left,' Johnny reminded Gavin. 'You had any since then?'

'No. Then again, I haven't had a woman in my bed since then either.' Gavin sat back on the bed, both hands fiddling with his long hair, as if trying to tie it into a knot at his nape. 'When did Andrew tell you about those?'

'I visited his house and we got talking. It came up.'

'Didn't he tell you that they appeared after Kylie left, maybe an hour after I woke up? I wondered then if they were some sort of stigmata or something.'

'The stigmata are reputedly signs of Christ's crucifixion, and usually only appear on holy men and women. I hate to tell you, Gav, but you're no saint.'

He laughed.

Johnny grew more serious. 'I've heard of cases of demonic infestation where victims have been scratched by unseen hands, usually the scratches appear in bands of three, denoting a mocking of the Holy Trinity.'

'Surely that stuff only happens in the movies?'

'Were you in the movies when it happened to you?'

Gavin stopped laughing. Johnny put his hand on his friend's shoulder. 'Are you going to be OK, Gav? You haven't been acting yourself since we saw Poppy yesterday.'

He exhaled in a judder. 'The truth, Johnny-boy? I'm shitting myself.'

'You're scared you might be next to die?'

'No, mate. I'm scared by how I'm beginning to think.'

Johnny nodded. 'Me, too, Gav. Me, too.'

Distracted by their talk, Johnny had allowed Kylie's video to play to the end. It prompted him to watch again. He hit the play icon on his phone and the video ran again from the beginning.

At the point where Kylie fell on the ground, thrusting her phone between her and whatever she claimed to have seen there was a definite warping effect of the video. On the small screen of a phone it had not been very noticeable, but on the larger screen in all its HD glory, the effect was evident, and to anyone that cared to study it they'd agree it formed the indistinct shape of a crouching figure that abruptly lunged towards the camera. Kylie had not been lying, there had been some kind of entity in the apartment, and while she scrambled backwards, dropping her phone in her panic, the figure turned towards the sleeping figure on the bed. And as Kylie half-skidded and half-fell down the stairs, her phone stayed propped on something showing a glimpse of the near invisible thing straddling the bed and its occupant. Now its form had morphed, its legs growing incredibly long to span the entire bed, and its upper body had gone bulkier. But its face, in profile, was most shocking of all, because it was not Poppy's face, neither whole nor deformed, it was another's face that they both recognized.

'Oh, for f—' Gavin croaked as it bent to whisper sweet nothings in his ear.

Johnny couldn't, wouldn't, believe his eyes. 'No way am I bloody having *this*,' he moaned.

THIRTY-EIGHT

Gemma Barker

'I'm not sure that this is a very good idea,' Gemma said as Andrew Miller negotiated the tight entrance to his driveway. Gates on each side barely left a space wide enough for a hand to slip between the gatepost and car's body, and it was fortunate that the wing mirrors sat higher than the posts otherwise they would have been knocked off.

'Nell's gone for . . . well, I can't really be sure of that, because it's doubtful she'll ever come back. You don't have to worry about anyone catching us together.'

Andrew set the handbrake and turned off the engine. Gemma was amazed that they'd made it back safely to his house as he had driven like a man possessed at times. He had decided he was on a promise, and he had not been shy about revealing that since Nell pushed him aside he'd felt like one of those involuntary celibates that he'd heard lurks in their mother's basement, perving on animated pornography day and night. Perhaps by dropping that little nugget he hoped to enthuse her that she was getting him in his entirety, that she wasn't the *other woman*, but the *only woman*. It would probably annoy him if she admitted to having slept with several different partners over the past years or so, because she was certain he'd got the idea that she was solely into him. Yeah, she liked him, but not at the exclusion of other dates, specifically ones nearer her own age.

This to Gemma, although she wouldn't tell him until after they inevitably split, was just a little bit of fun. A box to tick to say she'd dated an older man – and if he played his cards right, that she'd slept with an older man – but it was nothing more than that. He wanted sex, she wanted sex, so they were each doing the other a favour, right? She liked him, but that was as far as any kind of relationship would extend. Infatuation, love, they were for another person entirely, one she might dote on and settle down with to raise a family. But that was in the future. She was too young to be tying

herself down to one partner yet, and who knew? Perhaps in an hour
or two she might find him totally feckless in the bedroom, or maybe
a complete stallion. *Yeah, ride 'em, cowboy!*

She flushed at the latter thought. Fingers crossed.

The rain had become a constant drizzle.

Gemma remained in the car while Andrew got out. 'I'll check
the coast's clear if it will make you less nervous?'

'I think that's best,' she said.

He nodded, threw an elbow over his head like the villain tossing
his cape in an old black and white silent movie, and lunged across
the garden towards the house.

'Last chance to get out of this,' Gemma warned herself in a
whisper.

She wasn't a complete slut. She didn't sleep with loads of people.
This, to her reckoning, was the first time she'd been on a date with
a married man, although he was practically split up from his wife.
She didn't intend making a habit of getting between couples in a
relationship, and as she'd confided in her closest friend, Nicola at
work, this thing with Mr Miller was purely for the thrill of getting
away with it.

She couldn't see where Andrew had gone.

She waited.

The rain picked up a little, drumming on the car's roof like the
fingers of a thousand infants. The windscreen grew awash.

Through the rain he jogged, an indistinct blur of colour.

He went directly to her door, and grinned at her through the
rain-dotted window. He held up an umbrella. What a gentleman!

She got out of the car and huddled beneath the brolly. He wrapped
one arm around her waist, and kept her slightly off balance as they
trotted together through the rain.

'We've got the house to ourselves,' he reassured her, as they
approached the front door that he'd strategically left open.

Stepping out from under the umbrella, Gemma looked around.
She was in a mid-priced house, beautifully decorated and furnished.
Not bad at all, she thought. Mr Miller's wage must far exceed hers
for him to be able to live this comfortably, even if Nell also brought
in a decent salary.

'Does Nell work?' she wondered.

'Not since the accident,' he said.

She took it that he meant the terrible event that had wrecked their lives, and taken their daughter from them, so she didn't push for more.

'Nice home,' she said.

'Yeah,' he agreed. 'It used to be. Do you want to sit in the kitchen while I get us a bottle opened?'

'Sure.'

He closed the door, shook raindrops off the umbrella that he'd closed and set it in a rack beside the wall. 'Go on. Just follow the hall.'

She went ahead of him, suspecting he was watching the sway of her backside. She didn't mind, and again felt a little giddy with excitement. Back at the pub she had probably drunk more wine with her dinner than intended. She was tipsy, no doubt about it, and her inhibitions had lowered almost to the gutter. She giggled at the thought, and twirled her fingers in the air. 'Fetch us something expensive from the cellar, James,' she called in her poshest voice.

He followed her.

The hall smelled strongly of deodorizing spray from a number of air freshener devices timed to squirt the place every few minutes. A door opened into his kitchen and an adjacent utility area. There was also a sunroom, but all the windows had venetian blinds, currently closed. She headed towards a table surrounded by chairs, but apparently he had another destination in mind. He pulled out some high stools at a breakfast bar, and patted the cushion on one. 'Here,' he said. 'D'you need a hand up?'

'Please,' she said, and reached out to him.

A tingle of delight went up her arm to her brain as he held her fingers in his and helped her settle her backside on the stool. He crouched, intimately close, while helping hook her heels on to a rung. She thought she heard the breath shuddering out of him as he stood and turned away. He took off his coat, and dug several items out of his pockets and set them aside, then took his wet coat and hung it in the utility area. Gemma glanced at two matching mobile phones, his car keys, and some loose coins.

Two mobile phones, huh? She thought. She'd heard that cheating spouses often equipped themselves with a second phone, in order to contact their lover. She wondered if her number would end up keyed into Andrew's second phone, or if he was waiting to see how the night went before making things more official.

'Are you cold?' he asked.

'No.'

'Then why not take off your coat?'

'Help me?' she asked, playing the damsel in distress, the tall stool acting as her ogre's tower.

He helped her out of her jacket, and she knew it was deliberate the way his hands brushed her breasts. She didn't complain, which encouraged him to lean in and press a kiss at the corner of her mouth. She turned her face to him and they kissed longer and deeper. She could feel his urgency, but wanted to play things a little cooler. She had no intention of making love in the kitchen when a comfortable bed lay empty upstairs.

'Go fetch the wine,' she said.

'It's in the garage,' he said.

It was an odd place to store wine, but not totally unusual, she decided. Maybe he'd stashed it there, out of sight and mind of Nell, when planning to lure Gemma back here at his first opportunity.

While he was gone, she couldn't resist having a poke around.

She pulled his phone towards her, and tipped it, bringing the phone to life: typical bloke of the older generation, he hadn't made it secure with facial recognition or a pass code. She saw the messages listed from Nell, and read them. Yeah, sure enough, his wife had announced that she was going to stay with her sister for a few days, and that she'd call him in a day or two. She opened his photos, but there was nothing there of interest, only some weird video of a woman gasping and yelling and running out of a house.

She put aside his phone, and reached for the other. What secrets would she find on it?

Actually, the second phone held the same text messages as his first, only it appeared that they had been sent rather than received by the second phone. A quick scroll through the photos, and then bringing up a Facebook app, and she discovered that the phone belonged not to Andrew, but to his wife. How the hell had he ended up with Nell's phone in his pocket if she had allegedly sent him those messages?

Gemma dropped down from her high perch. Her tipsiness had drained away, replaced by a heavy feeling in her stomach.

There was something wrong.

Decidedly wrong, and that smell, the overpowering scent of flowers filling the house. On first smelling the cloying scent she'd assumed it was because the house had been locked up all day while the air fresheners had continued to do their work, filling the still air with chemical deodorants. Now Gemma wasn't as certain.

Wondering where Andrew was, and if she'd time to get out the house before he noticed, she began a swift trot down the hallway to where the umbrella had been discarded. The door sat open an inch, because he'd gone outside to enter his separate garage. Afraid of bumping into him on his return, she backtracked, then glanced upward. If she could get to the bathroom, lock herself inside and use her own phone to call a taxi . . .

She went up the stairs, feet drumming on each creaking step.

At the top she was faced by several doors. Two were obviously bedroom doors, the next partially open door was to a spare room and the fourth was to the bathroom, evidenced by the small window above the door, a feature of older houses like this one.

Gemma tried the door.

It was secure.

Not locked from inside though, this door was locked from without, and the key hung on a loop on the door jamb.

Using the small key, she unlocked the door, already dreading what she would find.

As the door swung inward, she was rewarded by the exact nightmare scenario she had imagined.

Nell had not gone to stay at her sister's house, Nell was home.

She was in the bath, naked, knees bent and protruding from the cold murky water, while her upper torso and face were submerged.

The stench that billowed over Gemma was putrid.

She slapped a hand over her mouth, halting a scream.

She couldn't alert Andrew of her discovery, not before she could ring the police and get them . . .

'You shouldn't have come up here,' Andrew growled from behind her. 'You've gone and spoiled everything, you stupid bitch.'

He had ascended the stairs in his stockinged feet, avoiding the creaks and squeaks he was obviously familiar with. In his right hand he carried a bottle of wine. He held it inverted by its neck. Like a Neanderthal's club, or a hammer.

He slammed it down, directly on Gemma's forehead, the thick base smashing her nose and breaking the frame of her glasses.

THIRTY-NINE

1988

A ndy stood, the sun blazing against his back. His T-shirt was misshapen where he'd pulled and twisted at it while trying to shed the dirt and grass chucked at him earlier by his mates. He'd warned them that his mother would kill him if he went home filthy, and he wasn't lying. Unlike his weakling dad, his mother was quick to lift a hand, or to swing a slipper, her slug-like tongue forced out the corner of her mouth in her rage. Sometimes she would strike Andy until he squealed for mercy, but sometimes his cries only encouraged further cruelty. He carried bruises and scrapes most days, but nobody noticed: when he was a rambunctious boy whose friends often targeted him for bumps and scrapes, his mother didn't need to fear her child cruelty being found out.

Where the sun beat on his skin he was red and tingled. His fair skin was burned, and would peel later. Andy would pluck it off in rags, his shedding skin almost translucent and gossamer thin: it wasn't the first time this summer that he'd burned.

The flying ants that were so prevalent earlier had all but disappeared, but they had been replaced by other swarming insects. Little gnats flitted about him in clouds, and moved with him, as if they were trapped in his bubble whenever he proceeded. They got everywhere, even on his tongue and he had to spit their tiny, bitter tasting bodies out.

For now, he stood, and he ogled the bare-breasted models Ian Nixon had clipped from newspapers and magazines and pinned to the tree trunks in his makeshift den. The models all smiled broadly, and the inviting tilt of their heads seemed to call to him, to reach out and touch. He touched, fingertips trembling and he grew aroused.

Distantly a dog barked.

He couldn't say if it was Mel and Poppy's Golden Retriever he heard, or a different dog entirely, but he snapped his gaze off the nude models towards the frog ponds.

He walked, almost as if being pulled along by a string tied about his chest, his features lax and little thought in his mind. For years he'd suffered blackouts and fits, and occasionally he seemed to march to a different drumbeat than everyone else. Before he left Nixon's den, he bent to one knee and inserted his hand under a fallen log and grabbed the hammer Nixon had secreted there.

Andy wended a path between the trees, clacking the hammerhead off trunks and branches, and found the cinder path and the first stile that allowed access to the field alongside the riverbank. He stood astride the stile a moment, the hammer swinging forgotten at his side. The sun again worked on his reddened neck with scorching fingers.

He grew lucid for the time being.

He recalled his pals all going home, summoned by the aromas of fish fingers, chips and baked beans, or in Brian's case a Vesta beef curry, his personal favourite for tea. Andy hadn't been ready to go home, not while he was still dirty and wet from playing in the ponds: he was prepared to stop out for hours, until his mother fell asleep in front of the telly when he could sneak in and change out of his soiled clothes. His tea would be there waiting for him, a plateful saved by his father. His dad was usually the equivalent of a wet lettuce when it came to standing up to his mam, but not at the expense of Andy starving to death.

At a loss, and with hours to spend alone, Andy had retraced their steps back to where he and his mates had spent their afternoon. Ian wasn't around when Andy went looking for him, to smooth things over. The others called him Divvy Nixon, but Andy wasn't like the others. He didn't want Nixon taking it out on his little cousin Johnny because Carl and Brian, and even Gavin when he followed the pack, got their kicks out of setting cheek at him. He took away the hammer, rather than allow Nixon to threaten Johnny, or anyone else, with it again.

Across the field he went, scrambled over the next stile and joined the cinder path, swinging the hammer at imaginary creatures, trolls and ogres and goblins. He voiced their roars, and the sounds of crunching bones and splattering blood, their dying screams: totally harmless imaginary fun.

He heard the tinkling laughter of girls as he clambered over the five-bar gate.

He'd assumed that Mel and Poppy would have left the area by now. After all, there was little to hold the attention of girls at a frog pond, not when they weren't prone to administering the same type of cruelty as teenage boys were, blowing frogs up with straws in their bums or lobbing them from their catapults.

He spotted the girls and he crouched in the long grass in front of the gate.

They were sitting on the right-hand embankment, and appeared to be weaving bracelets and necklaces from reeds plucked from the pond. They would try on their pond jewellery, then swap them about, admiring each by holding them up to the sun. It was pure innocence at play. Their dog still snuffled about in the bushes, and wasn't so old and deaf that it didn't register Andy's presence. It turned towards him and barked once, and Andy ducked down.

The girls looked in his direction but he couldn't be seen.

After a minute or so he raised his head and spotted Mel. She stood alone, with her head thrown back, holding above her another craft-made bracelet. It dangled from her wrist and she turned her arm about, admiring the way it looked. Andy couldn't help but admire her, he thought she was very pretty, and when he allowed his gaze to drop a little found her breasts looked nice the way they pressed against her shirt. He stared, and thought of those pictures of girls pinned to the trees in Nixon's den and believed that Mel could give any of them a run for their money.

'Ewww! Have you got a stiffy? Are you some sort of pervert or what?'

Andy jerked at the female voice.

He spun about and there stood the Golden Retriever and Poppy, less than ten feet away, having climbed up from behind the embankment alongside the gate. She looked at his face, then down at the front of his jeans again, and he was mortified, because she wasn't wrong. In his daydreaming he had become aroused again and it was plainly obvious who was the object of his desire.

'Hey, Melanie. Look! You've got a Peeping Tom, a dirty little perv called Windy Miller.'

Andy shook his head. 'No, it's not . . .'

But Poppy laughed at him, crowding closer. Bending to get a better look when he twisted his hips aside.

'Melanie. You should come and see . . .'

'Stop it!' Andy swung his arm at her, to push her away.

The hammer struck her head, and her thick red curls did nothing to cushion the blow. The claw end of the hammer shattered her skull, and in the moment Andy heard it *pop!* Almost like a deflating balloon the side of her head seemed to compress, and she sank down to her knees with a long wheeze emitted from a suddenly constricted throat. Her right hand probed at the side of her head, fingers trembling. They came away bright red. Against the set of woven bracelets on her arm, the blood looked extremely vivid: *red and green should never be seen*, Andy intoned.

How Poppy managed to crawl away, he couldn't fathom. The injury to her head was horrendous. Even her dog watched her quizzically, whining and rocking its heart-shaped head from side to side. When she began weeping, the dog went to her, brushing brusquely against her, as if urging her to stand. Andy stood with his mouth open, and the bloody hammer held raised beside his shoulder. Poppy mewled something, probably crying for help. Earlier, when those poor frogs had suffered enough, he'd put them out of their misery, and he tried to serve the same mercy to Poppy. He walked on stiff legs to her and struck her again, beating her already broken head further in. Poppy collapsed face down on the couch grass.

A scream, running footsteps, and Melanie launched at him. She thrust at his chest and face, pushing him aside, and when he thought she would go for his eyes with her nails, she dropped to her knees alongside her adopted sister. She cried out for help from God, from her mother, and even from Andy, but nobody was listening.

He stood as if in a daze.

Andy's hearing had withdrawn to a distant whistle as if all sound was being fed to him from the far end of a cramped tunnel.

He was lost.

He didn't know what to do, or what was expected from him.

Poppy's blood was splattered across his T-shirt and he knew that his mother would kill him if he returned home in that kind of filthy state.

He had to get cleaned up, but first he must clean up this mess.

He had no recourse except to hit Melanie too and after he'd played with her a bit, he laid her face down in the pond.

The senile old dog lay at the edge of the pond, watching him with wet eyes. He struck at it a couple of times, missing with each swing, until the old dog ran, tail tucked under its legs and hid shivering under the bushes at the side of the pond.

'Be careful. Don't get too close,' he cautioned the old mutt, 'or Ginny Greenteeth will drag you under.'

He trudged away, swinging the hammer, and after wiping his fingerprints off its haft with his T-shirt, he returned it to its hidey-hole under the log in Nixon's den. Nobody saw him squirm out of his bloody shirt and burn it on one of the smouldering fires at the rubbish dump at the foot of the lonning. Bare-chested he walked home, which wasn't unusual because lots of kids in his neighbourhood went without their shirts in the heat of summer.

FORTY

Jennifer Seeley

Seated in her private room, Jennifer Seeley faced a window that overlooked part of the North York Moors. Rolling hills, deep purple under the low clouds, undulated for miles. Lights were dotted about the landscape, but they were sparse and far apart. Groups of sycamore trees made darker blots against the terrain, but only the closest were visible. Beyond the horizon there was a sizable city, its street lights evident on the underbelly of the clouds. The rain currently washing over the north west was yet to make its way east over the Pennines; for the time being the night was still.

Jennifer didn't see any of that through her one healthy eye.

She had her eye open, but it had rolled up so that anyone viewing her would only see the white sclera. Her head had rolled back too, as far as the cushion of flesh over her neck would allow. Her jaw hung to one side, her bottom lip drooping and from it a string of drool stitched her mouth to her chest.

She dreamed.

Or perhaps she experienced a different process than other people did when succumbing to the place where her thoughts formed.

To look at her, an outsider might believe that Jennifer was devoid of intelligence. She sat most of the time either as still as a boulder, or she grew agitated and her body would jerk and spasm and she'd grow vocal, albeit not with words recognizable as the English language. And yet there were times she was highly cognizant, whether or not it showed externally.

Her carers could sometimes tell when she was aware of her surroundings, and they would do their best to engage her in one-sided conversation: they would just chatter, and it mattered not that half of what they said was rubbish because it still felt comforting to know that other people felt her worthy of their attention. Without dwelling too much on the distant past, it was more than what she had ever been the recipient of from her birth mother, or from the sour woman that had stood in as a surrogate for a few years before she was attacked.

Back then she had been Poppy.

But that ended when Margaret Bishop showed she was incapable of loving a severely disabled daughter, and had handed her back to her designated social workers to be homed elsewhere. Jennifer hadn't had a say in her situation, nor in the reversion to her birth name, and so much time had passed since then that it no longer mattered to her. Jennifer rarely, if ever, thought of Margaret in other than bitter terms, and she couldn't even picture the man who'd supposedly been her adoptive dad, she could only remember Melanie.

Melanie had been everything that Poppy wasn't, she thought. Pretty, popular, clever, athletic, a great dancer, a beautiful singer, but Poppy had not been envious. The opposite was true in fact; she had worshipped her sister, looked up to her, and one day hoped to be loved half as much as Mel was by all that knew her. She had loved Melanie more than she might have loved a sister of the same blood.

In her strange dream state, Jennifer laughed at the thought.

The same blood . . .

There was a time when Mr Choi visited her room and sat talking to her. He encouraged her to think in repetition, to conduct brain training exercises, and she embraced the challenges he sometimes set her. On other occasions he'd simply chat, treating her like an actual human being rather than a crippled empty vessel. Sometimes he would read to her, or tell her off-the-cuff anecdotes or humorous stories. On one occasion he'd told her the genesis of her family name.

Seeley.

He told her that in Scottish folklore a 'seelie' or 'seely' was a fey creature, a kind of fairy-like nature spirit, and that the name was derived from an ancient Anglo-Saxon term meaning 'happy' or 'prosperous'.

It was a whimsical story.

Until you understood that there were two sides to the seely fey, and that they were divided into opposing classifications, the Seelie and Unseelie Courts. The easiest way to classify one from the other was as good or evil, though Mr Choi warned they all could be dangerous enemies to those who offended them.

Seelies were magical trickster beings, and Jennifer learned of their ability to throw a glamour over those they intended tricking. In her damaged mind she wondered if she possessed the ability, and had sat for countless hours reaching out, and seeing if she could cloud people's eyes. She wished so hard that she could talk things through with her doctor, because she was certain that Mr Choi would assist her to develop her abilities if he knew what she intended. He was open-minded for a scientist, not a man to shy away from the weirder subjects, and who stoically believed her survival and recovery could be counted as miraculous.

For years, the exercises set to stimulate her helped open new or unused neural passageways, and she had discovered ways of using her brain that bordered on the paranormal, but was totally natural. It has been said that the human brain has ten times, a hundred times, a *thousand times* the capacity we put it to. With training her restructured brain showed it was capable of performing its own miracles.

In her dreams she visited people, and afterwards she could never be certain if the reactions of those she'd visited were real or simply the responses conjured from her own subconscious.

There was a TV and a radio in her room. Unless she was asleep they played constantly. She was able to absorb the images from a TV, even if she didn't always understand them. Radio, being audible, was easier to contend with, and she often learned more from listening than she did from the flashing and flickering colours on a screen. From her radio she had heard of the murder of Carl Butler, and the name of her childhood tormentor had brought back a flood of memories, and a heart-rending disappointment that after all these years, nobody had been prosecuted for the attacks on her or her beloved sister.

Some kid with learning difficulties had been blamed for the assaults, and in his fear of incarceration – and what would happen to an alleged sex offender inside – had taken his own life before Poppy, not yet Jennifer again, had been woken from her comatose state. Not that she had been able to tell a soul that he'd been wrongly accused, because she had lost the ability of speech, and of the motor skills necessary to write or to tap down a name on a keyboard. She was still incapable, decades later, of forming more than guttural or liquid sounds, or of making herself understood, so it perhaps was not unusual that justice was yet to be served.

In her dreams she'd roamed, seeking out the group of boys that had made the allegations against Ian Nixon, trying to warn them that they had been mistaken, and that a monster lurked in their midst. She had no way of knowing if her interactions were real, or that she'd actually reached them at all, and in those dreams she was often unable to control the manner in which they met. Sometimes the dreams were merely strange and she'd find herself in unusual locations, or misdirected instead to a person close to the intended recipient, and they were unhelpful, and then on others they ended up being too erotic than it was comfortable for her, or they were downright frightening.

With no way of knowing if anything was genuine, she had continued sending out messages, keeping them brief, with tiny snippets of speech dredged from that fateful day, where she tried to prompt the killer's friends into rethinking their involvement, to reassess the day, and hoping it would lead to them unmasking the monster.

Why not simply unveil him, tell them his name and point the finger of accusation at him?

She had tried, more than once.

But she had poor control over their interactions, and there had been occasions where her dreams had taken ridiculous turns and she had halted a moving car by the power in her hands alone, leaving an impression of her palms trapped between the layers of paint like a negative caught on film, and on another had vomited the contents of the murder scene all over a posh shop. Another time she'd tried scratching the name of the killer into the chest of one of the sleeping boys, now a man, but her motor skills control in her dreams was as ineffective as the chicken scratchings she could form when awake.

She had no idea if any of her messages were making it through. Until yesterday that was, when out of the blue she had been almost nose to nose with her attacker and two of his old friends.

Their presence at the institute was proof that their thoughts had been turned to her, not that they'd understood what she'd tried conveying yet.

She'd tried warning them then, but as it had since that awful day, her body failed her, her ability to speak failed her. Thrashing around, cawing like an angry seagull, she had sent them running. They had fled, horrified by the monstrous, demented thing she appeared in life.

She hadn't hurt Carl. She had not intentionally harmed Brian.

Johnny and Gavin – beyond those scratches on him – she would not harm.

For Andy Miller she'd make an exception if she could.

At least, she would try to stop him from killing again . . .

FORTY-ONE

Andrew Miller

I grabbed Gemma by her clothing and dragged her into the bathroom.

You might say that by then things had gone too far to ever expect to get away with murder again, but I wasn't ready for giving up.

From her place in the tub, Nell watched me from under the water. She eyed me with reproof, a look I'd grown used to lately. She had begun the process of decomposition, and already some of her bodily fluids had leaked into and mixed with the bathwater. Other than a slight sickly aroma, the smell hadn't been too bad, and I'd managed to keep it under control with the closed door and liberal use of air fresheners. Had Gemma not sneaked upstairs and opened the bathroom door, she would never have guessed that the sweet smell in the downstairs hall was that of putrefaction. The other day, I thought that Johnny's sharper nose had picked up on the odour of death, but he'd been too intent on revealing his crazy supernatural theories to give it much attention. Flaming egregores indeed!

I knew I couldn't keep the ruse going forever, and must move Nell's body at the first opportunity, but other things, other bodies, kept coming up. Brian's untimely death had thrown a spanner among my plans of disposing of Nell, because it had ensured visits to my house from Joyce and Johnny, and I couldn't risk the chance of moving her when any of them could turn up unannounced. And then there was this turn-about with Gemma, and the hot little vixen wanting my body. For a few days I'd been concocting a feasible explanation for Nell's disappearance and had used her mobile phone to message her sister, so that it appeared she was alive and well, and thinking of taking a few days away on a break. It had given me the idea to send more texts from her phone to mine, to make it appear that she intended staying away at her sister's house, but was in truth making plans to leave me and was heading to a secret location unknown to all but her. Those texts had come in handy when luring Gemma back to my house. I'd fully expected to entertain her and get away with moving Nell in a day or two and dumping her phone with her.

Gemma's head bled profusely. It was the way with scalp injuries, they bled like mad. I wasn't concerned that I'd bashed in her brain box the way I had with Poppy and Melanie, because I'd hit her on the forehead, the hardest part of the skull. The red dye she'd put in her hair was almost prophetic now; blood spilled from directly below the orange slash, now crimson, and made twin runnels either side of her swelling nose. Her glasses had fallen off when I'd manhandled her into the bathroom. She lay with her shoulders propped against the bath, head lolling, her breaths coming out in long rasps. Her bottom lip was bulbous, her nose turning purple-blue and spreading across her features. She wasn't pretty, not in the least. Suddenly I lost any desire I'd ever had to make love to her.

I roused her with a jab of my toe.

She whined as she gained consciousness.

'Not a fucking sound,' I warned her, and brandished the heavy bottle, 'or I swear to God I'll smash your skull to a pulp.'

'Andrew? Why?' she keened.

'You really want to hear?'

'What did you do?'

'To Nell? Why I came in here while she was bathing, grabbed her skinny ankles and dragged her underwater. I thought it a fitting way to die for her, seeing as how much she blamed me for Becky's drowning.'

'You . . . you murdered her?'

'Have you got soap in your ears?' I countered. 'Didn't you hear me?'

She wept, and I again threatened her with the bottle. It was expensive, a quality wine in a quality bottle: if I'd to make odds, I'd say Gemma's skull would break before the base of the bottle did.

'Don't feel sorry for her,' I spat. 'She betrayed me, more than one time. I suspected she was having an affair, and after *his* funeral, when we got back here, she admitted to it. No wonder she supposedly didn't want Carl in our house, it was because she knew they wouldn't be able to keep their flings a secret from me anymore. Sometimes old friendships are best left in the past, she'd gloated to me at his funeral, as if she'd got away with it scot-free. To think

I'd been totally loyal to her, abstaining while I waited for her, and she'd been running around behind my back with that little weasel. Well, what do you know? I admitted I'd suspected what they were up to and that I'd murdered him for it. That's right, I admitted beating that sneaky little bastard's brains in with a hammer from my garage. Here . . . look.'

From the back of my belt, I pulled out the offending weapon.

After killing Carl I should have got rid of it, tossed it away in a bin miles away from the old canal where I ambushed him on his way home from the pub. But I'd brought it back with me, washed it clean of his blood and hid it on one of the garage rafters, out of sight of anyone but the pigeons that sometimes roosted inside.

'Wh-what are you going to do with that?' she croaked.

'Was originally planning on putting up a new bookshelf this evening,' I said sarcastically, 'but my plans might have changed. What do you think I should do with it?'

I couldn't really say why I'd brought the hammer from my garage along with the wine, maybe there was part of me that had expected my crimes to be discovered, and I'd made a contingency in my mind to deal with Gemma. I couldn't state exactly what had motivated me to reach up and pluck it from the cobweb-covered rafter and stuff it down the back of my belt, because I'd acted under one of those fugues that had afflicted me since childhood. It was only when I'd returned to the kitchen and found it empty, and mine and Nell's phones disturbed, that my hand had crept to my lower back and found it tucked there.

'Please don't hurt me,' Gemma cried as I held out the claw hammer.

'Oh, but I must,' I said. 'I can't very well have you carrying back tales to Norman and ruining my good reputation, can I?'

'If you come near me I'll scream.'

'Funnily enough, that's what Nell said. Kind of compelled me to grab her ankles and drag her under water. The thrashing about that she made! Ha! You should have seen the bubbles. There was no need for the bath bomb she wasted.'

'Mr Miller, please. Andrew! *Andy?* You don't really want to hurt me. Come on, please put that down. Let's go downstairs and I'll clean myself up while you pour us some wine each, yeah? It's not too late to turn things around, we can stay friends can't we? We can still . . . you know.'

I laughed. 'Can you hear how ridiculous you sound? Do you really believe I'm so crazy that you can manipulate me into getting drunk and randy again. What then? You'd get me to drop my pants and then you'd knee me in the balls and run? Sorry, Gemma, but right now I'd be more attracted to a pig wearing lipstick than to your ugly face. In fact . . .'

I stepped backwards out of the bathroom and set aside the bottle of wine. With both hands full I'd probably have found dealing with her too difficult. By the time I stepped back inside, the stupid fool had tried lunging up and slapped at the window over the bath, perhaps thinking it was her best opportunity to try fleeing. What was she hoping to do, leap from the bathroom window in those heels?

I snapped out my left hand and grabbed her throat. I pushed, and her back bent painfully before she fully lost traction and her feet flew skyward. I bore down on her, pushing her down into the stinking water alongside Nell. Gemma screamed once, and then her head went under the frothing water. Bubbles erupted from her mouth, and I heard the gargle as the putrid water invaded her throat, and I grinned like a shark. I held the hammer poised in my other hand, should I need it. For the moment though, I allowed the Wicked Jenny part of me to do her worst.

FORTY-TWO

Johnny Wilson

'Gav, I need you to look at that and tell me exactly who you see. C'mon, man, because if it's only me seeing this I'm going totally off my head.'

Gavin pinched the bridge of his nose between his index finger and thumb. He'd shed his glasses rather than see clearly.

'Gavin, man!'

'It's probably like when you can make out faces in the clouds or the man in the moon,' Gavin said, but there was no dismissing what was there on the TV.

'You're talking about pareidolia,' said Johnny. 'That there is not like finding Jesus Christ's likeness on your morning toast. Look at it, Gavin, you can't ignore it, mate.'

He fed back on his glasses and settled them as he turned slowly to the screen. In the past minute or so, Johnny had fiddled with the remote control, trying to pause the video at the most pertinent spot.

Gavin looked again, and Johnny could tell he was questioning if he was still high from the cannabis or not, and desperately hoping that he was.

'Well?' Johnny demanded.

'Yeah. That's Andrew.' Gavin turned aside, shaking his head and muttering under his breath. He went to the window and slapped his left palm on the wall while he leaned out to suck in deep gulps of air.

Johnny eyed the screen.

Back when he'd been a member of the paranormal investigations team, most of their adventures, coined 'investigations', had been done for shits and giggles. The more he'd participated in the more he'd begun to doubt some of the evidence presented by other teams, because his own found their similarly recorded phenomena turned out to be technical glitches, artefacts on lenses, moisture in the atmosphere, dust particles and, yes, pareidolia, where the miraculous was formed from the mundane through the human brain's propensity to seek recognizable patterns. He hadn't grown completely cynical, but his scepticism had risen quite a lot, which he'd decided was no bad thing if he intended studying seriously. He had seen enough bogus 'evidence' to be able to spot similar, and had once upset a few believers at his work when he'd showed them that their glowing apparition caught on CCTV was actually a spider hanging close to the camera lens, out of focus and reflecting the infrared light. He tried to find a way to explain how the wavy image on Gavin's TV had morphed from the indistinct figure of a hag into an exact likeness of their friend, Andrew Miller.

Again, all he could go back to was an egregore, a thought form, given substance through the power of an incredibly powerful mind to scratch Gavin as punishment for a perceived wrongdoing.

Gavin pulled his hair out of the bun he'd formed at the nape of his neck. Seconds later, he began winding and tucking his hair again. He stared at the screen, swore colourfully several times, then turned to Johnny.

'What do you think this means?' asked Gavin.

Johnny felt too sick to reply, and Gavin understood his reticence.

'This is a sign, right, sent to us to tell us about Andy,' Gavin stammered.

'What about Andy?' Johnny demanded, wanting to hear confirmation of his own fears.

'I dunno. But there's something wrong, isn't there?'

'Yeah,' Johnny finally agreed against his better judgement, 'there's something wrong. Have you seen or heard from Nell lately?'

'Last I saw her was when we were at the Manor House after Carl's cremation.'

'Yeah,' said Johnny. 'That's my last time too. I've spoken with Andy, been at his house, but she was never there. Least, Andrew said she wasn't home.'

'You saying they've split up?'

'Come on, Gav, you know I'm suggesting more than that. Look at that image on the screen, it's a sign, man. Whoever the hag-thing is, whether Poppy or Wicked-fucking-Jenny, she was trying to tell you something, and I think it was a bloody warning about Andy. Or maybe it was none of them. What if Andrew's the source of the apparitions, and his mask slipped and showed his true face?'

Johnny had no idea; all he could be confident of was that things were decidedly messed up and he was going to lose his mind if they didn't get this cleared up quickly.

'What do we do?' Gavin asked.

Years ago, they would have thrown things past Andrew first, sought his opinion and his studied response before doing anything. That was back when Johnny needed a leader he could trust, but he'd grown up since then. 'I'd say we should go to the police but I'm reluctant.'

'You don't want to after blaming the wrong person before?'

'Exactly that,' he said.

'So, what do we do, Johnny?'

'I don't know,' he said, 'perhaps we should . . .'

Gavin's doorbell rang.

It sounded incredibly loud and sharp.

They both yelped in shock.

'Bloody hell, I almost had a heart attack,' Gavin wheezed, while clutching his chest.

Johnny shivered as he peered at the closed door leading to the stairs to outside.

'What if it's him?' Gavin croaked. 'What if he knows that we know and now he's come here to get us?'

'We don't know anything for sure.' Johnny frowned at him. 'Where's your intercom?'

Gavin nodded at the plastic box on the wall that Johnny had noticed earlier. He whispered, 'Grab something heavy, just in case.'

'You want me to smack Andy?'

'If he tries to hurt us, I expect you to bash his frigging face in.'

Gavin tossed about and came up with a work boot. At first it looked a stupid choice as a weapon, but it was made from sturdy leather and was capped with steel. Johnny nodded in satisfaction, then approached the intercom. He checked with Gavin and saw his friend had taken cover behind the bed, holding aloft the boot like a murderous glove puppet. Shaking with adrenaline, Johnny pressed the button.

'Hello?' he said. 'Who's there?'

'Pizza order for Hill,' a voice answered.

Johnny wheezed in relief. 'Don't know about you, Gavin, but I've lost my appetite.'

'Bugger that, I'm ravenous. We can eat on the way. We are going to go and check Andrew's the bad guy before we sick the cops on him aren't we?'

FORTY-THREE

Gemma clawed my hand, her nails digging in and drawing dots of blood. It was supposed to make me let go, but it only encouraged me to push harder. She fought violently for her life, and I thought about hitting her a few times to soften her up and make things easier on myself. But I didn't. I kept the hammer in reserve, using my greater weight and strength to keep her submerged. As she fought, the water sloshed, and Nell bobbed about, her face coming up out of the foam at one point, eyes rolled up, eyelids drooping so that she looked as if she was a Bloodhound. I used the handle of the hammer in my right hand to press my wife back down again. The stench rising off her exposed flesh was disgusting.

Craning away, I took a breath of cleaner air.

By doing so I'd released some of the pressure off Gemma, and she burst from the water howling and spluttering. She dragged in a noisy inhalation, though not enough oxygen to sustain her for long. I rammed her down once more, and this time the back of her skull rang off the bath. Her backside slid over the edge of the bath and she sat down in the murk. Nell popped away from her like a bar of soap squeezed from a giant's fist. Gemma's bared forearms beat at the sides of the bath. The noise was like some lunatic having a whale of a time on a kettle drum. It masked the knocking and banging noises coming from downstairs.

Gemma battled vigorously to live. I had to admire her will to survive; she wasn't going to die as easily as the other three females I'd killed before her. Correction, two and a half, because that horrible thing that was once Poppy Bishop still lingered. Gemma had a lot to live for, I suppose, and I can't blame her for trying, but I simply couldn't allow her to survive. If I could shut her up, she could be taken along with Nell and disposed of. Nobody from work knew that we had been on a date, and nobody at the pub on the outskirts of town had recognized us, so I felt assured that we wouldn't be traced together there. I was reasonably sure that she hadn't told any of our workmates about me groping her backside the other day, or that she was meeting me for a romantic rendezvous this evening. At work, I could look blank, and wonder aloud where she had gone when her disappearance inevitably came up.

Gemma drove her heel into my thigh. It was sharp and tipped with a steel seg.

It was as good as having a stiletto blade driven into the muscle.

I shouted in pain, and barely saved my genitals from similar abuse as she stamped a second time. My grasp broke free of her throat, and again she fought up, dragging in life-saving air. She battered at me with her fists, and knowing how painful a jab of her heels was, she again stamped, and this time holed my shirt and took several layers of skin off my ribs. Blood seeped through my shirt and trickled down my side.

Swearing viciously, I lunged in, and to empower my rage, my tongue stuck out the corner of my mouth. I grappled with her, but she wasn't a slouch, and she was desperate to live. She rolled sideways towards me, and I couldn't control the entirety of her weight: she was short in stature perhaps, but was no slip of a girl. She rolled out of the bath and dropped, thudding wetly on the floor. The impact resounded through my house, echoed a moment later by my front door being kicked open.

Gemma screamed at the top of her lungs.

Luckily her throat was raw from the toxic water, and any oxygen in her lungs couldn't be wasted on shouting. Her thin scream barely carried down the stairs, so I had no fear of any nosy neighbours coming to check what the fuss was.

However, somebody was there, and in the moment it didn't dawn on me who had come to Gemma's rescue. Actually, in hindsight, they didn't know about my workmate, they shouted my name and also for Nell.

'Up here,' Gemma screeched. 'Help me. He's trying to kill me.'

I heard swearing and exclamations, and then the pounding of feet up the stairs. I spun around to face Gemma's would-be saviours, lifting my hammer with the wicked claws poised like the fangs of a rattlesnake about to strike.

My shoulders dipped an inch when I saw who mounted the landing first. It was Johnny, and barely a couple of steps behind him, Gavin.

I wondered how I could blag my way out of this.

If it were only Gemma, I could swear to my friends that she was the nutter, and after wheedling her way into my affections she'd tricked me into bringing her home where she'd then gone crazy when I confessed I wasn't interested in her like that. Perhaps they would have believed me when we were thirteen, but these were not my boyhood chums anymore – all for one and one for all, and all that stuff – they were adults, and practically strangers. Once upon a time they might have died for me, as I would've for them, not now. And besides, Johnny looked past me to where the agitated water had tossed Nell up and she bobbed about like a rotting cork. There was no lying my way out of her drowning.

'Andrew, in the name of God, what are you doing?' Johnny cried.

'Aww, for fu . . .' Gavin tagged on.

'You shouldn't have come here,' I scolded them. 'What are you doing barging into my house? Did you two arseholes kick open my front door?'

'Andrew,' Johnny repeated. 'What did you do to Nell?'

'She got what she deserved. That cow was sleeping with Carl behind my back, but I found out and I made them pay.'

'It was you? You murdered Carl?'

'Who else? Sure as shit wasn't your divvy cousin this time.'

'It wasn't the last time either, was it?'

I aimed a facetious smile at him.

Gavin swore again, and backed a few steps downstairs. He wasn't for running though, I could tell, only getting to a more advantageous position to defend from.

Johnny didn't retreat. He stepped forward, extending both hands towards me. He glanced past me, checking on Gemma. For now, I ignored the slut. His gaze darted to Nell, and intense regret washed over his features. 'Please, Andrew. Put down the hammer, eh? It's not too late to stop this. You need help, mate, and I'm here to help.'

'Want to grab Nell's feet and I'll get her arms and we'll carry her out to my car then? I've a spade in the boot, you can help me dig her grave.'

He didn't answer, but his hollow features spoke a million words. His eyes welled with tears. 'What happened, Andy? What made you do this?'

'Blame my abusive mother,' I said flippantly. 'Or blame the Tories, or blame Labour if you prefer, cause it doesn't matter who's in, the government is shite. Blame the coppers for not fully investigating back when we were kids. Blame Poppy for not dying when I pounded in her bloody head. You saw her, sitting there like something out of a horror film. It's her, she's the one sending those visions, your fucking egregore. She's the one forcing me to do *this*.'

'No, Andy, mate. She isn't. She's the one who's been trying to warn us about you. *This* is all you.'

I knew his point was valid. Although it was Poppy's teasing of me that had first caused me to strike out with the hammer, she wasn't the one guiding me now. Everything I'd done since hitting her – the murder of Melanie, the beating to death of Carl, drowning my disloyal wife, and now trying to end Gemma's life – I was responsible for it all. Those fugues I sometimes fell into, those occasions of lost time, who knew what I was compelled to do during them, but it was only my own psyche speaking, not some crippled woman confined to a wheelchair a hundred and fifty miles away. This was my psychopathy acting out, nobody else's. 'Andy Miller,' I crowed, in an old hag's voice, 'I hear you've been very bad.'

'You have, too,' said Johnny, 'but it's not too late to stop. Please, Andy, man. Put down the hammer.'

'Can't.'

'You can.'

'No, I must finish what I started. I never wanted to hurt you Johnny but . . .'

'Like buggery,' shouted Gavin. He swung out past Johnny, arm whipping forward, and I was hard put to dodge the missile he hurled at me.

I knocked it aside with my hammer, and watched, bemused, as a scuffed old work boot clattered down the hall. 'Hey, Gav, you cowardly git. That could have fractured my skull if it hit me.'

'It was supposed to.'

'Some pal you are,' I said, and lunged.

My intention was to force down Johnny with my greater size, reach over him and rap Gavin on his skull: he'd pulled back his hair in a man bun, making a shiny target of his forehead. However, Johnny proved he was tougher than his slight build belied. He threw his shoulder into my gut, and wrapped his arms about me. He thrust with both legs, and I was driven backwards, and slammed against the door frame. I looked down at him, and genuinely felt a moment's pause: I'd told the truth a moment ago. I had always liked Johnny, had always pitied him, and for that split-second had no genuine desire to harm him. The hammer wavered in the air, but I pushed off the door frame, forcing Johnny back towards the head of the stairs. Even without bashing in his skull I could force him down the stairs; maybe he'd fall, get entwined with Gavin and the impacts with the stairs would do my work for me. But it wasn't to be.

I'd forgotten about Gemma for the moment, but she had every sense targeted upon me. As I bullied Johnny back, and into Gavin, she snatched up the bottle of wine I'd set down by the door frame and brought it whistling down on the back of my head. Glass and wine flew everywhere.

I collapsed, the hammer dropping from my spasming fingers, and the three of us cartwheeled together to the foot of the stairs.

Groaning, moaning, my old pals struggled to extricate themselves, while I lay there, unmoving and, a second or two later, was oblivious.

FORTY-FOUR

Poppy Bishop stood over me, staring down from beneath her mop of copper curls. She said nothing, only held me with a look of complete disapproval. It was a look I was used to, it was my mother's default face whenever I reminded her that I was her greatest mistake.

I lay there, on my back, having taken a spill from my old Raleigh Grifter. That bike, despite it being second or third hand, with mismatching parts, and spongy brakes, was my pride and joy. I hoped I hadn't caused any damage when I fell off, the decal on the frame was already peeling and faded.

'Help me up?' I asked and extended a hand. Flying ants landed on it.

'There's no help for you,' said Poppy, 'I've heard you've been very bad.'

'How do you know?'

Melanie moved in alongside her adopted sister, laying a hand on Poppy's shoulder. Her forearm was resplendent with woven bracelets, and there were necklaces about her throat, not simply woven from weeds but flowers too, and verging on being as magnificent as a Hawaiian lei garland. Her blonde hair caught the rays of the sun, but they sparked so sharply I had to turn my face aside or be momentarily blinded.

'Don't tease him, Poppy, he's not to be teased, but pitied.'

'Why are you saying that, Mel?' I demanded.

'Well, isn't it obvious? Just take a look at yourself.'

The girls huddled conspiratorially, and in the next instant they were several metres away, sitting on the bank of the frog ponds, and my bike had disappeared and I was on foot. Rather I was up to my knees in water, wading through duckweed, spitting out bitter-tasting gnats. The more I progressed, the more the weed ensnared me and tried dragging me back.

'Help me,' I called.

'Get stuffed,' Poppy called back from the other side of the frog pond.

'Better keep away from the water, or ol' Ginny Greenteeth will come out and snatch you.'

I turned, expecting my best friend, Brian.

Instead, it was Nell that faced me. Standing upright, naked, the skin had already begun to slough from her bones. Her eyelids were puffy, the bottom ones drooping and her sclera was jaundiced. With her tousled hair and fingernails all broken from fighting against the side of the tub, she looked like a witch risen from the depths of the murky water. She wiggled her fingers as though they were talons grasping at prey.

'I mean it,' Nell pressed on. 'Ginny comes for the naughtiest boys and girls, and from what I hear you've been very, very bad.'

Again, Melanie was beside me, radiant, the blasts of light propelling the image of my murdered wife away from us. I rasped my thanks, but she clucked her tongue and said, 'You'd best run home before it's dark, little baby, or you're going to be late for bedtime.'

I could hear laughter, a group of immature boys whooping and hollering. 'Don't pay any attention to that lot, Melanie,' I said. 'They're only kidding.'

'No, we're not.' And like Melanie there was Carl and he crouched, scooped up handfuls of duckweed and then flung them over me. The weeds writhed and squirmed with lives of their own, wrapping around and constricting me, and dragging me down. The Golden Retriever cowered at Carl's side. 'Go on. Git!' he snapped at the old dog. 'Or ol' Ginny will drag you underwater too.'

I fought against the coiling tendrils, pulling them apart, throwing hunks of weed off me, but the more I discarded, more flowed over me. Tiny hands, with hooks for fingers, snagged my clothing and I tore off my top and jeans.

I stood, knees knocking in the dimness in my Y-fronts.

'Where's your shirt?'

My mother was sitting in the gloom with the TV off. Waiting for my return.

I looked beyond her, out of the lounge window.

'Uh, I took it off, it was too hot,' I lied. It was an easy lie, because even this late in the day the heat was still atrocious. Outside, the tarmac had bubbled in places, and the grass on our front lawn was burned yellow. My Grifter lay on its spine, like a skeletal carcass on the Serengeti, missing its wheels and seat. The broken chain hung loose from the pedal. It was a pitiful sight and I wanted to cry.

'You got it dirty you mean and threw it away. Where have you been all day, down them bloody frog ponds again no doubt. What have I warned you about going to those ponds? You're lucky that Ginny Greenteeth hasn't come out and grabbed you. It's what happens to bad boys and girls.'

'Mam. I'm thirteen. I don't even believe in Ginny Greenteeth.'

'You believe in Santa Claus, don't you? Believe in the never-never. Believe in me paying your way on chucky, because how else am I supposed to afford a new shirt? Believe you're clever, do you? Well, you should believe me!'

She was in the chair and then she wasn't. She was there, inches from my face, her tongue nipped between her teeth, the squirming tip protruding and her eyes glaring as her palm rained on my head and bare neck. The slaps stung on my sunburned skin, but I endured them, it was the awful smell of her tongue that made me almost vomit.

I retched, and forced up on to my hands and knees.

'You're all a bunch of horrible little shits,' I groaned . . .

And that was the catalyst that brought me back from that fugue world.

Johnny and Gavin had pulled free from me, but I could sense them standing close, and I didn't doubt that they were prepared to kick and punch me back to the floor.

Let them try.

What was it that Johnny once said to me about Carl splitting my lip? 'You should have kicked his arse. You could have, you know, if you'd really wanted to.'

Well, he wasn't wrong. If I'd wanted to I could have battered Carl and given Brian a run for his money too. As far as Johnny and Gavin were concerned, I could've taken on both of them then, as easy as I could now. Especially when armed. I groped for the hammer I'd dropped, and it was almost as if fate led my fingers to the cool wooden haft.

'Stay down,' Gavin warned. 'Don't make us hurt you.'

'Don't make me laugh,' I growled and clenched the hammer tightly.

'We've called the police already,' Johnny called. 'It's done, over with, Andy, now just stay down. C'mon man, don't fight us again.'

'You called the coppers, eh? Nobody round here likes a grasser,

Johnny-boy,' I said. 'What's your dad gonna think of you doing it again?'

'Leave my dad out of this,' said Johnny, his voice husky.

'He's dead isn't he? Liver cancer? Shame he went to his grave hating his youngest son, eh?'

'Shut up, Andy.'

'Yeah,' a female voice piped in. 'Just shut up. If you don't think your friends will knock you out again, don't you worry, I'll bloody well do it for them.'

'Jeez, Gemma. At work everyone thinks you are all sweetness and light. Wait till they find out what kind of bitch you are with a few glasses of cheap wine on board.'

'I warned you to stay down.' Gavin stepped in tight, placing both hands on my back to force me down on to the floor again.

I only had to twist a little and his right foot was directly under my shoulder. I rapped the arch of his foot sharply with the business end of the claw hammer.

Gavin howled, hopping away and clutching at his foot. It had been barely more than a tap, but it was fast, and undoubtedly I'd broken the fragile tarsal bones. He fell against my lobby wall, then slid down it, buckling my umbrella beneath him. Johnny and Gemma both shouted in alarm, and in the confusion I powered up to my feet and turned to face them. In their naivety they'd pushed the kicked-in door shut, probably to stop me from escaping if I tried to make a run for it; they had cut off their own escape route.

From beyond them I heard the thin strains of approaching sirens.

'Blooming hell, Johnny, you weren't kidding about grassing me up. And I thought you were my pal. Well, there's nothing for it now. I'm gonna have to shut you all up.'

I stalked towards them in my socks, limping on my injured thigh, the hammer cocked.

A figure materialized from nowhere.

One second I was lurching at Johnny, intending smashing him to the floor before turning on Gemma. I would keep Gavin for last because he was in no fit state to run from me, easy to pursue.

And then she was there, one hand touching her breastbone, the other extended towards me. There was not a hint of aggression in her gesture, it conveyed only love.

'B-Becky?' I croaked in dismay.

My dead daughter smiled at me.

'Becky, love, I thought that . . .'

'Daddy,' she said, ignoring my words. 'You aren't to blame for what happened to me. It was purely an accident, out of your control, out of Mum's control. But for the rest you are responsible. You must stop now. Please, Daddy, do it for me before it goes too far.'

I wept openly.

I didn't care who watched, or who heard.

I cried, and it was through love.

'Becky, I should have been there. I should have saved you.'

'You couldn't, Daddy. Nobody could. It was simply my time. Now please stop what you are doing. Enough people have been hurt already. You wish you could have saved me . . . save them instead.'

I looked at Johnny, at Gavin, at Gemma.

They couldn't see or hear Becky.

They cringed away from me, expecting the worst to happen.

I looked at the hammer, and thought I shouldn't disappoint them.

'Go away,' I said.

My old friends thought I meant them, they even shifted as if about to obey my command. But then I slashed the hammer through the apparition of Becky, ripping it into tatters. My daughter was a young adult when she'd drowned; by then she hadn't called me *Daddy* for seven or eight years.

'You are not my daughter,' I barked. I tapped the hammer against my skull repeatedly. 'Get the hell out of my head, Poppy. I know it's you in there, creeping your way through my mind, showing me your lies.'

I don't know how, but I suspect that those mind-expanding exercises of the good doctor Choi had somehow given Poppy's psyche the ability to roam beyond the confines of her own damaged vessel, and wriggle its way into mine. She'd shown me a sequence of horrors a moment ago, but none had worked to halt me, so she had changed tack in a last-ditch effort at staying my murderous hand. Instead of the hatred and bitterness of that day, she had chosen the worst of my life and my love for my daughter to try pulling me back to sanity. Where hatred fails, love should prevail. Yeah, put that on a sickly sweet greetings card. Or else, where love fails, come here you grass and I'll knock the brain right out of your damned head.

I lunged through the dissipating shade of my daughter, and struck Johnny down. He fell with a cry, grabbing at his busted left clavicle with his other hand, and I lined him up for a second smack, just behind his ear. But Gemma crashed into me, screeching like a wild cat, and somehow Gavin found the bravery and mobility to scramble across and lock his arms around my knees. Again, we all went down in a bundle and the police sirens vied with dominance over our shouts of anger as we fought.

I flailed about with the hammer, and hit meat and bone, though I couldn't tell you where or on whom. They weren't finishing blows though, although they were hard enough to force my trio of antagonists to scramble away and seek cover. Gasping for breath at the exertion, I stood, and turned just in time for the door to be kicked wide a second time and I was greeted by yet another apparition. This time it wasn't a victim, an old friend or family member, it was a burly copper wearing a stab-proof vest and aiming a blunt-shaped yellow and black object.

'Police. Drop your weapon,' he roared at me.

Likely he would have ordered me to get down on the floor next, but I didn't wait. Roaring back at him, I launched myself with the hammer raised and was met by 1,500 volts pulsing through my body.

FORTY-FIVE

Today

Call it a sweet twist of irony, but I ended up in the same county as Ian Nixon had all those years ago, remanded into custody while cases were built against me. Whereas he'd gone to the young offenders' institute in Barnard Castle, I'd been taken up the road to the adult jail in Durham. I was within twenty-five miles of where he'd hanged himself on the strips unpicked from his tracksuit bottoms. I hadn't been given an opportunity to end it all with a noose made from my clothing, dressed as I was in a disposable paper suit: all my clothes had been seized in evidence at the police station in Cumbria where I'd first been taken after my arrest.

I sat alone in a holding cell, my fingers knitted on my belly, as I stared at the institutional paintwork on my walls. The colour was hard to describe, kind of somewhere between cream and aubergine, supposedly a calming hue, or it had been specifically mixed to make you heave. My cell came with a low concrete plinth on which there was a water-piss-and-vomit-proof blue mattress. A steel toilet, without a seat, and a tiny steel sink completed the furnishings. I'd been allocated five sheets of toilet paper, any more and I could try blocking my toilet or sink and flooding the place. The last thing I wanted was for the floor to be awash with toilet water.

I contemplated my bare feet. I crossed them, and uncrossed them a few times. There wasn't much else to occupy my thoughts. I switched from counting my toes to counting my fingers. For fun I counted down on one hand – ten, nine, eight, seven, six – and then up to five on my other hand, making eleven altogether. I stood up and walked around the cramped space, then went and sat on the mattress once more. I considered using the toilet, but was saving that task for when I grew truly bored; the highlight of my day!

I lay down with my head to the outermost wall.

If I slept I've no recollection of it.

After some interminable minutes I turned and lay with my face towards the steel door. Somehow, I felt vulnerable like that, so I turned my back to the door instead and lay curled up in the foetal position.

That time I snoozed and dreamed of my dad. Not the doddering old man he was now, but the younger fellow from when I'd been a teenager.

'If you're going to amount to anything you have to be a star,' he'd said in my dream, paraphrasing the words he'd used on me as I lay fascinated by the night sky. 'Stand out, don't conform.'

'Am I shining bright enough, Dad? Everyone's going to know my name now!'

'You are scintillating,' he agreed, then his proud features wobbled and collapsed. 'You've made our family name poison in everyone's mouths.'

I was wakened by a fist banging on the door.

Blinking the fog of disappointment from my eyes I turned towards it, and saw the letterbox-sized hatch open. It opened outwards: no sharp corners inside the cell for me to ram my throat into and bleed to death. For somebody responsible for a number of brutal murders, they were taking great pains not to allow me to self-harm. Of course, this was all about getting me to court, and sentenced, and incarcerated in Frankland for the remainder of my days. They'd missed the opportunity with Ian Nixon, so weren't taking any chances with me.

Eyes peered in at me.

'Are you OK?' asked the woman custodian. The prison officer was conducting her third welfare check since my arrival. HMP Durham was for category B prisoners, and was a reception prison. They wanted to ensure that I was fit and healthy for when I was subsequently transferred a few miles away to the high security HMP Frankland, where the worst of the worst category A prisoners were penned.

'Nice of you to ask,' I said, and sat up.

'Do you need anything?'

'A cake with a file baked in it? Ha, I bet you've heard that more times than you care to recount.'

'There's been a few times,' she admitted. 'Do you want a hot drink?'

She meant a lukewarm drink, because handing over a boiling liquid to a dangerous convict invited it being thrown back in her face.

'Coffee,' I said. 'Y'know what? Scratch that order. This is probably a good opportunity for me to quit my caffeine habit. Do you have hot chocolate?'

'Yep. Coming right up.'

'Does it come without somebody's spit in it?' I asked.

'Take it or leave it,' she said without confirming or denying.

'I'll take it.'

She closed the hatch.

I knew from experience that it wouldn't be long until she returned. I stood and approached the door. My thigh ached where Gemma's heel had stabbed it. Footsteps outside my cell heralded the officer's return. I bent slightly to see her when she had lowered the hatch enough. The hatch clattered open, and I looked into another set of eyes. 'Fuckin' *spinner*,' the owner of the eyes said. 'Eat shit and die, you fucking beast.'

I was momentarily stunned. This couldn't be any of the custodian officers, as the cells were under 24-hour CCTV surveillance, and none of them would risk their jobs like this. Had to be another detainee, or maybe one of the supposed trustees. Whoever it was, they cleared their throat and spat directly in my face.

Rearing back, I wiped the dripping saliva off my cheek and forehead.

'Just wait till you get across the road,' the spitter crowed. 'You know how they treat nonces over there, don't you?'

In the space of half a minute he'd accused me of being insane, wished me dead, called me a rapist, threatened imminent violence and alleged I was a paedophile. Spitting on me was simply putting the icing on the cake. He slapped shut the hatch and walked away.

'Bastard,' I called him, but mostly because I had to use some of my small stack of toilet tissue to wipe off his foul-smelling spit.

The female prison officer returned.

As the hatch lowered, I moved back this time. I should have shown more caution with my previous visit. When the female officer had conducted her first welfare check, she had ordered me to take a few steps back through an intercom. There was a fisheye peephole in the door and another in the corner of the cell at the foot of the bed, used to ensure a detainee wasn't hiding in a corner and about to pounce if an officer had to enter a cell for any reason.

'Are you OK?' she asked, like she was a broken record.

'Who was that who just spat on me?'

'Sorry?'

'Somebody just spat in my face. Look at me.' I indicated the smelly saliva still adhering to my cheek in places.

'Sorry. I don't know what you're talking about. There's nobody else in the corridor but me.'

'Some lad just opened the hatch, accused me of all sorts and then spat a mouthful of stinking phlegm on me.'

'I'm just going to put your chocolate here, OK. Wait till I step back before you take it.'

She set a small paper cup on the hatch, and then moved aside.

I reached for the cup, felt it was barely warm as I surmised, but took it anyway. The custodian closed the hatch, ending my investigation into who was responsible for spitting at me.

The chocolate flavouring was weak, poorly stirred into warm water, and clotted like purple sludge at the bottom, I'd bet. I'd no way to stir it except with a finger. I didn't want to do that after wiping another man's saliva off my face. I looked at the sink, but was loath to turn on the tap to wash my hands. For reasons that might seem quite obvious I had acquired a mild form of hydrophobia.

I wiped more with the toilet paper, then wadded it and searched for a bin. There wasn't one, of course. I moved to chuck the ball of tissue down the toilet. And halted. I unfurled the crinkled but perfectly dry tissue. Touching my cheek with a fingertip it wasn't tacky with residual saliva.

'What the . . . Oh, right. You again, Poppy?'

The guy at the hatch had not existed in reality. He was a thought form, an egregore. His spit had felt real, but like the time Poppy spewed pond weed in Helen's shop, its ectoplasmic substance couldn't be maintained forever.

My cell was abruptly filled with figures.

They swarmed around me, hags with green knotty sticks for arms and bundles of twigs for heads, weeds and stinging nettles for hair. Their clothing was uniform, like grey sacking, and their lower limbs were lost in a miasmic swirl of muddy colours and ill-defined shapes. They plucked and prodded at me, and I could do nothing other than stand there and endure the taunting. As each figure hove closer, they took on individual features, and it was a parade of my victims: Poppy as a girl, Melanie as a girl too, then Carl and my disloyal wife, Nell, and last, not Becky as I feared, but another young man, and it took a moment for me to realize that he was one and the same with the dirty divvy that just spat on me: Ian Nixon. How had he become one of my victims? It was obvious, I supposed. Had I owned up to my horrible crimes back then, he wouldn't have been arrested and taken to Barnard Castle; he wouldn't have hanged himself from his bed frame.

I endured their poking and shoving. I stood stoically while they transformed to ugly hags once more and pressed their hooked noses up to mine, breathing stinking breath into my nostrils. It was like drain water, or from a still pond. I knew what Poppy referenced. Each of these forms were the witch my mother used to threaten me with, Ginny Greenteeth, or Wicked Jenny as I'd come to think of her. But it was as I'd told my harpy of a mam, and I was older than thirteen now, that I didn't believe in her, so I was unafraid.

It was as if that thought was powerful counter magic against them. The figures swarmed me one last time, howling and jabbering, and then faded into nothing.

'Nice try, Poppy,' I said. 'Now back off.'

She wasn't backing off.

Johnny stood in front of me, his wavy hair lank, his left arm in a sling. Gavin was at his side, resting on a crutch, with his broken foot in a plaster cast. Gemma scowled at me through restored glasses. The dye in her hair was now blue.

'Would you have really killed us, too?' Johnny asked.

'We were friends,' said Gavin, and tugged at the end of his hipster beard with the tips of his fingers.

'I really liked you, Mr Miller,' said Gemma and the scowl reformed into a smile.

Guilt nipped me then, but only mildly.

'You lot got off lightly,' I told them. 'You should be thankful.'

These were not my friends and potential lover, these were figments, and as they faded out of existence, my words were wasted on them.

Instead, I said, 'Poppy. If you can find any forgiveness in your heart, then I'm sorry for what I did to you and Melanie. It was a moment of madness, and I had no control over myself. Are you capable of forgiveness? Can you find it within you to put aside your hatred of me and forgive me?' I raised the chocolate drink and took a swig. Around curdled lumps of chocolate powder and milk, I laughed nastily, then spat it on the floor. 'Or are you the bitter, twisted creature I believe you to be?'

It was all it took to find out.

Something squirmed in my throat. I gagged and coughed and spluttered. Something wormed downward into my gullet, while more of the same reached upward and poured from between my teeth. I chewed down on it, but it was tough and sinewy, and tiny filaments needled into the roof of my mouth and tongue and injected their poison. My hands went to my throat, and I let out a horrendous croak of dismay, because this was not happening! More of the sinuous weed spilled from me, out of my mouth and nostrils, and some of it looped around my neck and constricted. Dirty water the colour of weak hot chocolate spurted from me, and I fell to my knees.

The floor was wet with what I'd already spat out, but more filthy liquid kept spilling out and I was in a puddle of the stuff. My paper suit was tattered, falling to damp pieces. I collapsed on my side, hands trying to drag the spooling weeds from my throat, and drowned . . .

'Are you OK?' asked Janine Collins.

'Must've swallowed some of that pond weed,' a voice whispered back at her.

'Say again?'

She didn't really care one way or another, but if the murderous pig had done himself harm, it was for her to deal with the aftermath. Other officers would come to help, but she was the one tasked with the care and well-being of this particular detainee and the last she wanted was the paperwork and the verbal arse-kicking she'd get if he hurt himself. The prisoner was in transition, heading off to HM Prison Frankland as soon as they had a place ready for him, and hopefully it would be sooner rather than later.

She didn't like speaking with him.

He was creepy.

One moment he could seem perfectly normal. In the next, he could be distant, as if his vision was fixated on distant vistas of his making.

He could be polite, but he also had a facetious manner about him, as if it didn't matter that he'd murdered several people and tried to end the lives of three others when his crimes were uncovered. She kept things perfunctory, down to business, and faux friendly enough that he didn't grow vitriolic with her.

Earlier when she took him his hot chocolate, it was as if he had read her thoughts: she had considered picking her nose and stirring something nasty into his cup, and when he came out with that tale of some lad hawking phlegm in his face, it had sent an uneasy qualm through her. After leaving him, dabbing at his face with a small wad of toilet tissue, she had gone and checked the CCTV recording and nobody but her had visited his cell in the interim. There was one instant where the video recording wobbled, and an artefact like a watermark washed slowly down the screen, but otherwise there was no lad whatsoever. Still, she felt odd returning to conduct the next welfare check, and steeled herself for more odd behaviour.

She couldn't see him from the open hatch. She moved and peered through the fisheye lens in the wall at the foot of his bed plinth.

She saw the pale blue of his paper suit, and the rounded shape of one shoulder. He lay still.

'Mr Miller,' she spoke into the intercom, 'please stand and move away from the door.'

He didn't reply. He didn't move.

She pressed the intercom button again. 'Get up and move back from the door.'

He had not moved even a fraction. Bile flooded her throat.

'Oh, no.'

She hit the alarm buzzer beneath the peep hole, and waited for her colleagues to race to her assistance.

Joined by two burly colleagues, she used the master key to open the holding cell door and they entered cautiously, this time warning Miller not to move.

He would never move again. His face was turned towards them, and was as blue as his paper suit from lack of oxygen. His tongue and eyeballs protruded, small capillaries having burst in the sclera. Stuffed in his mouth was the tail of the tissues Janine had watched him dab at his cheeks with earlier, but the majority of it had been forced deep into his throat, perhaps blocking his windpipe.

Serial murderer Andrew Miller lay on the floor, dead.

They couldn't fathom how his paper suit had become so tattered that it had dissolved in spots, or why he smelled as if he'd taken a dip in a muddy puddle.

Approximately seventy miles to the south of the prison, Jennifer Seeley sat facing the window in her room. Her radio played quietly,

Yazz singing that the only way is up, an old song from her childhood. Outside, brief showers sent curtains of rain across the rolling
landscape, while the sun played hide and seek with the scudding
clouds. She saw none of nature's beauty. Her one seeing eye was
rolled up into her socket and her mouth hung open to one side. She
rocked back and forth in her wheelchair. She stopped and then her
shoulders rose and fell repeatedly.

Her nurse laid a comforting hand on her shoulder. 'What has
tickled you, then? You seem really pleased about something.'

Chuckling audibly now, Jennifer came out of her self-imposed
trance. Her vision focused and she saw the rain beading on the
window. She set her jaw more naturally and worked her tongue.
After a few trial words, a couple of wet slurps, plain to hear, she
said, 'I hear Andrew has been very, very bad. Wicked Jenny comes
for the naughtiest boys and girls.'